LAURIE KIRK'S writing journey began in 2021 when her mediumship kicked in and she discovered she is a womb twin survivor.

She wrote a TV pilot about the pain of losing him and her parents. And naturally it's a comedy. They all haunt her on the regular and she couldn't be happier about it.

She stepped into the horror/thriller genre with BABY MARVIN. It began its life as a feature script, but a novel was the obvious next step.

It explores duality, identity and the fractured self.

Originally from Florida, she and husband Mike moved to Pennsylvania in 2015 to escape the humidity. They live in the country with two of their five children. She spends her time writing, rescuing dogs and causing a commotion.

She is also constantly on the lookout for the perfect burger.

Obsession with duality and dead parents - Laurie is the Batman of the Poconos.

Published in 2026 by Dark Anthem Press

www.darkanthempress.com

Created and Printed in the United States of America.

First Edition 2026 - Published by Dark Anthem Press, an imprint of One Moorer LLC.

Cover design by Drew Foerster.

Identifiers: 979-8-9926547-3-8 (eBook)
979-8-9926547-2-1 (paperback)

BABY MARVIN

A psychological, supernatural thriller
about the good and evil that exists
in all of us.

By

Laurie Kirk

Dedicated to my brother Kyle

Thou know'st 'tis common; all that lives must die,
Passing through nature to eternity.
Hamlet Act 1, Scene 2

Dedicated to my son Christopher

My youngest child,
my inspiration for
Baby Marvin (but without the blood)

NOW

They graze, only their backs visible over the thick mist hovering near the rain-soaked ground. Heads popping up, the seven deer wander into the three-acre pumpkin patch, cautious but comfortable in this familiar yard.

The center of the pumpkin patch is disturbed, a shovel standing sentinel. The metal handle reflects a waning full moon grappling with receding storm clouds.

The deer avoid this strange area around the shovel, their instincts guiding them away from it. Something inexplicable happened here.

The deer chomp the impenetrable pumpkin rinds for a few moments. Then they freeze. They wait, white tails twitching.

Sounds approach. They tend to ignore breaks in the quiet but now they reconsider. Not the usual hubbub they are so comfortable with. These sounds bewilder them, placing them on alert.

A giggling baby.

A man's labored breathing.

Something dragging and scraping along the gravel driveway.

They recognize the man from a distance, they know him. But something is different—he's changed since they saw him last.

Always accompanied by glowing, radiant waves of gentleness, seen only to them, he's become - death.

They scatter into the surrounding woods.

The disparate sounds wind their way up the long driveway, approaching the house. The moon finally wins its battle with the clouds and lights up the old Victorian looming at the end of the driveway.

Dismal gray with white trim, a single floor lamp on the first floor punches a feeble, yellow glow out into the night.

The green-eyed baby, cherubic face lashed with dried blood, chortles and coos as he looks over the left shoulder of the weary man carrying him.

The man's right hand drags a gore splattered ax along the driveway, dust and rocks clinging to the sticky blade.

Bone-tired, he's too fatigued to carry it.

The front door hangs partially open, but it is not inviting.

Leaning into it, eighteen-year-old Marvin Damon drags himself inside the house. He leaves the door open behind him, the blood dripping from his shoulder leaving a crimson streak.

Almost an arrow, hideously guiding unfortunate visitors inside to a questionable fate.

Bleary Marvin takes in the dim living room with his gray-green eyes. He is unrecognizable amidst the ichor on his face, in his dark, wavy hair and on his white *Keep on Truckin* t-shirt.

He sets the baby down on the oak floor with great care, leaving a bloody handprint on the back of the light blue footed pajamas the child wears.

The six-month-old little boy is nonplussed by the horrifying situation; he sits up on his own and continues to be delighted by every new sight.

THUMP!

Startled, but lacking the energy (or will) to fight, relief washes over Marvin when he realizes the old bloodhound, Theodore, has slumped off the lavish sofa onto the floor. He had been dozing comfortably against a tufted pillow.

Hard of hearing and half-blind, the curious dog waddles over to investigate the strange little creature on the floor.

The baby reaches his podgy hands out toward the animal and squeals with joy as Theodore licks the blood from his face.

Marvin flips the wall switch on. The well-kept living room has the modern conveniences of the current year 1968, but overall reflects a style more reminiscent of the 1940's.

Not a surprise as the new mid-century designs are quite a departure from the more traditional themes of a home like this.

And, as his mother once declared regarding mid-century modern, *"That style is more suited to the baseborn. Not for us, darling, not for us."*

A smashed movie poster frame leans against the far wall, *the feature wall*, glass scattered around it.

Jimmy Stewart grins up in his finest golly-gee manner at the shadow of a huge rabbit. *HARVEY starring Jimmy Stewart.*

An autograph, "Annette, Best Wishes, James Stewart."

Two official looking documents lay discarded in the midst of the glass shards. This area of ruin contrasts with the rest of the pristine room.

Regaining some of his strength, Marvin looks down at his right hand and notices the ax.

He stares at it in disbelief, not realizing he still had it in his hand.

"I did it," Marvin whispers.

Silence, then -

"*We* did it," a voice corrects him.

PART 1

HAPPY BIRTHDAY MARVIN

1
BEFORE

Early morning sun streams into his bedroom.

"Revolution" by the Beatles blares from Marvin's radio alarm clock.

Shoot! I forgot to turn it off. Hopefully she didn't hear it. He didn't need the musical reminder to start his day. He's been awake for hours.

Smiling, looking out the open window at the autumn-tinged forest, he's been anxiously waiting for the sun to peek through the fiery trees.

He sits up on his elbows, his grin widening. His green eyes shine, not a hint of gray on this, the most special morning of his young life.

The calendar hanging next to his bed is turned to October 1968. From the First National Bank Downtown, the image reflects the same colorful collage framed in his window.

Days one through twenty-eight are crossed out neatly with a diagonal line. The twenty-ninth is circled in red with a smiley face and "18!" written in Marvin's careful script.

He pats the calendar before rising and stretching his six foot two inch tall frame. Grabbing the Monkees t-shirt and jeans draped across the foot of his bed, he heads into the bathroom.

His mind races as it has for the past few hours. It's finally here. Everything changes today.

A poster of The Monkees hangs on the wall behind his bed. Their records are most prominent in his neat stack next to the turntable.

A poster of the movie Psycho stares down the innocent boy band from the opposing wall, Norman Bates daring them to book a room at his motel.

The walls are a pale blue. The multitude of items covering them makes it difficult to tell the actual color of the room without close inspection.

There are sketches on graphing paper, notebook paper, even napkins. All are furniture ideas. Chairs, tables, bed frames, side tables.

His drawings are sometimes very detailed and deliberate but a few are haphazard and drawn with whatever he had handy when that bolt of lightning struck his artistic mind.

One napkin has a coffee ring and smudge of blueberry pie on it, along with plans for a rocking chair.

His tidy, wooden desk has a stack of more drawings, one written on an old piece of wallpaper. A ledger lies open, his pencil on top of it. The desk of a much older man, the desk of someone who runs a business and household with conscious skill.

As Marvin emerges from the bathroom, his mother's voice drifts up from the kitchen, "Come on down, Precious Pumpkin!"

A wave of dizziness surprises Marvin. His bright green eyes cloud to a light gray. He clutches his dresser with one hand to keep himself upright. He puts the other hand on the small poster next to his mirror.

The black and white poster has President Eisenhower holding four year-old Marvin in front of the White House. Surrounded by government officials they stand under a banner announcing, "SAFE DRIVING DAY 1954—PRESIDENT EISENHOWER WELCOMES NATIONAL SPOKESMAN BABY MARVIN."

Marvin has a two-inch diameter dot on each cheek and a smaller one on the end of his nose, giving him an adorable clown-like appearance.

He and the President smile broadly and wave to onlookers.

As the dizziness abates, Marvin stands tall and looks at himself in the mirror. The image blurs. *Maybe it's time for a pair of glasses, I do spend a great deal of time doing detail work.*

As the handsome boy in the mirror becomes more crisp, he feels like he's looking at someone else. This is not the first time that this has happened to Marvin.

Numerous times over the years, he's become fixated on his mirror image as everything else around it swirls and swims out of focus.

He often sees himself multiplied, six images turning around and around. The disorientation always reminds him of one of his favorite TV shows, *The Twilight Zone*. He would not have been shocked to see Rod Serling stroll into the room with his typically dour expression and announce that he had entered *a fifth dimension, one that is not known by man.*

He's never told his mother about these occurrences. He learned early on that the only news that Annette desires to hear is pleasant news.

So, he's kept it to himself, along with his plans for the future. But - something is different this time. It's him, but it's *not* him. Closing his eyes, Marvin shakes his head and looks again. His own slightly worried face stares back at him, eyes back to bright green.

Her voice, shrill and unpleasant, "Marvin!"

With a displeased glance toward the sound, he keeps his voice cheerful.

"Coming!".

Briskly striding out of his bedroom, Marvin stops suddenly and takes a deep breath. He hates this part of his day most of all. His bedroom is situated at the end of an interminable dim hallway.

He's forced to pass the four empty bedrooms every day on his way to the stairs.

The doors stay closed, blocking out any light from their windows that could have made the hallway less tomb-like. Always a reminder of how alone he's always been.

How many times has he imagined rushing out of his room in the morning and across the hall to jump on one of the beds of his many siblings, laughing and joyfully waking them so they can start one of their fun-filled adventures for the day?

Staring at the closest oak door, he pictures what his life could have been.

"Marvin!" She's getting angry. He doesn't care. He doesn't have to care anymore.

"Can't find my shoe!" The lie slides out of his mouth with such ease that it disturbs him. But not much.

"OK, well hurry, I have a surprise for you!"

An unpleasant but commonplace odor smacks him in the face. Focused on the only open door on the second floor, Marvin picks up his pace and follows the familiar stench to the end of the hall, past the staircase.

The smell of cigarette smoke is stronger as he reaches his mother's darkened bedroom. Peeking in, he sees the lit cigarette propped carelessly on an ashtray next to the canopied bed.

Shaking his head, he rushes in and stubs it out muttering to himself, "You're gonna burn the whole house down, and us with it."

He rubs his hand over a dent in the finish of the ornate bedside table. An expert craftsman, of course he notices it. Smelling his hand, even more disgusted now that the abominable smell of the cigarette is on *him*, he grits his teeth and grabs a bottle of lotion that she keeps on her dresser with her myriad of beauty products.

On a visit to New York City once they had visited Macy's Department Store.

Seven year-old Marvin had considered the counters of women's toiletry items and wondered why they didn't have as many as his mother did on her dresser. But even at that tender age, he knew better than to ask her.

Lavender, one of the scents he most associates with her, glops out on his hand as he covers the distasteful smell of the cigarette. Better, but now his hand smells like he's been smoking lavender. He's going to wash his hands when he gets downstairs.

His eye is drawn to the china doll perched on the bed. An eerie copy of his mother, the doll stares at him with bright emerald eyes. Her porcelain skin is surrounded by jet black curls, lovingly kept in place by a fuschia bow.

His mother calls the doll Josephine, and in one of her particularly bad drunken rants, rambled about the doll being named after her father. Her father's name was George but he didn't contradict her at the time.

It's always been best to just smile and nod along when she's drunk. This miniature of his mother saddens him and also infuriates him for some reason.

Storming over to the windows, he throws back the heavy curtains. He opens one of the windows to freshen the space with crisp autumn air. Sunlight streams in to brighten the gloomy room.

Dark damask wallpaper and cherry wood furniture set a somber tone, reminiscent of a funeral home.

The only source of lightness in the room is a poster of four year-old Marvin.

A close up of his smiling face, sporting his facial dots, SLOW DOWN, DAD! EVERYDAY IS SAFE DRIVING DAY!

Marvin smiles at his younger self and shakes his head. He runs out before the harpy shrieks at him again.

2

Annette Sinclair-Damon struggles to make edible pancakes while alternately passing her cigarette from her pursed red lips to her left hand.

An enormous two carat diamond ring weighs it down, much too gaudy for everyday but she doesn't care. She earned it. But that's the past. Her only concern right now is splayed out in front of her.

Her yearly attempt to play mother and create breakfast for her one and only child is not going particularly well. A stunning, forty-five year-old beauty, her talents lie elsewhere. The plate of uneven, slightly burned pancakes attests to this fact.

She would be much more comfortable having breakfast with Joan Crawford and Bette Davis and being served by accomplished chefs on a veranda overlooking the Pocono Mountains. *As if they'd be caught dead out here in this dismal hick town.*

Nearly finished ruining the pancakes, she finds herself surrounded by a colossal mess. Batter lays puddled near the stove, flour and sugar both spill out of their paper bags. A large spoon stands upright in the mason jar of homemade pumpkin puree retrieved from the pantry.

Unsightly globs of pumpkin dot the white counter in a design reminiscent of a child's finger painting. Annette is untalented *and* untidy. Ironically, she herself remains impeccable, untouched amidst the gooey chaos. Domesticity itself seems repelled by her.

She sighs as her attention is drawn to what she refers to as the *feature wall* in the living room. Naturally, a home this large and distinguished has a feature wall. The kitchen and living room are connected and open, the feature wall visible to the inept chef as she flips the final batch of smoldering pancakes, slopping half of one over the side of the skillet onto the stove.

Most Victorian style homes have distinct, condoned off rooms on the main floor, little boxes separated by doorways of varying design leading to more little boxes. But Annette wanted openness and airy space. She wanted to float from one room to another, lighter than air.

I won't live in an ant farm!

So, her then-husband obliged by having this house specifically created for her. He had little concern for such matters and truly wanted nothing more than for her to shut up about it and get about the business of giving him children to fill the outlandish home.

He's long gone and she's stuck here, living in the middle-of-nowhere; Stroud Junction, Pennsylvania, in a home designed to be filled with hordes of children.

The aforementioned *then-husband* was born and raised in this unfortunate part of the country and wanted his children to be reared here, in the fresh air, away from the din and crowds of New York City.

Annette wholeheartedly agreed, certain that after the birth of the one and only child that she was willing to ruin her figure for, she could convince him to move back to where the action is. Simulating a barren womb after Marvin's birth would not have been a problem.

Growing up in Vaudeville teaches you a thing or two, or even three; a phrase she has uttered to Marvin on more than one occasion, resulting in the inevitable eye roll from the boy.

The feature wall that Annette curated with such pride and joy is adorned with carefully selected items.

A movie poster from HARVEY starring Jimmy Stewart is signed, "*Annette, Best Wishes, James Stewart*".

An eight by ten photo of her with Jimmy Stewart at the premiere hangs next to it.

The beginning of the end.

A huge sigh, sneer and a tut (her customary trio of derision) at the affable Jimmy Stewart escape her before her gaze falls on two framed portraits.

John F. Kennedy and Robert F. Kennedy gaze out at her, smiling. Both portraits are draped in black funereal bunting. She's in mourning. First Jack five years ago and now Bobby. Her grief hits her at the depths of her soul.

She was inconsolable when Bobby was cut down a short time ago. Jack's death was horrific but Bobby, her Bobby - it's not just an emotional loss, she's unsure what she'll do without that extra -

Distracted by several photos of her as a small child, posed adorably in her dance costumes. Her vaudeville career was short-lived. Born too late to fully take advantage of the celebrated form of early 20th century entertainment, she set her ambitions on something new. Motion Pictures.

Her mother was a seasoned performer and had introduced her doppelganger daughter onstage after her performances to enthusiastic applause. Tiny Annette would join her mother to sing and dance her miniature heart out. She wanted her mother's adoration and that was the way to get it.

Another way to garner her mother's love was to accept and love her mother's various suitors. Most were decent and even, kind, men. She called them all 'Father'. But one was - she absently reaches up to touch the back of her shoulders without realizing she's doing it. She shudders.

An absent father's lack of love and appreciation created a chasm in her that was never to be filled. Unlike other "trashy" women, she never sought that love with a myriad of men. She filled her aching heart with an ambition to be loved by live audiences and later by movie goers. They couldn't hurt her. There was no cost.

"Then-husband" came about as a result of her foray into films. A former actor and successful director, he used his connections to get her cast in "Harvey".

A champagne fueled celebration of that game-changer is what led to her pregnancy. And the eventual descent into hell that is Stroud Junction, Pennsylvania.

A black 1940's style asymmetrical button dress with long sleeves hugs her perfectly, as do all of her expensive clothes. An ebony pillbox hat completes the dramatic widow look. Her jet black hair lays in a soft bob, ala Marilyn Monroe. *That slut, going after not one but both of them.* Marilyn's portrait does *not* adorn the feature wall.

Annette dabs her eyes with a handkerchief (black, of course). A photo of her as a teen with Jack and Bobby, arms around each other. She can't look away. Tears course down her cheeks before she focuses on a huge poster for Safe Driving Day.

A duplicate of the one in Marvin's room but twice the size. A brief hint of a smile before –

Her acting headshots!

Six of them, lined up to remind her of what could have been. Yet she doesn't take them down. They help her focus on the future that she's going to have to create for herself. Her career was going so well if not for - WAIT! He's coming. Finally.

She's been holding onto this silly pill for an eternity. The prescription bottle sits next to the sink, carefully staged. The disastrous pancakes done, she arranges a vase of red roses until he comes in.

She always keeps red roses in the house, from the yard when they're blooming, from the florist otherwise. They hold great meaning for her. She beams at him as he lumbers in. She throws up her hands in greeting with the pill visible between her fingers. Her cigarette burns down to the nub in the ashtray.

"Happy birthday! I'm making your favorite, pumpkin pancakes!"
"Thanks, Mama."

She holds up a finger and gestures for him to wait as she goes to the sink to fill a glass with water. Pretending to take the pill, she drinks a bit and pours the rest of the water out into the sink where it goes down the drain with the palmed pill.

Performance over, she whirls back to see her son stubbing out the remains of her cigarette. He's always hated her smoking, from the time he was old enough to express his opinion, which was at an unimaginably young age. She keeps her smile intact until she sees the expression on his face. Different. *How is it possible that he actually looks older since yesterday?*

Taking in her outfit with that head tilt of his that never portends a positive comment, "Isn't it time to stop mourning? Everyone else has moved on. You look like a widowed Scarlett O'Hara."

The off-hand reference pleases her momentarily. Always sold by her agents as a "young Vivien Leigh" she is possessed of the same dark hair and green eyes that charmed Rhett Butler and Stanley Kowalski years ago.

And it worked. She had booked the role of her life, in a movie with Jimmy Stewart no less, when she fell pregnant. Fiddle-Dee-Dee. She'll think about her career tomorrow.

Time to focus on Marvin.

She snaps back to reality, confronted by the true intention behind her son's acidulous comment.

Stop mourning? How can he say something like that? He knows how I feel about the Kennedy boys. But he doesn't know the whole story.

"*Everyone else* didn't know the Kennedy family personally. Spending all that time with them in Massachusetts, they made my childhood -"

"Bearable. I know, I've heard it all before." Marvin grins as Annette scowls.

"I'll thank you not to smirk. You don't know as much as you think you do."

Marvin, jabbing "Jackie just got married again."

Annette scoffs, disgusted and dabs her eyes again. Marvin stares for a moment and heads into the formal dining room, shaking his head. The wood paneled dining room features a crystal chandelier and a mahogany dining table long enough to land a small plane.

Another reminder of the siblings he should have had. Golden cherub candle holders, lace tablecloth, expensive silk napkins. Maple syrup in a crystal decanter. Fine Havilland china place setting for one at the end of the table.

Marvin sits as Annette puts a plate of the more appetizing pancakes in front of him. Marvin has no interest in the food and even less in the finery. Annette glides to the far end of the table with no plate of her own and sits.

Unsure what to say to her son, she grasps at anything she can, hoping to make a connection with him on his special day.
"I can't believe you're 18 already. Thank God you're done with that school. I'm sorry you had to spend the last few years there. Honestly, a public school. Oof."

This again?

"I graduated months ago, you're beating a dead horse. And I really liked school. It was good to be out of the house. To be around people."

She's not listening to him, "I couldn't afford a private tutor anymore. Times being what they are."

Marvin shoves food into his mouth, grimaces slightly and talks with his mouth full, "Good. Mr. Gray treated me like something was wrong with me."

How are these pancakes burned and raw at the same time?

He forces himself to swallow, grabbing the syrup and pouring copious amounts over the ruin on the plate.

"He worked with Bobby's children. He came highly recommended."

"As did Hermann Göring, I'm sure," he retorts.

Annette is completely flummoxed. This is not how she wanted the morning to proceed. Not looking forward to this day, she's been preparing to deal with him differently. As an adult. But still her child. A difficult balance. But he's woken up a different person. Her Vaudeville roots, as always, will come in handy now.

Time for –

ACT TWO: ANNETTE CHANGES THE SUBJECT.

"What would you like to do today?"

Marvin, decisive, "I'm getting my driver's license."

Knowing this conversation would rear its ugly head again sooner or later, Annette lies.

"Absolutely not, darling. Those streets are not safe. Why, I barely escaped a terrible collision just yesterday."

They both know she hasn't left the house in several days. She rarely leaves the house at all. She spends her days dressed to the nines, meandering around, smoking and drinking and watching TV while thumbing through fashion and Hollywood magazines. Both let the deception sit for a moment, Marvin half-smiling defiantly.

Annette, always calculating, decides why tell one lie when you can tell two for the same price.

"And I have no idea where your birth certificate is anyway. I can look for it later."

Marvin's eyes get more gray by the second. Silence again before he breaks the stalemate, "I'm buying a truck for my business."

Annette, horrified, "Your business!? Don't call it that, Marvin. It's just temporary. I'm going into New York to meet with my agent soon and I intend to speak to him about you again. You're much too talented and handsome not to be in show business. It's in your blood after all. From both sides. You can't ignore destiny.

I'll take care of it, then you can put this other nonsense aside."

"It's not nonsense. I'm a very successful carpenter. And I love what I do, creating things with my hands. I love seeing people's faces when I bring their ideas to life."

"Yes, you're very talented at that -" she waves her hand, swatting away the word like a pesky fly, "Woodworking thing. By the way, my bedside table needs repairing. I don't know what happened to it."

He knows. Too many empty tumblers dropped on it as she passed out.

"I'll fix it tomorrow. I need to get my license, get a truck and work on expansion plans for the gardens today."

Annette huffs and exclaims loudly, face to the heavens, "With your talent? Furniture? Gardens? Like I said before, nonsense."

"This *nonsense* keeps the lights on. We don't have Kennedy money after all."

"Oh really," Annette states. Marvin hears her but ignores her.

She continues, "We need to move away from here, you've never lived in New York City. That's where the action is. The excitement." She gestures around at the house, "Living out here in the wilderness isn't ideal for an acting career."

"Pennsylvania is my home. I love it here and I'm not leaving. You're free to do as you please since I'm an adult now. I don't need supervision anymore."

Her face falls and he feels sympathy for her.

She doesn't know who she is unless she's acting or planning a career for me. But she needs to find out.

Marvin, quieter, "I think New York would be great for you. We could sell the house, it's too big anyway. That would set you up well financially."

Biting the inside of her cheek, she looks up at him with glistening eyes, unsure.

Marvin, empathetic, "My going out on my own has nothing to do with how I feel about you. I know that taking care of me without my father has been difficult all these years."

She blanches at the mention of his father, lowers her eyes to her folded hands on the table. "Thank you for that. I—I will think about what you've said. I suppose I've never considered life beyond you."

She regards him with a genuine smile, full of warmth, the smile he's always craved but seldom witnessed in his young life. Now is a good time to drop another bomb on her.

Why does every conversation have to be a chess match?

"Carey is coming by to get me."

Picking through the edible sections of pancake, he waits for an explosion but Annette is uncharacteristically calm at the mention of her least favorite person. At least he thinks Carey is her least favorite person, it's hard to tell. She doesn't particularly like anybody.

Sensing a dynamic change, and not wishing to destroy the wonderful moment they just shared, she carefully calculates her response in a way that expresses her opinion without being too overt.

"Oh. I have to be honest, Marvin. I never liked that *boy*."

Marvin works to control his temper but his eyes darken, "That's rude. He's my best friend."

"I'd just prefer you not spend time with a mentally deranged person. Wouldn't you agree that it's reasonable for a mother to feel that way about her only son?"

The phony smile is back.

Yet another reminder that he's all she has. Marvin stands, smiles and drops his napkin on the unfinished plate of - *could it even be called food?*

"Of course, I agree that I shouldn't spend time with a mentally deranged person. That's why I'm leaving. Enjoy your day."

As he storms past his dumbfounded mother, Annette reaches out to frantically claw at his arm. "Wait, I -"

Marvin stops, hoping against hope that his mother will apologize for insulting his best friend. They had experienced a bona fide moment back there, but predictably, her smile belies her intentions. She releases his arm and pats it.

"I need some money."

Marvin pulls his wallet out of his back pocket, thumbs through the sizable wad of cash and holds out a ten dollar bill.

She stares at the money, her hand to her throat as if he was handing her a dead rat.

Feigned disgust. Tragically, she's not wearing any pearls to clutch. "I'll need more than this."

Marvin drops the bill on the table and heads out. She hears his booming voice from the living room as he heads out the front door.

"I'm not paying for any more widow's weeds." SLAM!

Infuriated, Annette attempts to light a cigarette with her gold lighter. She's shaking so badly she needs to use both hands. After a particularly long inhale with her emerald eyes closed, she gets up and glides to the drink cart in the living room.

As she selects the perfect scotch bottle for this occasion, the grandfather clock facing her chimes nine times, outraged at her behavior.

It's nine a.m. you splifficated harridan, how dare you drink alcohol this early!

She pours her preferred scotch into the tumbler while glaring at the ancient mahogany judge. Her expertise at the perfect pour without having to see the glass is impressive.

Temptation to throw the tumbler through the smug face of the clock overwhelms her. But how would she explain *that* to Marvin? One final glower at the old fuddy-duddy as she holds her glass up in a mock toast.

Satisfied that she's let that clock know who's the boss, she drains the glass and slams it on the table before tucking the money into her bra.

3

Autumn.

The grand Victorian house is luminous in the daylight.

Clear cerulean skies frame the Pocono Mountains in the background. A scene worthy of the high standards of First National Bank's calendar.

The pumpkin patch in the front yard is brimming with orange, umber and copper orbs and is undisturbed. Late blooming red rose bushes run along the south side of the house.

Several areas of the twenty acre property are sectioned off for various fruits and vegetables. The vast majority of the acreage is untouched forest.

The house is hemmed in by eight foot tall thick hedges, erect soldiers guarding the front of the property from the street, as per Annette's demands.

We don't need a crowd of looky-loos peering in, do we?

Closed in, boxed in, only a narrow driveway in or out. Situated at the end of a winding dirt road, it is by far the nicest house anywhere around, out of place in a working class neighborhood. The only vehicle is Annette's black 1958 Buick Riviera.

A detached two-car garage with roll-up doors is Marvin's destination as he races out the front door and across the gravel driveway, kicking up dust and small stones, a huge smile on his face. His sanctuary, a place away from his cloying mother. He first converted the dusty old building when he was a mere sprout of eleven.

Mr. Garcia had lived most of his life down the street from Marvin. Dead for the past seven years, he had introduced Marvin to the world of carpentry. The boy was mesmerized by the craft and skill that Mr. Garcia had used to repair the very dining room chair that newly adult Marvin had expressed his opinions from that very morning.

Unable to sleep that night, filled with visions of the things he could create, he began to visit Mr. Garcia as often as he could and became his unofficial apprentice.

His sudden death from a stroke was devastating for Marvin and he was concerned that his dreams for a career in carpentry were gone with Mr. Garcia.

Never in particularly good health. Mr. Garcia always made sure to have his affairs in order and his wishes known.

When a lawyer came knocking one week after Mr. Garcia's passing, Marvin discovered that he had been left all of his old friend's tools, books and drawings.

A lovely, handwritten note came with the news:

Dear Marvin, I'm glad to have known you. Go make beautiful things. Your Friend, Mr. Garcia.

Annette was none too happy about Marvin's newfound hobby. Terrified of the assortment of sharp implements and vexed by the constant noise, she hoped to persuade him to put this *nonsense* aside.

But Marvin was focused in a way that she had never seen and she knew she couldn't talk him out of it. She assumed he would tire of it sooner or later after the grief of losing his friend passed. She was wrong.

A chopping block made out of an old oak tree stump rests next to the building, a neat pile of freshly chopped wood behind it. A dozen felled oak trees are strewn around the area, waiting to be stripped and made into wooden planks by the young carpenter.

The ax in the chopping block has a stripe of black paint on its handle. His attention is drawn to it. Picking it up, he tests the blade gently against his finger. Dull. Marvin props it on his shoulder as he raises both doors of the garage by hand.

A red painted wooden sign with black wood-burned letters lets everyone know that this space is: MARVIN'S WORKSHOP

Converted into a well-provisioned woodshop, it has every tool that a furniture maker could possibly need. Table saw, chisels, clamps. Electric sanders and hand saws. Hammers and tape measures are held by hooks on a corkboard screwed into the back wall, along with screwdrivers and a sliding bevel.

A hand plane sits on his work bench, partially covering his latest sketch, a dining table labeled, "Mrs. O'Neill - not *too* fancy".

The treasured note from Mr. Garcia hangs on the back wall,

framed. A constant reminder that his future is in this room, not in stuffy, smoke-filled audition spaces filled with glowering casting directors.

A low section of ceiling showcases two perfectly straight rows of old glass baby food jars. The lids are screwed into the ceiling board and the jars contain various types of nails and screws. The jars sit at Marvin's eye level and he need only reach up and unscrew the see-through jar to get to its contents.

Marvin had found dozens of his old baby food jars shoved into the dark corner of this very garage years ago when he took it over as his own.

Why did she keep these? Why does she do any of the things she does?

His ingenuity kicked in the moment he picked one of them up and gazed into the spherical face of the infant adorning the label. A lopsided grin spread across his face as then twelve year-old Marvin bounced the jar up and down in his palm. Always thinking. Always planning.

This system of his own making has received praise by other wood workers in the community over the ensuing years and has been copied by most of them.

Several partially finished chairs and tables are stacked up. Carefully designed plans are tacked to the walls with exact measurements.

Measure twice, cut once.

Bags of lye for soap-making are piled nearby. A lathe for fashioning table and chair legs has a baseball bat held in its grip. Another opportunity to create a source of income.

Scores of white ash trees are hidden in the forest on the property. And people really seem to treasure things that are handcrafted, made with care and love.

This is how Marvin creates things. His well of ingenuity and creativity is almost as extensive as the spring of his genuine love and affection for people.

The incongruity between Marvin and his mother is profound, and a source of gossip for the small town.

He must take after his father. Poor thing, being raised by - her. That boy must have a wonderful guardian angel.

The bat that sits near ready is just another example of Marvin's thoughtfulness. It's a gift for someone very special.

The twenty by thirty feet room has a window on each side for natural light but being nestled in the woods keeps the workspace dim even on the sunniest days, such as this one.

But Marvin dares not fell the trees surrounding the building. He's not skilled enough to keep one from crashing through the ceiling. That would be a "serious bummer".

As a result, Marvin installed a lighting system. He flips the light switch. Two fluorescent bulbs up front flicker and come on lethargically, the other two in the back continue to wink at Marvin incessantly.

Sighing, Marvin checks a tall corrugated cardboard box in the corner next to the door for replacement bulbs. Empty.

Why do they always go out at the same time?

He'll pick some up later. He's been so distracted lately planning his new life that small details have been eluding him. Two years in the making, everything is coming together. He's flipped calendar pages and slashed days as they passed.

The one saving grace is that his mother has no idea what he's been up to. If she had any social life at all, if she had any friends to talk to, she might have overheard something.

Something about his dealings with the local real estate agent and preparations for his driving test. Something about the business license in the works, the new place he plans to live.

But he can't worry about what she knows or doesn't know. He has to remain focused, this is a delicate time, so many balls to keep in the air. Balls in the air, HA!

The memory of the juggler on Johnny Carson last week leaps to mind. An enraptured Marvin was frozen with anxiety as the man juggled a dozen balls before moving on to bowling balls, chainsaws and axes. Marvin sympathized. That's what he is engaged in these days, juggling axes. With one hand. Blindfolded. Standing on one foot. With his mother at the ready to push him over.

The comical image leads him to glance at his other ax, this one with a red stripe on the handle, hanging inside the door on pegs. The black one is his favorite, it holds an edge better than the red one ever has. But he keeps the red one because you never know when you'll need an extra ax. It's best to always be prepared.

Marvin lives by the famous Boy Scout maxim, even though he was not permitted to join the local troop by his snoot of a mother.

They let just about any picaroon into those groups, darling.

Young Marvin had no idea what a "picaroon" was, much of his mother's archaic language eluded him, but he was certain he did not wish to associate with or, worse yet, be considered one.

KNOCK, KNOCK, KNOCK.

These sounds shift Marvin back to the present moment. They come from his homemade steamer. Used to bend and shape wood, the six foot long converted metal wash tub has an airtight lid. A water tank heated by propane is attached and the misty dial hovers around 350 °.

Marvin turns the tank off, the *THRUMP* sound broadcasting to him that the flame has been extinguished. The knocking slows as the system shuts down.

This is his pride and joy, he spent months designing and constructing the steamer. When he first turned it on he was distressed to hear the constant knocking sound. It felt imperfect somehow, less than. But Miss Jezzy set him straight.

"Oh honey, stop takin' on, it's just talkin' to you."

He smiles at the memory as he sharpens the ax on the grinding jig. When he's happy with it, he walks back towards the steamer. Focused on the ax, he trips over the large floor fan that he uses to clear out sawdust. Sighing, he rights it, sets the ax down and puts a heavy work glove on his right hand.

Using the gloved hand, he opens the steamer and leaps back to allow the scorching, humid cloud to escape. When it's clear, he glances at the curved wood inside. Happy with it, he smiles and leaves the lid open to cool. Grabbing the sharpened ax, he heads to the door prepared to leave but something stops him.

It's missing.

A solitary nail sticks out next to the red handled ax pegs. Marvin searches for the item that should be hanging there. There it is! Must have fallen off. He picks up the plague doctor mask, stares into its face, smiles at it and shakes his head.

Her voice, a memory "Don't open -"

4
1962

"-Your eyes yet.

"I won't!"

Twelve year-old Marvin sits on Theodore the dog's future napping place wearing a blue pointed party hat with an elastic strap under his chin.

Helium balloons in every color float untethered about the living room. All alone he waits, eyes closed. He hears shuffling sounds from the next room.

Annette swoops in, wearing a bright red dress with black polka dots (since the Kennedy brothers are still alive) her heels clacking on the wood floor, taffeta rustling. She plops on the couch next to him, placing a package in his lap. Blue paper covered with stars topped with an oversized red ribbon.

Marvin opens his eyes and rips into it.

Annette proudly exclaims, "Happy twelfth birthday!"

Marvin opens the box and immediately looks confused. He's a little bit frightened as well.

What is this?

He lifts a plague doctor mask out of the tissue paper lined box. Annette, downcast at his reaction. She was prepared for exclamations of joy and gratitude. She had thought long and hard about this gift.

"You said you needed a mask for dust or something. For your workshop. Isn't this what you meant? Is this alright?"

Marvin beams a great smile, his face lighting up as he puts it on.

He replies in a muffled voice, "It's perfect! This is the best birthday ever! Thank you, Mama!"

Annette smiles and claps as he hugs her, crushing the mask against her shoulder.

5

Marvin hangs the plague doctor mask up carefully, resting his hand on it for a moment, reliving the good memory.

He heads out of the workshop, pulling the doors closed behind him.

Swinging the ax around with his right hand, Marvin picks up a small pumpkin from a pile next to the chopping block. He uses these pumpkins to test the blade and his flexibility.

He tosses the pumpkin straight up into the clear air.

SWISH!

He slices it cleanly in half with one hand as it drops back down. He's slender but strong. Much stronger than he appears. Driving the ax deep into the chopping block one-handed, he heads up the driveway.

His usual group of deer have gathered in the pumpkin patch again. He considers them "his". He is accustomed to them and they to him. And it's hunting season, they know they are safe here.

They can have a few pumpkins, but I'll have to chase them off if they get greedy. We need the money.

Marvin and the deer look at each other, he nods and salutes. The deer watch him walk past, mouths gnashing the pumpkin vines.

A car horn scatters them.

Guess they won't have a chance to be greedy today.

Marvin hurries to meet the white V.W. Bug pulling up at the end of the driveway. He knows Carey will stay on the street, not wishing to get any closer to Annette and the house than he has to.

Carey waves enthusiastically at Marvin through the open passenger window. Warm for October, he has all of the windows open.

Leaping into the passenger seat, Marvin greets his oldest friend with an exuberant wave.

Eighteen year-old Carey smiles, perfect white teeth gleaming against his brown skin. His smile reaches his sepia, soulful eyes.

Those eyes quickly turn dubious, "Your mother know where you're goin'?"

Marvin just stares at him, smiling, but Carey is unconvinced, "Well, you need your birth certificate. You know that, don't ya, dopey?"

Marvin waves his hands in front of him like a magician preparing for a trick. As Carey prepares to speak, Marvin holds up a finger to silence the grinning boy.

Leaning up a bit in his seat he waves his hands as if conjuring a spirit while widening his eyes comically. He reaches behind him and pulls out a manila envelope that was tucked into his jeans, hidden by his t-shirt.

"Ta da!"

Laughing, Carey reaches behind his seat to the floor and produces a small box with a crumpled red bow on it.

"Ta da yourself. Happy birthday."

Marvin feigns dramatic crying and appreciation as Carey punches him in the arm.

Opening the box, Marvin's eyes widen, "Is this-?"

He holds up a small gold angel suspended on a chain.

Carey interrupts him, "Michael. The protector. Also, the divine judge of humanity. You'd know that if you went to church."

Marvin shoots him some side-eye, "Do you really think your grandmother didn't teach me everything about the Bible? I'd like to have gone with you but-"

"Your mother would spit nails if you went to a colored church."

Marvin puts the necklace on and pulls the rearview mirror his way to admire it, "Doesn't matter anymore. I can do as I please now."

Carey watches Marvin regard the necklace then slowly begin to turn the mirror back to its proper place. He stops and glances at his reflection one more time. Too long this time, like he's searching for something.

Marvin has always had an odd fascination with mirrors. Carey has caught him staring into them over the years, for as long as he can remember.

Not admiring himself, Marvin doesn't have an ego, particularly for such a goodlooking boy. It's as if he's looking into another world, seeing something that no one else sees. A hypnotic stare.

But this time is different.

Carey's concern rises as Marvin's eyes darken and his expression changes to one that Carey isn't familiar with. And Carey knows every possible expression that Marvin's face could possibly wear. They have known each other since they were babies.

He can't decide what emotions he's seeing. It's not Marvin at all. It's as if someone else is wearing Marvin's face. Carey has seen the changes that come over Marvin when he's angry, his eyes turn more gray than green but this-

Carey stops himself from this silly cogitation. Smiling, he remembers what his Grams would say, "Your crazy train done jumped the tracks."

Marvin is just distracted, but that's understandable. Lots of changes coming his way.

Carey clears his throat and Marvin snaps back to the moment, eyes bright green again.

Marvin declares, "And I'm protected. Thank you."

Almost as if no time had passed since he put the necklace on.

Carey nods slowly. Marvin doesn't realize what just happened. Carey debates whether or not to ask Marvin if he's OK but the enormous grin on Marvin's face puts his mind at ease.

Get that crazy train back on the track, Carey.

He pulls the mirror back to its original place and turns the radio on. The boys speed off, kicking up dust and singing loud out of the open windows.

Annette looms on the front porch, having watched the entire scene. Although the driveway winds through some trees, there is a small window of visibility if she stands on the far left side of the covered porch. She discovered this years ago.

It's important to keep an eye on your child, isn't it?

She takes a huge drag on her cigarette, turns slowly and enters the house.

6

Chortling to the point of being out of breath, Marvin and Carey barge into the department of motor vehicles.

They are both doubled over clutching their middles until they are immediately quieted by the annoyed glances of the few patrons in the waiting room.

The boys settle down into hard, blue plastic chairs that seem designed specifically for discomfort. They've had to travel two towns over, this being the closest office to their small borough.

As a result, there are no familiar faces in the room.

The workaday room is painted the most unattractive shade of gray humanly possible. The color of prisons and asylums. The people waiting and the employees also appear gray and colorless, seeming to move in slow motion.

The boys feel like Dorothy after she'd gone from vibrant Oz back to the somber palette of Kansas. Annette would refer to places like this as "the doldrums".

Looking around, desperate for something to amuse him to break up the interminable wait, Carey sees something on the wall behind them and nearly bursts out laughing again. Holding his hand over his mouth, he stifles the giggles. Marvin looks at him like he's crazy. Carey points behind him and Marvin turns to look.

An old black and white poster shows the interior of a car, the camera shot from outside the front windshield looking in. Little Marvin is seated in the center of the backseat with his "Mom" and "Dad" in the front seat.

Right out of central casting, the mother is blonde and gorgeous, the father handsome and distinguished. "Dad" drives but glances at Marvin in the rearview mirror. "Mom" looks somewhat concerned about the speed with which "Dad" is rocketing down the highway, her lips pursed and her eyes laser focused on the road.

Marvin's little eyes are wide as an owl's and his mouth is forming a perfect O. The dots on his face are dull gray (like the rest of the room).

The phrase *"Slow Down, Dad!"* is stretched across the bottom of the poster. Marvin rolls his eyes at his distressed young face.

As an elderly woman shuffles away from window number two, the clerk motions to the boys. Marvin leaps up and is at the window in two long strides, looking back over his shoulder at the female fossil who has just renewed her driver's license.

She can barely make her way out the door that chivalrous Carey holds open for her. She pats Carey's arm on the way out, grateful.

His mother's warning echoes in his head, *Those streets are not safe.* She *may* have a point.

Marvin absorbs the vision before him. The clerk sports "Betty" on her name tag. Either sixty and looking about her age or forty and having been bashed around by life, she has a platinum blonde beehive hairstyle that rises to meet the heavens. Her makeup skills could best be described as liberal.

His mother doesn't wear this much makeup in a year. Marvin is mesmerized by the pink lipstick surrounded by smokers' wrinkles. This is not a color of pink that is found anywhere in nature. He files the color away in his carpenter's memory.

He's been commissioned to create a toy box for an angelic little girl one town over. This might be the perfect color.

"Help you?" sounds more like a gravelly threat than an entreaty to provide a service.

Marvin focuses on the task at hand as she takes a drag on her cigarette and chews gum at the same time. He tries to hide his disgust at this nauseating combo as he produces the envelope containing his birth certificate and an application form that he had previously filled out.

Betty the pink-lipped wonder (Or salmon? Coral?) finds a third document in the envelope and looks at it with knitted brows.

Marvin takes it from her gently and puts it back in the envelope, "Sorry. That's something else I have to take care of later. It shouldn't have been in there."

Betty has been around the block more than a few times. She's dealt with her share of raucous, rude and frankly disgusting teenagers. This polite boy is a welcome reprieve.

Finally smiling at him, Betty looks past Marvin to the poster on the back wall. She squints for a moment, then looks back at

Marvin. To the poster, back to Marvin, three times.

This isn't unusual for Marvin but it happens less and less as the years pass. And it doesn't bother him at all.

He's very proud of his past as Baby Marvin and well aware of the privilege that was bestowed on him at such a young age.

During his year as Baby Marvin he constantly peppered his mother Annette with questions.

Do you think people will drive safer now, Mommy? Am I saving lives? Are you proud of me?

His tiny enthusiastic inquiries were always met with the same expression. Head tilt. Pursed lips. Tut tut.

It's just a job, Darling. You're an actor, don't take it so seriously.

Betty notices Marvin's name on the documents for the first time. Marvin breaks into a huge smile, then opens his eyes wide and forms the O with his mouth.

"Slow down, Dad!"

Nodding, she numbly hands him his documents again and points back to the waiting area. Turning away from the counter, he encounters his young face again.

Looking around at the gray box of a room, he is reminded of another-

7
1954

-Bare-bones room on the tenth floor of a skyscraper in New York City.

The space is filled to the brim with people.

A dozen mothers fuss over their young children. The sixteen children range in age from three to six and most are dressed in their finest Sunday garb. Crinoline underskirts and bowties abound. One group of three toe-headed brothers is dressed in matching bib overalls with red t-shirts.

Several of the children play on the floor in spite of their finery. The mothers watch them like hawks, swooping in to adjust a bow or strap, give a spit wash, or comb hair that will be sticking up again within moments of the women returning to their seats.

A ten by two foot professionally made banner on the wall is much too large for the small room.

"SAFE DRIVING DAY AUDITIONS. WORK WITH PRESIDENT EISENHOWER TO SAVE LIVES. THE COUNTRY NEEDS YOU"

Beneath the banner, a beleaguered young woman with a cigarette balanced on her bottom lip shuffles papers and children's photos at a cheap, fold-up card table.

A handwritten sign taped to the front announces: "REGISTRATION, please have headshots ready!"

Annette bursts into the room dragging four year-old Marvin behind her.

As an adult, she obviously outpaces him. But she's also tall, five foot ten in heels, so her pace has always bedeviled poor little Marvin. He spends an inordinate amount of time hustling his tiny legs, trying to keep up with her.

Annette's bright green couture dress hugs her figure perfectly, highlighting her eyes. She stands out among the other mothers, looking like a movie star with a rented child.

Accustomed to being the most beautiful woman in every room

she enters, she removes her over-sized sunglasses and floral head scarf with great flair as though playing for a camera.

Glancing around the room, she is astonished to see a lack of recognition in the eyes of these dullards.

How dare they not recognize me! I've been in several major motion pictures. For Heaven's sake, I was in HARVEY with Jimmy Stewart!

Marvin wears crisply starched gray shorts and a white button up shirt with dark gray suspenders. He marvels at the group of children and the wonderful noises that they create.

He never gets to spend time with other children, only Carey.

Eyes moving around the room, he notices a boy standing in the corner, apart from the other children, with his hands in his pockets.

The boy looks at him with a hint of a smile. Looking at the boy, really seeing him clearly, Marvin is overwhelmed

"Mommy, that boy-"

Annette shushes him and directs him to a pair of chairs near the other mothers (but not too near, she's not here to engage in meaningless blather).

The women glance at Annette and feign warm smiles but have no interest in her. She's never gotten along with other women, she assumes they are all jealous of her. Some are, she is a striking woman, but most just sense an unhappy narcissist and want nothing to do with her.

The genial children notice Marvin and wave. A five year-old Asian boy wearing a newsboy cap gleefully approaches, much to Marvin's delight.

Annette recoils as if a rabid coyote with snarling teeth was bearing down on them. Marvin starts to go with the boy, excited, but Annette stops him, shooing the disappointed Asian boy away.

She leans close to Marvin, "These aren't your friends, darling, they're the competition. You need to focus on besting them."

Glancing to the corner of the crowded room again, Marvin notices the boy that waved is gone.

Annette checks in with the clerk, handing her a black and white professional photo of Marvin. She regards the other photos that are scattered on the rickety table. Most are not terribly well thought out. Not even remotely flattering.

These people are clearly amateurs. Hopefully we'll have a leg up on them in that respect at least.

She parades back towards Marvin in a straight line, disturbing the various groups of children. Not one to have obstacles get in her way, she inadvertently knocks some blocks over and nearly steps on a coloring book.

Well, they shouldn't be making a mess in the first place, this is a place of business not a nursery school.

A dowdy, pan-faced mother scoops up a tearful little red-headed girl with freckles and faces Annette as she sits down.

"Do you mind?!"

Annette, cold as ice, "Actually I do."

The perturbed mother comforts her daughter and sets her off to play with another child. She looks with pity at Marvin.

Scanning the room, Annette takes in the competition.

The red-head will be puffy-faced now due to that crying jag, she's out. The fat one won't be a problem, they can hardly use him as a spokesperson but that blonde girl could be trouble for us. Also, that swarthy boy is handsome, but surely they won't take one of-them. It's America after all. Same for the Asian. But still-

Annette is worried for the first time since she meticulously put Marvin together this morning, taming his thick, wavy hair and selecting the perfect outfit. Not too dressy but certainly not the run-of-the-mill garments that some of the other urchins are wearing.

He needs something else. Something-

She is astonished at her insecurity. Imagine being concerned in this room full of country bumpkins and rabble. He's the best looking child here, by far. But she just doesn't know what they're looking for.

Then, an idea. The idea that would change everything. The idea that would charm the President and the entire nation. And she, as Marvin's mother, would ascend to heights never before dreamt of. Grabbing Marvin, she hustles him into the restroom right off the main room.

The restroom has a built-in sink with an adequate sized counter so Annette picks Marvin up and sets him on it. She then proceeds to dump her purse out into the sink.

It must be in here somewhere! Oh, where is it?!

A satisfied grin spreads over her face when she finds her prize.

Encased in an ornate gold case the name is in raised scripted lettering on the side of the tube. REVENGE RED.

She removes the top from the lipstick, stares at it, then at her bewildered son, "This is what success looks like."

She hears the clerk from the other room, "Marvin! Marvin Damon!"

Five casting directors wait in the cramped, secondary audition room. A long wooden table has them all on one side, awaiting the next national treasure to walk through the door. So far - bupkis.

It's been a long day and they have nothing to show for it except for a couple of headaches and one fairly bad case of indigestion.

The three men and two women have nearly lost hope that anyone worthwhile will come through that door.

One man stares out the window, *Would it kill me to jump from this height?*

Another gulps his fourth cup of coffee, *Or is it my fifth, who the fuck cares?*.

The two women huddle together over the latest issue of LIFE magazine with Grace Kelly on the cover. The third man has his head down on the table, banging it repeatedly.

"There's no amount of money worth this," he mumbles into his folded arms.

"Some of them cry, some huddle against their mothers. And how 'bout that kid that wet himself. That was the highlight."

They come to attention as they hear the clerk call out for a child named Marvin Damon. The clerk comes in alone and hands Marvin's headshot to the man on the end, then turns and leaves.

Good looking kid. At least this picture wasn't taken by Dad in the backyard. Why is the last name familiar?

They all take their seats and brace themselves. One man does the sign of the cross.

Marvin Damon enters the room well ahead of his mother, who closes the door behind her. The beleaguered row of people alternately gasp and smile.

Already a handsome child, the red dots on his cheeks and nose give him an elfin look. Adorable, like one of the munchkins from THE WIZARD OF OZ.

To top it all off, Marvin approaches each one of the delighted casting directors and offers his hand in a professional handshake as Annette looks on from her perch at the door like the cat who caught the canary.

If she knows anything, it's presentation.

Annette knows the handshake is just the icing on the cake. The deal was sealed the moment they saw that face. Her son's face. His face is going to be everywhere.

Marvin will be a household name. But not *just* Marvin. She needs to think of something more. A hook, if you will. Thinking back to her childhood in Vaudeville, she remembers the wide variety of names, some descriptive, some ironic.

Then it hits her, sending a shudder down her spine.

"Mr. President, I'd like to introduce you to my son, Baby Marvin."

8

Sixty year old Jezebel Franklin rocks contentedly on her front porch.

"Miss Jezzy" to anyone and everyone, she reaches down to scratch her leg, revealing her name clumsily carved on the back of the rocker. MISS JEZZY.

The name Jezzy was chosen by her at a young age out of necessity. Good Christian parents named her Jezebel because it was a Bible name. However, since they were mostly illiterate, they hadn't actually *read* the story.

"I got named after a nasty nocount who done got et by dogs." While bent over, she pats the head of her beloved bloodhound, Theodore, always at her side. Mostly blind and deaf, he wags his tail, still a happy dog.

Her small, craftsman house is tidy and well-kept. Isolated, at the end of a dirt road, it's situated in a clearing surrounded by forest. A recently harvested vegetable garden takes up one whole side of her one acre yard. Black-eyed Susans grow wild everywhere and sit in a vase next to Miss Jezzy's iced tea. Sweet tea, of course.

Her formative years were spent in Savannah, Georgia, as Jezzy Washington. She only moved north to Pennsylvania after marrying Theodore Franklin, a kind but weary man, twenty years her senior. Their union produced one daughter, Susan, named for her favorite flower.

The death of Susan's father during her childhood left a gaping chasm in both of their lives. Susan, unfortunately, filled it with the company of young men who had no interest in her heart or soul. Miss Jezzy chased more than one off with her favorite shotgun but in spite of her efforts, Susan became pregnant at fifteen.

Unwelcome at the local hospital back in 1950, Susan labored at the very house Miss Jezzy rocks in front of. Miss Jezzy and the grisled midwife fought hard, and the always thoughtful Dr. Reeve rushed to the scene but Susan was lost soon after the brown, fuzzy-headed bundle emerged. Miss Jezzy named the boy Carey and became his primary guardian.

Thick glasses hide the all-knowing, kind deep brown eyes that are beloved by this community. These eyes have known pain and loss but remain filled with joy and hope.

She is famous for saying, "*The past is the past, no damn sense worrying about it. We'll just keep on a-movin.*"

She knows she is part of God's plan and trusts in Him.

What Miss Jezzy lacks in eyesight, she makes up for in hearing. She stands as she hears a car approaching. Clasping her hands together in glee, she watches as her beloved boys pull into the driveway, scattering a few chickens.

Marvin drives the V.W. and honks the horn wildly.

"Now don't tell me that's my Marvin driving that car! I never seen such a thing!"

Marvin parks, rushes her on the porch, sweeping her five foot tall frame into a big hug. He pets the dog as Carey gets out of the car.

Marvin exclaims, "Finally! Now I can buy that pickup truck from Mr. Jacobson."

He walks over to her rocker and examines it with his usual critical eye, "I wish you'd let me make you a new rocker."

Miss Jezzy ambles over, quick and spry in spite of her age, swatting his arm and interrupting, "Don't you dare touch that chair! That was the first project you ever made in that wood shop of yours."

Shoving him aside, "Go on, get away from there."

Marvin shows her his two empty hands then waves them around and snaps the fingers on his right hand, pointing as the brand new driver's license appears in his left hand.

Miss Jezzy stares in amazement, "I can't believe that woman let you do this."

Marvin states proudly, "I found my birth certificate and did it myself."

Leaning close to her, "It's my eighteenth birthday, you know".

Scoffing loudly, Miss Jezzy waddles into the house, her yellow floral house dress disappearing into the rear of the house along with the wisping sound of her slippers on the old wooden floor.

Reminding Marvin as she always does, "You can go on and plant me when I quit knowing things."

As the two boys wait on the porch, Marvin gives Carey a quizzical look as if something is wrong then proceeds to pull a quarter out of his ear. Carey laughs and punches him in the arm as they loudly fight over the quarter.

Miss Jezzy's voice as she returns, "Don't be causing a commotion on my porch for the whole world to hear!"

Marvin and Carey look around at the remote location and giggle quietly.

She emerges from the house with a beautiful, handmade sweater that brings out Marvin's green eyes. Stunned at the exquisite gift, Marvin holds it up to himself.

He marvels, "Miss Jezzy, you didn't make this?"

Carey proudly chimes in, "Yes she did. Took her months and months with her eyesight being so bad."

Miss Jezzy turns to him, hands on hips, "Not a thing wrong with my eyes that these glasses don't cure."

Marvin grabs his stomach and doubles over in fake pain, "I'm starving, is there anything to eat. My mother tried to poison me with her yearly breakfast."

He collapses on the porch and plays dead. Theodore leans over and licks his face until Marvin pops up again.

"Lord a-mighty, get on in the house, we'll take care of you. I wouldn't let that woman cook for Theodore."

Looking down at the dog, "Would I?"

He woofs at her, thumping his tail on the weathered wooden boards of the porch. She motions to him and he gets up and heads inside the house behind her.

Miss Jezzy's small kitchen is covered in baskets of produce, cartons of eggs and dozens of jars of piccalilli. Her specialty, the piccalilli keeps "the lights on" as Marvin says. People come from miles away to buy a jar.

The option of shipping them has become a recent consideration but Miss Jezzy is hesitant, concerned about jars breaking and people ending up with a box soaked in vinegar.

She grabs the nearest jar and sets it aside, "You take this home with you."

Marvin snorts, "My mom hates that stuff".

Miss Jezzy snaps her gnarled fingers, remembering, "Oh, that's right!"

She grabs a second jar and puts it with the first one, a huge smile filling her face.

Marvin and Carey sit at the small table in the kitchen and pick up forks already laid out on red checked napkins.

They both bang the forks on the table and shout, "Food! Food! Food!"

Miss Jezzy turns, hands on ample hips, "They done away with slavery."

The laughing boys put their forks down as Miss Jezzy roots in the overflowing refrigerator and brings out a container of chicken salad. Carey hops up and grabs two plates and some fresh brown bread. Both boys create gargantuan sandwiches leaving Miss Jezzy shaking her head.

"I should have some girls up in here, they ain't gonna eat me outta house and home like you two do."

She hugs Marvin as he takes enormous bites of his sandwich, notices his angel necklace and pats it. Her emotions are getting the better of her for some reason unknown to him.

"You're a good boy, Marvin. It's time for you to be on your own now. Get away from that woman. She's a nasty piece of work, always has been. I know 'bout as well as anybody does."

Marvin has always known about the contentiousness between his mother and Miss Jezzy but this comment shocks even him, "Is this what being an adult is? Getting the unvarnished truth?"

"Sure is, and there's a whole lotta truth to be told," she retorts as she sits with the gobbling boys.

Carey inquires, "Can we cut up that pound cake, Grams?"

Miss Jezzy looks over her glasses at him, "We? You mean me? Yes, I'll cut it up."

She rises and heads to the corner of the kitchen, retrieving a round cake platter with a buttery yellow pound cake proudly perched on it. Setting it on the table, she goes to the knife block and removes an oversized butcher's knife and begins to slice the cake, gesturing to Carey.

"Last time I let you cut the cake it ended up all cattywampus."

Noticing the knife, Marvin quips, "Remind me never to make you mad."

She plops two jumbo pieces onto their plates and sits back down, chuckling, "You still gonna stay here til you find a place of your own?"

Marvin, excited, "Yes, unless you changed your mind."

"I may do that with all the food you're eating. Gonna have to get me a job to pay for it all at this rate."

"You know good and well I'll pay my way," he smirks.

"I know, I know, I'm just joshing you. What about your workshop though, hate for you to lose that."

"I found a great space downtown for a really good price and some folks to help me move everything. I do still plan to live out here somewhere, in the country. I'm not cut out to be a city boy."

"Outta kick that woman out and keep the house for yourself. You take care of everything anyhow. Let her get herself a job and live somewhere else."

Carey nearly snorts pound cake out of his nose, "I don't see Mrs. Damon doing anything other than acting."

Miss Jezzy scoffs, "Then she can go act on the street corner for nickels."

All three laugh as Marvin leaps up, plate in hand and heads to the sink.

He begins to wash it but Miss Jezzy stops him, "Leave it, I'll take care of it. You go on and get your truck."

Marvin slings his new sweater over his shoulder and grabs the two jars of piccalilli, on his way to the door.

Carey, "Want a ride?"

Marvin waves him off, "Nah, it's only about half a mile. And it's a nice day."

Miss Jezzy follows Marvin to the door. She shares her feelings more constructively.

"There's a lot of truth in this world for you to learn. My years in your house were a blessing, in spite of your mother. Taking care of you, watching you and Carey grow up together. I hated leaving you alone but I had no choice in the matter."

She takes his face in her hands. Both Marvin and Carey are

unsure why she's being so intense today.

She looks deep into Marvin's bright eyes, "You're a wise old soul, Marvin. That's why I talk to you real. Like a friend."

Carey never misses a chance to jab at his grandma, "Grams, you don't have any friends. You keep outliving all of them."

"It's not my fault they're too damn stupid to live longer. I don't need friends anyhow, I have the two of you. And Marvin, it's time I told you-"

Her words are cut off by the unmuffled sounds of a speeding car. As the road is largely untraveled, they are all curious and come to the door to look towards the dirt road. Skidding to a stop in front of the house, a puke green, dented 1960 Chevy Biscayne thrums and belches blue smoke.

John and Roger Carter, seventeen and sixteen, glare at Miss Jezzy and the boys. They sneer and drip with disdain. Rocking the greaser look, complete with leather jackets and ducktails, they are an unattractive combination of anger and dimwittedness.

Acne scars ravage both of their narrow, feral faces. Their rage is directed at Carey, who cowers behind the front door.

John snarling, "Hey, faggot!".

Younger brother Roger, not to be outdone, "Coon faggot!"

John turns his vitriol on Marvin, "Hey Baby Marvin! Clown boy! You a faggot too?!"

A sneer at Marvin's Monkees t-shirt, "Nice shirt, asshole."

Marvin's eyes darken to gray as he descends the front porch steps.

Everything moves in slow motion for Marvin. A loud pulsing heartbeat swims in his ears as he looks down and sees his feet moving along at a snail's pace. Lullaby music, distorted into an eerie out of tune dirge, assaults him. A baby crying but immediately cut off. These strange sounds drown out the boys in the car.

Suddenly dizzy, a voice whispers in his ear, "Do it".

Marvin sees one of the jars of piccalilli he held rocket towards the car through the open driver's side window, shattering on the dashboard.

Shards of glass and the vinegar-soaked concoction spray everywhere. John clutches his eye, fury filling his face. Both brothers yowl in pain. Marvin smiles, the remaining jar tossed up and down in his left hand, casually.

Hand over his bleeding eye, John screams a warning at them, "You're dead, clown boy! You all are!"

Miss Jezzy grabs the second jar from Marvin's left hand, "Careful, we got another jar right here! Or should I get my shotgun?!"

She motions as though she's going to throw it. The boys speed off, spraying gravel and leaving a cloud of dust.

Miss Jezzy gives the jar back to Marvin and shifts her focus to teary-eyed Carey; she knows how those comments hurt him. She realized he was different a few years ago. It's not what she would have chosen for him but it wasn't up to her.

She loves him unconditionally and he's a precious child of God. Unlike those - well, they're children of God too. But way lower down the totem pole in her opinion.

Carey stands quietly, as always. He's been taunted by John and Roger since he was a small child. Never one to fight back, he has internalized the feelings of anger as a way to cope.

He remembers his rearing as a Christian, a living, breathing example of Christ's teachings. Forgiveness above all. But still - he wishes he had Marvin's strength and size.

Marvin has always been Carey's hero. A brother, a best friend. He spent several months wondering if his feelings for Marvin were more than that, but he disabused himself of that notion long ago.

Even if Marvin suffered from the same "problem" as he does, it wouldn't change things. They've never discussed the issue. Carey was initially afraid to share his confusion with Marvin.

But he suspects that Marvin knows. Marvin's mother certainly knows, she's always been ready with a pointed jab or muted utterance over her shoulder as she leaves the room.

His grandmother knew before he did.

She's always had great intuition. He knows she loves him regardless but he also knows that she had hoped for a normal life for him. She's taught him everything he knows and he'll make her proud someday, career-wise, if nothing else.

He's going to be a lawyer. And he'll take care of his grandmother in the style she deserves. He stares at the dust cloud that settles in the road.

Big-hearted in spite of everything, Carey comments, "Maybe if they'd had a mom, things would be different."

Miss Jezzy shuts him down, "Nonsense! You never had a mama and look at you! Marvin's mama is slick baggage. Look at him! And my mama didn't even have time to do nothing for me, since she worked her hands to the bone. Don't be talking to me about mamas. Having or not having a mama don't make nobody a decent person."

Marvin sighs and shakes his head, "Their mom didn't die all that time ago, you know?"

Carey and Miss Jezzy stare dumbfounded at this, knowing that Mrs. Carter had indeed succumbed to cancer fifteen years ago. She left her sons in the care of a man who preferred alcohol and gambling over all else, except beating on her from time to time.

Jezzy had known Ernestine Carter, found her to be a kind woman with a good heart. Her efforts to help with the two dark haired little boys after their mother's death were rebuffed by a profanity-laced rant from their father that nearly knocked her over. Prayer for the boys had continued over the years but to no avail. They were ruined.

Marvin continues, noticing their confusion at his remark, "She took one look at their faces and ran off. Been hiding ever since."

They all laugh, Marvin having lightened the mood.

Jezzy chuckles but regret gnaws at her.

More prayers incoming, Lord.

Then anger at the sight of her grandson's soulful face, "Those two better hide cuz if they show up around here again, they're gonna get an ass full of buckshot."

Marvin puts his hand on her shoulder, "Don't do that Miss Jezzy. The Sheriff is a decent man but still."

She finishes his thought, "He'll haul me off."

"Something like that. Even in 1968".

Carey slumps down on the stoop dejectedly, "This is my fault. They're after me."

Miss Jezzy pulls him to his feet again and hugs him adoringly.

Taking his face in her hands, "Well now, which is it? They had no mom, you're different or it's Tuesday? Lord almighty Moses. If it wasn't you, they'd go on terrorizing somebody else. You're just an easy target."

Carey smiles and hugs his grandmother as all three ponder what just happened even though it feels like a million years ago.

Carey finally sighs, "Perhaps they're coming to grips with their own latent homosexuality."

Marvin explodes into guffaws as Miss Jezzy shoves Carey back into the house.

"Go get started peeling those potatoes! No more of them books!"

She turns a rueful eye towards Marvin, "Trying to explain everything. Honest to goodness. Damn nonsense. Evil is evil."

Marvin nods and grins slightly, "There's good and evil in all of us, Miss Jezzy. Both just need a reason to come out."

Miss Jezzy, hands on hips, stares him down, "Not at my house."

Marvin kisses her cheek, takes the jar back from her and heads off down the steps with his new sweater slung over his shoulder.

Waving to her over his shoulder, "You go rest before you have a heart attack or something."

Miss Jezzy scoffs as she scoots into the house, "Piffle, Imma outlive all of ya".

The screen door bangs shut behind her like a gunshot.

9

Smiling broadly next to his new truck, Marvin waves to Mr. Jacobson as the elderly man limps towards his house with the help of a cane.

He slowly makes his way up the steps as Marvin observes, concerned, "Need a hand, Sir?"

Mr. Jacobson turns and shakes his finger at Marvin with a sly smile on his face, "Stormed Normandy back in the day, should be OK with these here steps".

Marvin shrugs and nods as Mr. Jacobson chuckles, "Thank you though, Son, you take care. And watch that accelerator, she's got a load-a giddy up".

"I will. Thank you. I wish you'd let me build you a rail to help you up those steps."

Mr. Jacobson turns, mildly annoyed at the reminder of his condition, until he sees the half smile on the boy.

Pondering, he finally states, "That'll do just fine. Thank you, Marvin."

Marvin replies, "I'll be by next week," before the old man slips through his front door.

Marvin slides his hand along the bright red hood of the Chevy C10 pickup truck. Mr. Jacobson took good care of it, it gleams in the autumn sun. Marvin processes what this purchase means for him.

One step closer.

Hopping inside, he takes in the clean smell, a combination of Lysol cleaning products and Mr. Jacobson's Old Spice after shave. He adjusts the side mirrors and finally grabs the rearview mirror, adjusting it.

Marvin rears back in his seat, heart pounding out of his chest; the reflection staring back at him is not his own face. It looks just like him but the reflection has a slight smile. Terrified Marvin knows good and well that he's not smiling right now.

The image fades back into his own wide-eyed likeness as he hears a voice.

His voice, "You did good, Marvin."

The same voice that encouraged him to throw the piccalilli jar.

Marvin's head is on a swivel, looking out the window, into the back seat, under the front seat.

Searching for the source of the voice, he finds nothing. And he smells something new, underneath the cleaner and Mr. Jacobson's aftershave. Something familiar.

Musky. Spicy. Vanilla. What is it? Different after shave? I know that smell.

Marvin shakes his head and closes his eyes briefly as dizziness overtakes him again. He opens his eyes, everything is fine.

The mirror image is normal and the strange smell is gone.

Marvin unconsciously touches his angel necklace, taking a deep breath.

10

Annette flounces down the sidewalk past the classical revival style homes that line Main Street.

Still dressed for a funeral, she's added black gloves and a handbag to finish the look.

Formerly the residences of the wealthy, most of the homes have been converted into business fronts. A lawyer, dentist, real estate office.

A homemade flyer nailed to a telephone post grabs Annette's attention:

FARM STAND TOMORROW! End of Maple Lane, All welcome!

Ugh, he's inviting anyone and everyone to come to my house. Who knows who might show up? I certainly don't care to associate with some of the people in this town. To think I have sunk to this low. To having Marvin, a former child star, purveying things to people at the end of my driveway. Selling fruits and vegetables like a disgusting migrant farm worker.

Furious, she rips the flyer down, crumples it and throws it on the sidewalk. A woman and her young son pass her carefully, the mother holding tight to her boy, not wishing to upset the poor unhinged widow.

The tan home that Annette approaches has a small sign on the front door. DR. MICHAEL REEVE, M.D.

ANOTHER DAMN FLYER!

Ripping this one down as well, she steels herself before entering the front door. Shoulders back, she prepares to perform. She'll need Dr. Reeve's help later on, when it's time to enact her plan.

A deep breath later, she turns the knob and enters the empty waiting area. A glance at her watch gives her pause. She's late, it's time for his "rounds".

I'm sure he won't be happy.

He's one of the few people who actually intimidates her. She rushes towards his partly open office door so that he knows she did her best to be on time.

Dr. Reeve peruses patient charts at his massive oak desk. His mane of silver hair gives him an air of authority, a distinguished lion leading the pride of this small town. Hearing a rustling outside of his open office door, he leans back in his chair, preparing for what is likely to be an unpleasant encounter. He truly loves and cares for all of his patients.

He considers them family. He's been invited into more homes than he can count and he and his wife have reciprocated as well. He's had most of his patients over for dinner.

With one exception.

Already annoyed at her impending arrival, seeing Annette sweep in with her usual grandeur pushes him over the edge. He glowers at her, then leans forward to look through a patient chart without speaking to her. She stands erect waiting for attention. Their usual power play.

Dr. Reeve, gruff, "You're ten minutes late."

Still standing, she exudes shock, "Am I?"

Not looking up at her, "You're not my only patient, Annette. I have people to visit and you've set my schedule back. Next time, I'll leave your prescription out on the sidewalk."

Annette, flustered at how this situation is proceeding, plops down in a chair. She really hadn't intended to be late, but it was unavoidable.

She prepares herself to gain some sympathy, an ally. Staring at the top of his head, she calculates.

"I'm so sorry Dr. Reeve. It's just that - well, oh - never mind."

Unmoved by her display and losing what little patience he has left, Dr. Reeve states very clearly, "Coy doesn't work on me. What is it? Are you still feigning grief over Bobby Kennedy?"

Truly taken aback, her first genuine reaction, "Well! I - what a thing to say! He was practically family."

"Your mother worked for them when you were a child after she quit vaudeville. You've put on airs ever since. Enough is enough."

He slams a chart down to emphasize his point as she dabs her eyes with the handkerchief she always has at the ready.

Doc Holliday couldn't draw a pistol faster than Annette Damon whips out a handkerchief.

"Well, as a matter of fact, that's not the issue at the moment."

Sniffle, dab.

"Well, what is it? Kindly get to the point, I'm busy."

His dark eyes bore into her.

Annette stands abruptly, smoothing her skirt and begins wandering through the room. She glances at Dr. Reeve's medical degrees and his personal family photos on the wall. A scowl, unseen by the doctor, at the image of his high and mighty wife.

She acts like the matriarch of this silly town. As if that's some sort of accomplishment. Of course, with a face like a horse, you have to get whatever attention you can.

A section of patient photos displays smiling, plump babies alongside cap and gown snapshots of the same babies years later. Marvin and Carey's graduation photos are the most recent additions to the collection.

Ignoring Carey, of course, she closely examines Marvin's photo. She has been cropped out of the photo! Marvin had been standing with his arm around her.

Well! I mean…

Setting aside her hurt pride, she proceeds, "I'm rattled. Marvin was not himself this morning. He was…horrendous."

That's a perfect word. An expensive education has its benefits.

Finally, Dr. Reeve offers his full attention, "Marvin? Marvin was horrendous?"

She nods as he looks back at the chart, "I sincerely doubt that."

This will be more difficult than I imagined.

Annette turns on a dime and sits back down, staring at the doctor the whole time, "I'm sure it's nothing. It's just…".

Pause for effect.

"It was just so bracing, the way he…loomed over me. His father used to do that. He's so much bigger and stronger than I am."

Dr. Reeve, still not looking up, sighs "Marvin wouldn't hurt a fly".

So much for all that money I paid to Lee Strasberg. Time to tell the truth, "Well, I beg your pardon, but he woke up this morning a different person. Turning 18 has him full of vinegar."

Dr. Reeve looks up, curious.

Might have to lead with the truth in the future.

He sets the chart down and folds his hands on the desk, "He's 18 today?"

She nods.

"It's time he was evaluated. He's old enough now to understand your condition and what it might mean for him".

Back to her carefully prepared script, she waves off his concern, "Oh, I'm sure he's fine."

"You just expressed concerns over his behavior. Is he fine or isn't he? Make up your mind."

Realizing his abruptness, he continues with more care, "Are there any symptoms?"

"I...I don't think so."

Dr. Reeve scrutinizes her, "Would he tell you if there were?"

"Well, I'm his mother!"

Pause for effect, "Although…"

Checking his watch, he realizes this conversation has gone on far too long.

Always a damn chess match with this woman, "Yes."

Annette leans forward, "He's been more withdrawn lately. I'm not sure why."

Dr. Reeve continues to stare at her, trying to discern if she's being completely honest with him. She stares right back. She knows exactly what she's doing.

Rising slowly, "May I have my prescription now, please? Since your schedule is so terribly full?"

Reaching into his desk drawer, he retrieves a pad, scribbles on it and hands it to her. When she grabs it, he holds onto it for a long moment disarming her.

"I want to talk to Marvin."

Annette snatches the paper and heads to the door. Hand on the doorknob, "I'll keep a close eye on him and let you know if I notice anything unusual. Perhaps today was just an anomaly."

She rushes out, heels clicking on the wood floor as Dr. Reeve stares after her.

He stands, stretches and pulls open the antique wood file cabinet in the corner of the room.

A quick glance at Marvin's graduation photo brings a smile to his face. He noticed how Annette stiffened when she saw she had been cut out.

He had no desire to see her face every day in his sanctuary. This place of healing, both for others and himself. He could have retired years ago but he is too dedicated to helping people.

And his wife made it clear that he would get under her feet if he was home too much.

Smiling again, he finds the two files he wants. He sits down with them.

MARVIN DAMON and *ANNETTE SINCLAIR DAMON*.

He picks up Marvin's file and thumbs through it.

11

Annette hurls herself out onto the stoop.

Slamming the door behind her, hurrying away from Dr. Reeve's office, she retrieves her sunglasses from her pearl-handled black handbag.

She takes a deep breath and calmly sashays down the steps and onto the sidewalk. A casually dressed man passes her and tips his hat politely.

She attempts a smile but he sees it as a sneer.

Seeing her destination, Annette jaywalks across the empty two-lane street.

Sheriff Steven McClane watches Annette commit the misdemeanor from his table at The Junction Diner. Having also seen the rude encounter with the hat-tipping man, he shakes his head as he gulps down the last bit of the blackberry pie in front of him.

Owner and proprietress, Marion, approaches his table with her arms folded.

He doesn't notice her at first, his attention focused on scraping up every last bit of Marion's renowned flaky crust while gazing out the window.

As her shadow falls on him, he finally looks up.

Marion's husky smoker's voice chastises him, "If you lick that plate, I'm gonna charge you double."

The forty four year-old Sheriff stands and smiles, displaying the dimples that make any woman with a heartbeat swoon.

But, at seventy, Marion is not most women. Not only is she old enough to be his mother but she's devoted to her husband and only has eyes for him.

The phrase *if only I had a daughter* leaps to mind every single time she encounters the six foot tall, blue eyed Sheriff.

He's what she and her friends used to refer to as the "cat's meow".

He leans down to kiss her cheek, "Can't charge me double, you don't charge me anything at all. Which I'd argue with you about but I know it's no use."

He reaches down to the empty plate and drags his finger across it, then pops it in his mouth to get one last morsel. He smacks his lips.

Marion reaches up to straighten the collar of his uniform shirt. The light blue, long sleeved shirt sports his gold badge and his nametag, along with a Pocono Township patch on the sleeve.

She teases, "You picked this color for your uniform just to bring out your eyes, didn't you Steven?"

That smile again, "Of course. Gotta charm the bad guys."

He pops his non-regulation Sheriff's Department cowboy hat on top of his wavy dark hair streaked with gray and strolls to the door.

He tips it at her as he pushes the door open and heads out onto the sidewalk.

Marion watches with disdain as he heads towards the pharmacy that Annette Damon just entered. She shakes her head, grimacing. Maybe it's just a coincidence? Of course it isn't.

His on and off fling with Annette years ago is the worst kept secret in the county.

She actually got down on her arthritic knees back when she found out about it and prayed that it wouldn't last. Thankfully her prayers were answered.

But Steven was hurt in the process. Used and tossed away, a sweet man like that. Typical of that woman.

She acts all highbrow but she's no better than anybody else. Worse in fact.

It's a shame because Marvin could have used a real daddy, such a treasure that boy is.

It does warm Marion's heart to know that Steven continues to look out for Marvin and to give him some attention. They have dinner together here in the diner frequently.

He's picked up a lot of Steven's habits over the years, which is a good thing. Annette, of course, wouldn't lower herself to step foot in the diner anymore which is fine and dandy with Marion.

She gave Annette a nice big piece of her mind back when the affair with Steven ended and was greeted with that smug head tilt and frigid smile.

Her only other waitress, Linda, steps up beside her. Both watch the Sheriff cross the street.

Linda leers, "He looks good walking away, don't he?"

Marion turns on the young girl, "Hush your mouth! He's too old for you. Go on and start the pot roast for dinner service."

Linda slumps away. Marion immediately regrets taking her aversion to Annette out on the girl.

She'll apologize as quick as a wink, set things right.

Marion picks up the dirty pie plate and finds a ten dollar bill folded up underneath it.

12

The bell over the pharmacy door jingles when Annette enters.

The pharmacist, Dr. Christopher looks up cheerfully from his perch in the back of the building.

"Hello, how are you?"

Annette simply raises her hand in a half-hearted gesture. Noticing an elderly lady slowly inching her way toward the counter with her cane, Annette picks up speed and sweeps in ahead of her, nearly colliding with her.

The woman harrumphs loudly.

Dr. Christopher, a slight frown on his lined face, looks over his glasses at her, "What can I do for you, Mrs. Damon?"

She holds out the prescription and he takes it from her, examining it and then his watch.

"Be about twenty minutes."

She wanders away down an aisle, keeping an eye on the pharmacist.

He always says it will be twenty minutes. Do they teach them that in school?

The elderly woman she cut off shoots her an icy glare as she makes her way out the door with her prescription bag, the bell jingling.

Annette turns away from her to peruse the magazine rack. Seeing a wood-working magazine, she picks it up. The bell over the door jingles again as Annette puts the magazine back in the wrong place as she speaks to herself.

"Not after the way you treated me this morning, thank you very much, Marvin."

A familiar lazy cackle immediately grabs her attention. Looking up, she watches Miss Jezzy warmly greet Dr. Christopher. Sneering and rolling her eyes, Annette turns her back on them and finds a Vogue magazine to thumb through.

"Guess they let anybody in here."

The low country voice that Annette abhors.

Annette turns with a plastic smile to face Miss Jezzy, "They certainly do. Why I remember the wonderful old days when it was whites only in here. But times do change, don't they, Jezebel?"

Miss Jezzy won't be baited, "That they do and usually for the better. Like Marvin, for instance, getting his license and buying a truck. Guess he'll be moving on soon. Who you gonna mooch off of then? Marion's hiring down at the diner. Even wash a dish?"

Annette seethes behind her phony smile, "Why no, I had a girl to do that for me. Until, I sadly had to let her go. She was stealing from me."

Miss Jezzy, stoic and calm, "I never took a thing from you. You wanted an excuse to get rid of me because I saw what a sorry excuse for a mother you were. And still are."

She gets very close to Annette and puts her finger in her face.

In spite of the height difference, Miss Jezzy has the upper hand, "Marvin will thrive on his own. He's a fine boy in spite of you. And he deserves to know the truth."

Annette spits with rage, "You will keep your good-for-nothing mouth shut or I'll have you run out of town! You and that abhorrent grandson of yours. Don't think I can't do it. There are people in power who will do anything I ask."

"Mrs. Damon," Dr. Christopher speaks sternly, "Your medicine is ready."

He holds up the prescription bag. Annette glares one last time at Jezzy and stomps off to the counter, grabs the bag and heads out.

"Marvin will be by to take care of the charges!"

She slams the door, the bell celebrating her exit, as Miss Jezzy shakes her head, "Mm, mm, mm."

13

Annette stands on the sidewalk in front of the pharmacy rooting around in her handbag.

Finding a cigarette, she puts it between her ruby lips and searches for her lighter.

CLICK, HISS.

She turns to the sound. Steven leans against the wall next to the door with his lighter extended towards her.

Caught off guard, she can't help but notice his devil-may-care attitude. As if he just happened to be inclined against this particular wall at this precise moment.

Butterflies fill her stomach, but then they always do when she sees him. It's been over a year.

And he's actually getting better looking with age, ugh!

Always weak for blue eyes and dark hair, Annette takes her cigarette out of her mouth and smiles disarmingly.

"You haven't smoked for years, why do you carry that?"

He lights the cigarette in her hand and stands tall in front of her, "Never know when you might need a lighter. Now, for instance. You find yourself fishing around in that purse of yours, which I happen to know is filled to the brim with junk, and some brigand shows up behind you. Said brigand snatches your purse because you're distracted and runs off with it."

She laughs at him, letting her guard down, "Brigand! Honestly, Steven, where did you come up with that word?"

"It sounded high class. I know how you like high class shit."

"Well you just ruined it with vulgarity but I appreciate the effort."

They stare at each other for an eternity until she snaps back to the here and now.

"Thank you for the light and for protecting me from the random highwayman who was likely lurking in wait for me."

She starts away and he gently grabs her arm, turning her towards him.

"Have dinner with me."

His face is open and earnest.

She struggles with herself, drowning in his blue eyes, wanting to accept the invitation but afraid of where it would lead.

The lightning strike of their first meeting had become a distant memory. After the Baby Marvin phenomenon had died down, she had considered the possibility of marrying again.

She was still young then and Marvin did need a father. And Steven saw something in her, something no one else saw. A kind, gentle, funny woman lurked beneath the brittle and angry surface.

She had learned in her teens to conceal that vulnerability. Toughness was the only way forward. Toughness kept her from shying away from auditions that she wasn't suited for.

Toughness kept her distant from the pain, the burns, the insults. As a result, she had no friends. It's always been safer that way.

Secretly, she thanked God that she hadn't given birth to a daughter, a daughter who would be used up and spat out by the myriad of men who would undoubtedly line up for the privilege.

Her mother hadn't been able to protect her and she was sure that she would have failed as well. But she had been blessed with a son. A son with no father.

Their affair had sated her but she had started to become dependent on him, not just for sex but for companionship. Steven McClane isn't the type of man to trifle with, he's a man to marry and build a life with.

He would have been a wonderful father to Marvin, he already is in most ways. But making it official? She would have been left out in favor of her son soon enough.

Her relationship with Marvin is, and always has been, her number one priority. Nothing can interfere. Not Steven, not anyone.

She can't let him in again.

She touches his arm affectionately, "I can't, Steven."

"Why not?"

"You know why. It's not just dinner. I can't get into a relationship right now."

"I know you care about me."

"Of course I do. It's just - I have to focus on Marvin right now."

Finally frustrated, he lashes out, "Marvin is grown now, Annette. Are you really planning to spend the rest of your life alone?"

She reaches up and kisses his cheek, heading off down the sidewalk.

"Yes I am."

Her hands tremble as she passes the bank, then the laundromat. He's not following her, she would sense it if he was. She's grateful, but also disappointed.

She could have made a life with him but she wouldn't allow it, she cut things off before that could happen. But it's still painful because this is the one time she has doubted herself, her decisions.

She hopes more than anything that he finds a woman who can love him in the way that he deserves. It will hurt like hell to see him with someone else but he deserves the best.

And she's not it.

14

Miss Jezzy leaves the pharmacy in a glorious mood, humming to herself.

She lives her life as an amiable, happy person, a good God-fearing woman but today she is over the moon.

Marvin is crossing the threshold of independence at long last, her precious Carey has decided on a career, and she got the opportunity to tell Annette exactly what she needed to hear.

And all in one day! The Lord is hard at work here in eastern Pennsylvania on this good day.

Her firing at Annette's hands wasn't a shock. She knew that Annette both hated and needed her. Incapable of caring for Marvin and taking care of the enormous house, she was dependent on Miss Jezzy.

She pawned Marvin off on her and barely contributed to his life at all. He was an ornament that she displayed to attract praise when she needed it. And, good God in Heaven, did she need it.

She hoped against hope that Annette would get over her negative feelings but her hopes were dashed on that fateful day eight years ago.

One day, in the midst of washing dishes, Annette had bustled into the kitchen and placed a check on the counter. Confused, Miss Jezzy had inquired with her eyes. Annette's reply had been terse and to the point.

"Your services are no longer required, Jezebel."

Hiding her devastation, she wiped her soapy hands on the yellow dish towel she had tucked into the waistband of her white apron. She picked up the check with a trembling hand.

In a rare display of altruism, Annette continued, "This needn't affect Carey's schooling. He can hardly start at the public school this late in the year. He's quite a sweet little thing and isn't any bother at all, I hardly know he's here. So, he's welcome to finish the school year with Mr. Gray."

This had always been Miss Jezzy's worst fear, that one of Annette's mood swings would affect her tender-hearted grandson.

Knowing that he could continue his education for the time being set her mind at ease.

He was a bright child, she had high hopes for his future. She'd frame her leaving and his move to public school in the fall as a mutual decision.

Annette agreed to this explanation. A few short years later, Annette's attitude would dramatically change when she suspected the truth about Carey.

Formerly tolerant and even occasionally kind to the boy, she became rude and belligerent. Thankfully, Carey was out of Mr. Gray's tutelage by this point.

Of course, he and Marvin still spent time together but they had become accustomed to being together all day every day.

One other positive aspect of her previous employment was that Annette paid well. Very well, in fact.

Jezzy put aside every nickel that she could to build a better life for herself and Carey. Raising him alone, without his mother was never something that Jezzy considered a burden.

He was a blessing, she bore him no ill will for his mother's death.

When a fellow parishioner mentioned to her that the baby would grow up knowing he'd killed his mother, Jezzy put that woman smack dab in her place with a stream of expletives that was still talked about to this day.

Jezzy dressed Edna down a peg or two.

Letting the pharmacy door fall closed behind her, Miss Jezzy sees Annette about a block up.

She's fixin' to jaywalk again. Be a shame if a car ran her over.

She immediately chastises herself for such an unChristian thought. But only a little bit. That woman would have tried the patience of Jesus Christ himself.

"I can practically hear you wishing a truck would mow her down."

The voice startles Miss Jezzy and she turns on a dime to find Steven still leaning against the pharmacy, arms crossed, right foot propped up on the wall. Her face lights up when she sees him. Hand to her throat, she bats her eyelashes and grins.

"No such a thing. And what the Sam Hill are you doing there?

Holdin' up that building? Why aren't you arresting that woman for crossing that way?"

"And do what with her? Send her to Alcatraz?"

Miss Jezzy sidles up to him and puts her finger in his face, "For starters. That woman is a menace. In every way."

"Why are you acting like a bear with a sore head today?"

"Anytime I have to deal with that woman, I get aggravated."

She crosses her arms and scowls at the slim ebony-clad figure disappearing around a corner. Once Annette is out of sight, she takes Steven's arm, yanking him off the wall.

"Come on now, quit lollygagging. Buy me a cup of coffee."

They sit in the very same booth Steven occupied barely half an hour ago. Marion set about fixing Miss Jezzy's chicken and waffles after remarking that Steven was back so soon.

"I'm not giving you another piece of pie, you'll end up with a pot belly, eating so much."

Miss Jezzy assures her, "Don't worry about him. He's got too big an ego to let himself go."

Steven rolls his eyes at the two hens, discussing him as if he's not sitting right there.

Marion heads off and Miss Jezzy pats Steven's arm, "You remember Marvin's birthday?"

"Of course I did. I sent him a card and a note. Told him I'd take him shooting and fishing. Maybe we'll shoot the fish. Who knows?"

"He's fixin' to move in with me until he gets settled someplace permanent."

"He told me. I'm just worried about -"

"If you say 'Annette', I'm fixin' to flip this table. The Lord Jesus got nuthin' on me."

"Sorry. Old habits."

"You know how many women would love to be your gal?"

"No."

"Plenty."

"Plenty's not a number. How many? Six? Thirty-seven?"

"Stop your joking. I'm serious. You need to find a nice gal and settle down and have some kids of your own."

"I've got Marvin and Carey, two fatherless urchins. I don't need kids of my own. I don't want little kids at this age anyway. And as for Ann -"

Miss Jezzy grabs the table with both hands, threatening. He reaches over and puts his hands over hers gently and gazes deep into her eyes.

"As for Annette, it's pretty much over. Has been for a while."

"Oh, dear Lord. 'Pretty much'. I will never understand as long as I live what you saw in that woman. Other than her looks."

"You don't know everything about her. She's got a good heart. But she keeps it hidden."

"Damn straight she does. Couldn't find it with a treasure map with a big ole X on it."

Marion brings the chicken and waffles and a decanter of syrup. She places the enormous plate in front of Miss Jezzy.

He jokes, "Thought I was only buying you a cup of coffee."

Miss Jezzy drizzles a substantial amount of syrup over the plate of food, "Didn't get to eat nothin' today. Those boys cleaned me out earlier."

She digs into her food. Steven reaches over to grab a piece and she slaps his hand.

"Get your own."

She smiles at him. Since his mother's death twenty years ago, she's been the one to advise, nurture and console him. His puppy dog expression melts her heart. She gestures at her plate and he rips a waffle in half, shoving it into his mouth.

He yells to Marion, mouth full, "Can I get another piece of pie?"

"NO!" comes the response from the kitchen.

He shakes his head at the situation, being at the mercy of these two women. Miss Jezzy chuckles.

"You get you a wife and we'll leave you alone."

His expression turns dour, but only briefly. Something outside the window needs his attention. He pretends to check his watch, stands and fishes his wallet out of his pocket.

He throws a five dollar bill on the table and kisses Miss Jezzy on the cheek. He's learned to keep people calm amidst a storm that's brewing near them.

And this situation is about to become a full-force hurricane.

"Carey coming to get you?"

He keeps his eyes focused on the street. Miss Jezzy can't see what he sees unless she cranes her head around and he prays that she doesn't. He desperately doesn't want her to see what will happen out there if he doesn't intervene.

"Yes, any minute now. You go on and keep the streets safe from trashy people jaywalking."

Still staring at the street with steely blue eyes, in full law enforcement mode, "I will."

Carey had pulled up and parked on the street in front of the bank almost ten minutes ago. This is where he always meets his grandmother when she runs errands. She used to walk the mile to town but her age has slowed her down a bit.

"Just a bit, though", she'd always say.

He had dropped her an hour ago and then spent his time waiting in the library. Although the library is small with a limited inventory, the librarian always keeps something on hand for Carey.

The seventy eight year-old former teacher loves nothing more than seeing young people devour books. She considers the advent of television years ago to be an abomination and refuses to have one in her small apartment over the library.

Carey has his nose buried in a book. *In Cold Blood* by Truman Capote. He alternates between modern fiction and law books. Engrossed in the story with his windows down, he doesn't notice John Carter swaggering towards him from the opposite side of the street.

Sporting an eye patch after an unpleasant visit to Dr. Reeve, John needs to let off some steam.

John and Roger's father had difficulty understanding the passage of time, among other things. His bourbon-soaked brain thought his grown sons had been beaten up by a four year-old child. Their explanation that Marvin was not only several inches taller than them at this point but that he had an arm like Fran Tarkenton fell on deaf ears.

So, a beating had ensued. For a man who was falling down drunk most of the time, he had one hell of a right hook. When he wasn't using his belt.

Dr. Reeve had fixed him up alright but he was not enthused to deal with yet another of John's injuries. He had interrogated him about it, peppering him with questions. Everyone knew that he and his brother were regular victims of their father's outrage.

John hated that.

Being looked at with equal parts derision and pity. Of course, he doesn't know what derision means. But he overheard the word once associated with him and his brother.

He can't believe his luck! That faggot is sitting right there across the street, reading some dumb book, thinking he's smarter than everybody else.

His father once said that it was a national tragedy that coloreds were allowed to learn to read. On this, he and the unfortunate man who spawned him agreed.

John had considered retribution against Marvin directly but feared that Marvin's snooty mother might still be fucking the Sheriff. He might even be at their house. He didn't wanna end up getting shot by that pompous ass in a cowboy hat.

Dealing with Carey would be so much sweeter anyway. He'd been itching to do it ever since his dad beat the shit outta him. Just a little beating for Carey, no big deal.

Queer coon needs to get used to it after all. Maybe he'll even run off when this is over. One less pervert in town. People around here will probably be grateful.

He crosses the street about fifty yards up from Carey and makes his way towards the car. He's unsteady. Half drunk and vision in only one eye.

But maybe that's for the best. He's moving more carefully than usual and this situation calls for nuance.

He actually knows what that word means, he heard it on the radio last week. Before his father threw a beer bottle at him for waking him out of his usual stupor.

He's gonna have to be careful though, he's out in public, can't do too much damage. But he'll get his point across. Starting with taking that book and using it to wipe his ass later. Maybe he'll make the faggot watch while he does it.

Suddenly he's grabbed by the back of his shirt and dragged into the alley between the bank and the shoe store. He's slammed into the wall of the bank, his head painfully striking the bricks, blurring his vision, increasing his panic.

Who the fuck?

"Whatcha doin', Johnny?"

The irate Sheriff snarls down from his position above him. Taller than John by four inches and about thirty pounds heavier, he knows he has the upper hand.

Not to mention the revolver strapped on his left side gives him authority.

"Nothing! Just walking! Is that a crime now!?"

Steven lets go of the boy, putting his hand on the red brick next to his head.

Looming over him, "Walking's not a crime, Johnny. But I know damn good and well you were headed over there to Carey to fix him up."

John stares at his shoes, mumbling, "Marvin fucked up my eye."

Steven jerks John's head up by his greasy black hair and stares at the eye patch, "You still got an eye under there?"

John nods and Steven continues, "Then shut the fuck up and go home!"

John regains some shred of dignity, "Ain't you gonna do anything about Marvin!? It's a crime to go throwin' shit at people, ain't it?!"

"Depends. What did you do to Marvin?"

"I didn't touch him."

Steven leans closer, a wolf about to strike a lamb, "Ah, but you did *something*, Johnny. I know you. And I know Marvin even better. He's not off throwing things at people who don't deserve it."

John mumbles, head down again, "Marvin ain't so perfect, you're just saying that because you're fucking his -"

Pushed over the edge, Steven grabs the boy's lapels and lifts him off the ground, "What did you say to me, you little shit?!"

"Nuthin'."

He puts John back down and backs away, calming himself down. He crosses his arms and looks heavenward, "You know, John, it really isn't a great idea to question my integrity, my professionalism.

If Marvin deserves it, I'll drag his ass to jail. Just like anybody else."

The skinny boy hangs his head, staring at his sneakers. They are worn, his right big toe threatening to poke through.

Steven's sympathy for the boy emerges after he takes a deep breath, "Look at me."

John looks up at him, wincing, expecting a beating. He always expects a beating. The Sheriff has never done more than drag him out of a fight or push him along to get him out of people's way.

Beatings are routine. Abused by his uncles, grandfather and mostly by his father, it's just a part of his life at this point.

Steven's adrenaline has subsided and he takes in the defeated boy in front of him.

"You don't have to go home. I can find you and Roger a place to stay. You just say the word."

John's expression morphs from wounded animal back to predator.

He spits on the ground and whispers, "Fuck you."

He leaves the alley and heads back the way he came, away from oblivious Carey.

Steven stares after him knowing that the storm isn't over.

15

The rising sun peeks through the woods across the street from Marvin's house.

It's less of a street and more of a dirt path.

A four by five foot hand-painted wooden sign is next to the road-

FARM STAND TODAY
hosted by Marvin and Carey!

Several years old, the letters are multi-colored and were painted by the much younger duo. Affection for the sign has kept them from updating it. And customers enjoy remarking on how much the boys have grown up.

The stand is a make-shift counter with half a dozen long weathered planks balanced on two sawhorses. Less fresh produce as the growing season winds down, but there are tomatoes, onions, potatoes and squash.

Bars of homemade soap in a pyramid on the corner of the stand. Dozens of fresh brown eggs are available, stacked on wooden crates next to ten jars labeled "Miss Jezzy's Piccalilli".

Marvin had begged Miss Jezzy to allow him to put her picture on the jars.

But she staunchly refused with her arms crossed, "Who am I? Aunt Jemima?"

As Marvin and Carey happily arrange the stand, Annette watches from the house, her perpetual frown firmly in place. She stares out the front window. Her view is obstructed by the hedge but she can see movement and knows what's going on.

Ugh, a farm stand, honestly, what a waste of his talent.

She sees Marvin rush toward the house, to the workshop, to grab a wheelbarrow. The smile on his face would warm the heart of most mothers.

But Annette isn't *most* mothers.

The idea of her son taking joy in such a trite task, like a common cottier causes her stomach to clench. What's next for him?

Marriage to some drab and filthy bare-footed children?

Marvin rolls the wheelbarrow down the driveway, stopping at the pumpkin patch. He loads it up, cutting the thick stems with a short, curved, razor sharp blade in a sheath attached to his belt.

As he returns to the stand, an old Cadillac pulls up nice and slow, keeping the dust to a minimum. Dr. Reeve steps out of the car, stretching his back. Carey waves at him as he finishes bagging up some eggs for a pretty, well-dressed young lady who ignores him.

The young lady only has eyes for Marvin and smiles at him beguilingly as he strides up with the wheelbarrow.

Carey, unfazed by her rudeness, "Thanks, Diane, you have a good day now."

She snatches the bag without making eye contact with Carey, swishing over to Marvin in her attractive brown knit set, long blonde hair pulled in a side ponytail, "Hi, Marvin."

Marvin lacks his best friend's patience, "Are you hard of hearing?"

Taken aback by the question, Diane stammers, "What do you mean?"

"Carey just spoke to you and you ignored him."

Waving Carey off like a mosquito, "He's only a worker. And I need to talk to you."

Marvin controls his anger with a slight grin that doesn't reach his graying eyes, "He's my partner and my best friend. And he's just provided you with a service. The proper response is, 'Thank you'."

Diane huffs, flirty mood gone.

Marvin puts his hand on her shoulder and leans down close to her face, "School's over now. You're not prom queen anymore. This is the real world. You have to treat people well if you want to get along."

Angry now, she glares up at him, "I get along just fine."

Releasing her shoulder, Marvin stands straight and folds his arms, "Not around here you don't. Don't come back here until you learn some basic manners."

Seething, she backs away, "I can't believe you'd defend that nig-"

Marvin is on her with lightning speed, hand gripping her chin, rough, "Say that word and you'll be sorry."

She sees the gray has clouded his eyes. A shiver passes through her.

Dr. Reeve approaches the young people. He's raised six children of his own and been caretaker for dozens more. Convincing preschoolers to take harsh tasting medicines, wrapping sprains amid screams and consoling hysterical mothers is part of the job. He knows how to handle difficulties like this one, to diffuse situations.

"Marvin, I could use your help over here."
Turning to the frightened young girl, "Diane, best get home now. Give your parents my very best please."

She hustles away towards her expensive sports car, tossing the bag of eggs at Carey. He catches them without breaking anything, which is a miracle in and of itself but Dr. Reeve isn't interested in Carey's quick reflexes.

He observes Marvin.

Marvin's eyes are flat, lifeless, gunmetal. He watches the rude girl speed off, turning his head in a robotic motion.

He's a different person.

Once Diane's car is out of sight, Marvin turns to Dr. Reeve. The sun glints off of his green eyes, he snaps back and becomes his normal friendly, animated self.

Does he realize what just happened?

"Sorry about that Dr. Reeve, thank you for the help."

Staring after the dust cloud that Diane has left in her wake, "My pleasure, Marvin. That girl is a spoiled little brat, always has been. You'd do well to stay away from people like that if you can."

Over his shoulder to Carey, smile broadening, "Carey, my boy, I'll take those eggs since they're available. And bag me up three jars of your grandma's piccalilli, if you please."

Focused on Marvin again, quieter, "Been a while since you had a checkup."

Marvin, slightly taken aback, "Well I appreciate your concern but I'm fine."

Something occurs to him, "Did my mother say something to you?"

Dr. Reeve waves off any concerns, "Only that you're 18 now. An adult. You can make your own decisions. Including when you want to see a doctor."

His smile is a little too forced. He realizes it but it's too late now. He's not handled this conversation the way he planned to.

Dr. Reeve is lying. But how do I know that?

Marvin replies, "Well, I'll come in if I feel bad, I promise."

Slapping Marvin's shoulder, Dr. Reeve walks over to a now-smiling Carey. Another car pulls up and a small boy leaps out of the passenger seat followed by his mother, desperately rushing to catch up to him.

Marvin brightens as the young boy leaps toward him, "Hello Bobby! Hi Mrs. Bonilla!"

The out of breath, young, caramel-skinned woman reaches Marvin.

Giving her son a chastising look, "Hello, Marvin. Carey. Doctor Reeve. Bobby said you have a present for him. Been talking my ear off."

Dr. Reeve surveys Marvin.

Carey notices, "Everything OK, Dr. Reeve?"

Dr. Reeve smiles, reaching for his wallet, "Of course, my boy."

He pays Carey, takes the bag and heads to his car.

Marvin swings Bobby around in circles, "A present? Did I say that?"

The joyful little boy squeals, "Yes you did, Mr. Marvin!"

Marvin walks slowly behind the stand, picks up something and hides it behind him as he walks back to Bobby, "Close your eyes."

The excited child closes his eyes, bouncing up and down. Marvin pulls a brand new ash baseball bat out from behind his back, "Ok, open your eyes."

Bobby, saucer-eyed, opens his mouth in an exuberant scream. He reaches for the bat, jumping up and down. Dr. Reeve scrutinizes from his car, ostensibly looking through a folder that he has with him.

Marvin gestures for Bobby to stop and leans down, looking him in the eye, "Now, hold on. I made this for you and I want you to be the best baseball player in the world. But, it's important to be careful with it. You can't go swinging it around without your mother's permission, you understand?"

Bobby nods enthusiastically as Marvin hands him the bat. The little boy is enraptured with it.

Marvin shakes his finger at the child, "Now if I hear that you're not treating this bat with respect, I'll come and take it back. Right, Mrs. Bonilla."

She replies, hand on one hip, "Oh absolutely. What do you say, Bobby?"

Bobby, dancing around, "Thank you, thank you, Mr. Marvin!"

Mrs. Bonilla grasps Marvin's arm and leans close, "I have to pay you something for that Marvin, the amount of work--"

Marvin waves off her concern, "I'd never have thought to use my lathe for bats if it hadn't been for Bobby. I was just making boring old chair and table legs."

Mrs. Bonilla, truly touched, "Well, you're too kind. Bobby, go on and pick out a pumpkin. Carey, please bag me up two dozen eggs."

Carey nods in the affirmative as Bobby pores over the bounty in the wheelbarrow.

Marvin stops him, sweeps him up onto his shoulders and heads into the pumpkin patch in the front yard, "Special customers get to pick one right out of the patch!"

Bobby yells, delighted.

Dr. Reeve smiles, seeing Marvin with the little boy. Maybe Annette wasn't creating drama when she mentioned her concerns.

Marvin had become another person when he confronted Diane. A mask had come off.

In all his years, he'd only seen one other person exhibit a dead-eyed expression like Marvin had.

Ed Gein.

16

Annette, perched on the sofa, the drink cart within easy reach, disguises her scotch with ice in a tall glass.

See sips her "iced tea" slowly, pacing herself.

Always calculating, always thinking ahead. It's what made her an exceptional actress, the ability to almost see the future, anticipating her partner's movements and line delivery. Her responses were always lightning quick and appropriate to the moment.

If only -

A glance at the *Harvey* poster, her big break, ruined by an unwanted pregnancy. She's done her best, learning to love Marvin. Everyone loves Marvin, a truly kind, wonderful boy. Because of her.

In spite of her?

If she's honest with herself, it's his relationship with Steven all these years that's helped him to grow into manhood. She owed Marvin that relationship. She owes him much more than he realizes.

As Annette reminisces, Marvin and Carey enter cautiously hoping she's upstairs. They manage to hide their disappointment at the sight of her on the couch.

Marvin grabs two glasses from the kitchen cabinet and fills them with water for him and Carey. Silence looms as Annette stares at the two boys, smiling like a shark.

Carey learned manners early in life, "Hello, Mrs. Damon, how are you?"

Annette pauses before answering, her phony smile frozen in place, "Fine as wine, Carey. And how's business today?"

"Very good day, Ma'am. Marvin's a natural with people, you should be very proud."

Annette seizes the opportunity to perform, leaping up, slightly unsteady, drink sloshing in her hand, "I couldn't be more thrilled, Carey. Honestly, to have my only child, the most talented and handsomest boy in the entire state of Pennsylvania, the son of not one but two movie stars, making a living selling pumpkins and soap. It's just simply more than I can fathom."

She gulps her drink and comes closer, making Carey nervous. Marvin tenses, at the ready. She's unpredictable when she drinks.

"Yes, Ma'am. I should go."

Carey turns toward the door.

Annette sets her glass down on the kitchen counter and takes Carey by the shoulders, feigning affection.

Her breath is sharp, medicinal, "But you already know he's a handsome boy, don't you, Carey? You've always known, hanging around here all these years. Watching. Hoping against hope."

Marvin remains calm, some pity for his mother in his eyes, "That's enough. Leave him alone."

Annette laughs and sits back down, "There's no future for you, Carey, not with you being - like you are. Not here. Maybe in New York City where they're more degenerate."

"Enough!"

Marvin pulls cash from his pocket and hands it to Carey, gently guiding him towards the back door.

"I'll see you later, take a pumpkin to Miss Jezzy and we'll carve it."

He smiles at his downtrodden friend and squeezes his shoulder. Carey skulks out, ashamed, defeated. Marvin turns on his mother, furious, eyes darkening.

Annette spreads her arms dramatically, spilling her drink, "How marvelous! A real family!"

Marvin seethes as Annette leans on the kitchen table, "That woman was always trying to take you away from me. All those years she worked here, plotting against me. That's why I finally fired her."

Marvin grabs her glass and pours it down the drain, "I thought she was a thief. Try to keep your story straight."

Leaning on the sink to gather his strength, Marvin turns around, calm, "Miss Jezzy is the best person I've ever known. And Carey is the brother I always wanted. Living in this large house, just you and me, it's been awful."

Taken aback briefly, Annette focuses on his angel necklace, "What is that around your neck?"

"A gift. The angel Michael."

Scoffing, "The angel of death? Charming."

Marvin grins, his eyes flat, "Among other things. Including divine judgment."

Leaning very close, he forces her to back up, "Stop drinking."

He hurtles out the door, slamming it behind him.

She heads to the phone, weaving. Picking up her address book, she thumbs through the pages, squinting through her drunken haze.

Shaking, she picks up the receiver and dials it wrong. Hanging up angrily, she watches Marvin out the front window as he races down the driveway. Carey is quite a bit ahead.

Maybe he won't catch him.

A deep breath, she dials again, keeping an eye on Marvin.

A male voice answers, "Hello".

"Max, it's me."

A long pause, "Who is this?"

I can't believe this, after all we've -

"IT'S ANNETTE, YOU IDIOT!"

17

Marvin sprints down the driveway, finally catching up with Carey next to the pumpkin patch.

Out of breath, "WAIT!"

Carey stops, his back to Marvin. Sensing Marvin right behind him, he finally turns, tears streaming down his face.

Marvin leans, his hands on his knees, catching his breath, "Don't listen to her. She's especially hateful when she drinks."

Marvin stands tall as Carey breaks down and weeps into his shoulder.

Carey, near hysterics, "I don't want to lose your friendship. It's the most important thing in the world to me."

Marvin pulls Carey up from his shoulder and faces him, "What? That's silly talk."

Sniffling, "I don't want you to think I feel - about you - that I-"

Marvin looks directly in his eyes, "I know how you feel about me. We're like brothers. Been bonded our whole lives. Nothing and no one breaks that bond."

A sniffle and a cough, "But your mother-"

Marvin glances back at the house, knowing that she's watching before he even sees her, "My mother is a lost soul. And no longer my problem."

"I just wish I was normal like you, Marvin."

Marvin turns back to him, slack-jawed with astonishment, "Like me? I spent a year of my life hanging out with the President of the United States. I traveled the country made up like a tiny clown, trying to get people to stop having a lead foot. I was once in a parade in Georgia sitting next to Miss Piggly Wiggly 1955. I'm hardly the barometer for normal."

A huge, brilliant smile as he punches Carey in the arm.

This brings a grin to Carey's face although he's still pensive.

"I don't know how to love anyone being like I am."

Marvin shrugs, sure of himself, "The same way anybody else loves. The right person will come along. And he'd better treat you well or I'll kill him with my ax and bury him in my pumpkin patch.

I need some good fertilizer."

Carey doubles over laughing. Marvin leans down and cuts a large pumpkin with his knife and hands it to Carey.

Marvin puts his right hand up in a vow, left hand on the pumpkin, "I swear that we'll be best friends and take care of each other forever."

Carey mimics the vow, "I swear too."

Marvin points his finger at Carey, "And I swear that we will both find our happiness. I don't know what it'll look like, but we'll find it. Together."

The boys hug as Annette glares through the window at them, drink in hand, finished with her phone call.

Someone moves in the shadows behind her.

18

The rural post office rests at the end of an ancient cow path.

An impassable swamp when poor weather hits, the hours of the post office are variable.

During spring rains, it's more than likely that patrons will find a hand painted wooden sign at the turn off to the path.

SWAMPED IN. NO MAIL TODAY. GOD BLESS.

There is no mail delivery, customers pick up their mail at this converted two room wood cabin that dates to the mid-1700's.

Old man Blarney had built and lived in the cabin; his eccentricity was widely admired and sometimes feared. Upon his death during the Revolutionary Way, it was discovered that he wished his property to become a postal drop location for the new pony express system.

A hand-scrawled will left under a rock on his kitchen table attested to the fact. He also bequeathed a sizable amount of money to renovate the building. Unfortunately, the township lacked the foresight to use some of the funds to shore up the route leading to the new post office and mail distribution has suffered ever since. Horses always loped through, no matter the conditions but since the advent of the automobile, things had gone downhill.

Even in 1968, folks are still known to remark to friends and relatives, "Send it by carrier pigeon and it'll get here faster."

Mr. Williams leans against the counter. Sixty-five years old, his reading glasses are perched on his nose as he looks through a stack of mail. His coal black face is lined with wrinkles but his years disappear when his candescent smile emerges, as it does now.

His favorite customer, Marvin Damon, bounds in the front door like a young colt.

"Hello, Marvin, how are you this fine day?

Marvin, innately capable of shaking off recent negative experiences, waves, "Great! How are you?"

Removing his glasses and setting them on the counter, he sighs, "Getting ready to retire this week."

"Oh no!" Marvin exclaims as he reaches the small counter in two strides.

"It's time, Marvin. I'm ready. Gonna spend more time with the Missus."

He pauses then grins, "We'll see how that works out, me being home all day."

He chuckles, then stares at Marvin, pensive, reaching behind him to find the Damon's mail in their customary slot in the wooden apparatus that serves as a letter sorter.

"Are you feeling OK, Mr. Williams? You're not retiring because you're sick, are you?"

Mr. Williams hands him several pieces of mail and puts his grizzled hand over Marvin's, "No, no, no, no, I'm fit as a fiddle. Bit of rheumatiz but that's about it."

"Then what's wrong?"

Mr. Williams, amazed at the boy's perception, "I've known you your whole life, since you were a little tiny sprout trying to peek over this very counter. You've grown into a good, fine person, Marvin. And I'm ashamed to say that I've done you wrong."

"What are you talking about?

Mr. Williams holds up a finger, a gesture for Marvin to wait a moment, then passes through a doorway into the back room, limping slightly, "Glad you came in today. Didn't wanna have to come out to your house. Considering. But I suppose I coulda left this with Miss Jezzy. She'd have seen you got it."

Curious Marvin hears the shuffling of boxes and rifling of papers with an occasional mutter of annoyance from Mr. Williams as he conducts his search.

Before Marvin can call out to inquire if the man needs help, he comes back to the counter with a brown paper parcel wrapped in twine.

"Marvin Damon" is written on it in his own shaky scrawl.

He sets it down and pushes it towards Marvin as though it's filled with the most delicate china, "I'm glad I get to give this to you myself."

Marvin picks it up gingerly, afraid of it. His heartbeat has quickened and his breathing has shallowed a bit.

Mr. Williams looks at him with warm brown eyes, "You're nearly grown now-"

"I just turned eighteen," Marvin interrupts, uncharacteristically due to his nervousness.

His eyes remain glued to the package. His stomach drops, whatever is in this package leeches through the innocuous looking box and absorbs into his hands, traveling through his body. He is reminded of the time he got a shock from a bad outlet at home but this isn't a sudden jolt, this is a continuous thrum.

Mr. Williams notices the boy's reaction.

He's for sure got the gift. Just like my grandmama, a seer. Wonder if he knows he has it?

He continues, "So much the better."

He hesitates, not wanting to cause Marvin any more heartache than necessary. Well aware of what the box contains, he presses on with his story.

"Your mother came in for the mail two or three years back and there was a letter for you. She was furious when she saw it and forced me to hold it back and any more that came for you. I didn't want to do that. Tampering with the mail is illegal, not to mention, it just ain't right. She seemed to reconsider a bit, but then she looked at me and my blood ran ice cold. The expression on her face was-well. She said if I didn't do as she asked, she'd accuse me of-accuse me of something that would get me fired at the very least. And everybody knew she was-friendly with the Sheriff. So, I did it."

Marvin, now grasping the package with his fingers claw like, is completely dumbfounded.

His eyes aren't right either.

Mr. Williams smiles warmly, "The world's changed a great deal, Marvin, mostly for the better but some things remain the same. A woman like your mother saying that a black man had-done something-untoward-way out here in the middle of nowhere without witnesses. Well, I had to protect myself."

Marvin finally understands the implications, "But why?"

"I can't speak to that. That's between you and your mother. All I know is, I'm leaving here and she can't threaten me anymore. But I kept everything aside and saved it for the day I could do right by you. To spite her, I guess. But mostly because you're a good boy. And everyone deserves the truth."

Marvin slowly turns to leave with the package. Mr. Williams pops the other mail on top of it, the boy having forgotten it.

Mr. Williams regrets the somberness of the mood and calls out in his friendliest civil servant voice, "Well now! Since you're grown, you can call me by my Christian name. It's Gabriel."

Marvin turns, his smile is back and his eyes bright green, "You're my second archangel in as many days. In the Bible, Gabriel delivered God's message."

Mr. Williams laughs, "Yes sir, he surely did. And this time he's doing it from the post office. Now you listen, come by the house sometime and see us. We'll have some lemonade, I remember how much you liked it. And we'll talk about the new dining room table my wife wants you to make us. Gonna spend all my retirement savings."

Marvin strides back over to the counter and shakes Mr. William's hand, a wave of nostalgia and sadness suddenly washing over him.

I'm never going to see him again.

19

Annette is posed in her bedroom.

Wearing only her black slip, she is draped across her black swan chaise lounge next to the floor-to-ceiling windows. The sight of her in this repose sets an expectation that either Cary Grant or Gregory Peck are due to storm into the room at any moment to confront her regarding her latest debauchery.

The heavy brocade drapes are closed, the room lit only by a lamp on her bedside table. A long cherry wood table behind the chaise features several of her headshots from the past.

And, naturally, more Kennedy photos.

The large close-up of Baby Marvin smiles down from the wall next to the windows.

His innocent smile proclaiming, "SLOW DOWN, DAD!"

She glances at the poster as she gropes around the cherry table for her scotch glass.

Old cigarette burn scars pepper her upper back. Her manicured hand finds her glass as her gaze rests on her headshots. Grabbing one, she flings it across the room, shattering it.

A telegram lies discarded on the floor, slightly crumpled, "….sorry to have to release you from your contract at this time…"

Marvin storms in with the opened package from Mr. Williams, ready for a confrontation, but stops when he sees his mother's condition.

Annette's scars are visible to him for a moment before she groggily notices him. Knowing the unfortunate incident that produced them, he calms himself.

Assuming that wasn't a lie too.

She sits upright, "Who set your hair on fire? Rushing in like that."

Her accent drifts to more mid-Atlantic when she's drunk. An anomaly that Marvin never understood.

Who is his mother? Is this really her and the rest a fiction?

Marvin gestures to the broken photo, "I thought the house was falling down."

Annette mutters to herself, gulping her beverage, "May as well be."

To Marvin, "My career is officially over, my darling. And naturally, yours is too."

Screaming at the telegram on the floor, nearly toppling off the chaise, "Couldn't even tell me in person! Cowards! Bastards!"

Marvin, weary of a lifetime of her delusions, "I don't care."

Annette's eyes widen as he sets his package on her dresser. Barely able to speak, "How can you say that?"

Marvin looks at his four year-old face on her wall and smiles.

He remembers, mostly talking to himself, "I had fame for a brief period of time. I met a lot of really wonderful, interesting people. It was fun too, seeing new places, being in parades, visiting The White House. I remember Mrs. Eisenhower caught me sneaking some of her 'Million Dollar Fudge'. I was afraid I'd get in trouble because I'd heard that someone important was coming to The White House that day and I told her that I was sorry. And do you know what she said?"

He looks at his mother as she shakes her head, bleary-eyed.

"She said that *I* was the important person. And she winked and handed me another piece. An amazing memory. I'm grateful to you for that, although I question your motives."

He continues, "I remember how you behaved when I filmed the first television commercial, the one that became the poster. I remember how you berated everyone because you wanted to portray the mother and they had already cast someone else. She was quite a lovely woman, I can't remember her name, but she looked at me with a kind of pity that I didn't understand at the time. But I grew to know exactly what was on her mind at the time."

"That was a misunderstanding, I was told-"

"No, you weren't. You wanted me to have a career in show business. To help you. Or worse yet, to pursue politics. To impress the Kennedys."

Annette, thunderstruck, "I wanted you to follow in my-"

"Footsteps? What footsteps? It's time you admitted that you never had much of a career."

Reeling, Annette attempts to stand, "HOW DARE YOU! I WAS IN-"

Marvin has heard this all before, "*HARVEY* with Jimmy Stewart. Mother, you were an extra with no lines. You were always an extra. Which is fine. But now you've become a pitiful background actor in your own life."

Marvin has crossed a line, his behavior, although unusually defiant, has come nowhere near this level of brazenness and he knows it. He remains calm in spite of the new information that he has thanks to Mr. Williams.

He continues, "You tried, you really did. And you have a great deal of talent. I commend you for that. But nothing came of it and nothing ever will. It's time for you to move on.

"Nothing! NOTHING! What do you call this house? Your lifestyle?"

Marvin, patience wearing thin, "My father's money. Until you spent it all. On nonsense."

Walking across the grandiose room to her closet, he flings open the double doors and disappears inside, gesturing to the racks surrounding him.

She's screaming now, "I need those things!"

Marvin appears holding a red sequined strapless gown with a train, "For what? The Oscars you aren't invited to?"

He holds it up, shakes it, then throws it on the floor.

Grabbing a light green chiffon gown, "Or the auditions that never come in?"

He snaps his fingers, his eyes blazing, "Oh wait, I know!"

He disappears again into the back of the closet. The rustling of fabric and the clacking of wooden hangers barrage Annette's ears before he emerges holding a mink coat.

"Maybe the parties that the Kennedys never invited you to because they forgot about you years ago?"

He drops the coat, stares at her, then turns and rips down the rod nearest to him, spilling dozens of yards of expensive, vibrant, colorful gowns and dresses onto the floor.

Stepping on them, he sprints to her dresser.

A dozen gold hand mirrors glow against the dark wood. He picks them up, one at a time and smashes them against the dresser, glass pelting him but miraculously, leaving him uninjured.

"You don't need all these mirrors!"

After smashing the last one, his attention is drawn to the enormous gilded mirror on the wall above the dresser.

Annette watches in horror as her mild-mannered son, glass shards glinting in his dark hair, fixates on it.

He's spellbound, his face expressionless. Is he even breathing? He was huffing and puffing before, but now - that angry boy is gone.

But this hypnotized version of Marvin? Why does he frighten her even more?

She whispers, "Marvin?"

He turns rapidly and rushes her, kneeling on the floor next to the chaise. Already afraid of him, she goes rigid when Marvin takes her hand, gazing into her eyes.

Mournful of what he's lost, he confronts her, "Do you know how old I was when you started putting all of the household bills on my desk? Thirteen years old. That's when I became the adult in this house. I scrambled for the longest time to make a go of my business so that I could keep us off the streets. And do you know what? I did it. I created something special, something that, in spite of you, I don't resent. I love carpentry. I love building, creating. Maybe I owe you a debt of gratitude after all."

On the heels of this last comment, Marvin's head snaps to his right, distracted by - something. He tilts his head.

Listening to something?

Annette follows his gaze and sees nothing, hears nothing. She desperately wants Steven right now. He could always talk to Marvin in a way that she couldn't.

God help her, even Jezebel would be a welcome presence.

Turning back to his mother again, Marvin inquires, "Why didn't you tell me about my trust fund?"

Caught, Annette snaps back to sobriety.

Her fear dissipates and she sits up snarling at Marvin's back as he turns to retrieve his package from the ruin of the dresser.

Annette replaces her initial snarl with wide-eyed innocence when he turns around, "What are you talking about? You know about your trust fund."

Marvin stares into the mirror over the dresser again. Perplexed, Annette observes him.

He has that look on his face again, what is he seeing?

Marvin's focus shifts from his own reflection to his mother's, "It's due now that I'm eighteen. Not when I'm twenty-two like you've always told me. And it's considerably more than you told me. I have the statement from the lawyer."

Annette stumbles up, grabbing her cocktail, "I must have made a mistake. I'm not infallible, Marvin. Raising you on my own has taken a toll on me mentally over the years. Or maybe there's been a clerical error? The people who do that sort of thing are hardly the best and the brightest."

She heads to the door, eager to leave the room.

Marvin is accustomed to navigating her lies, "Was it a clerical error when you lied about my father being dead?"

Annette freezes in the doorway, barely able to breathe, "Who told you that, dear? What an unkind thing to do, telling you something like that."

It's that damn darky postman. I'll fix him for this.

Marvin walks up behind her, she can feel betrayal seeping from his pores. His heavy breath is on her.

He leans close to her ear, "My father tried to contact me for the past couple of years. You had Mr. Williams hold back the letters."

Still speaking in low tones, his anger is rising, "He's a decent man and you threatened him."

"You're not actually going to believe that nig-"

Savagely spun around, she finds herself facing Marvin. He towers over her, figuratively and literally.

The back of his hand hovers near her face, the threat of a smack silencing her. Her glass shatters on the wood floor.

Marvin, barely audible, "Don't ever use that word."

Annette nods and takes his hands in hers.

After a deep breath, "Your father abandoned us when you were a baby. I told you he was dead. I thought it was the best thing for you at the time and I could hardly undo it once it was done."

"You denied me a chance to get to know my father."

She drops his hands and braces herself in the doorway, "Father?"

Clawing at the scars on her back, drawing blood, "THIS?! THIS IS A FATHER!"

He shakes her briefly. She regains her composure.

He leans close again, "That was some random man, not your father. And not *my* father."

He brushes past her into the tunnel of a hallway, heading towards his room.

Annette yells after him, "He went along with it. Staying away. You don't want to know him. Mental illness runs in his family."

Marvin stops short, his back still to her, "*His* family? Interesting. Just so you know, I'm moving out shortly. You can't keep me trapped here anymore."

"Oh, can't I?"

Her confidence sets Marvin back on his heels for a moment but he recovers. In spite of everything, her presence is powerful.

Still facing away from her, "I got my license and a truck. I'm making arrangements to live on my own."

Annette steps into the hallway, "How did you get a license? You need-"

Spinning to confront her, he points at her, "My birth certificate? Took me a while but I found it."

Stricken, Annette hyperventilates and leans against the dark floral wallpaper in the hallway. She clutches at it to remain upright but fails, her nails tearing into it as she slips to the floor.

Turning away from her again, Marvin sets his shoulders back and strides to his room.

He calls back over his shoulder, "I'm glad you're sitting. I was afraid you'd pass out." He goes into his room and slams the door, rattling the entire upstairs.

20

Marvin enters his room again a short time later, calmer than before, chugging a Yoo-Hoo.

He had retrieved it a few minutes ago after making sure that Annette had gone back into her room.

Slipping down into the kitchen he grabbed his favorite drink and creeped back upstairs so that he didn't disturb her.

She's likely unconscious right now.

His dark blue bedspread is covered with the daily mail and letters and documents from the opened package courtesy of Mr. Williams.

He flops on his belly, propped on his elbows, draining the drink. He sets the empty bottle on the floor and picks up two birthday cards that were with the regular mail.

He opens the first, recognizing the withering handwriting of former President Dwight Eisenhower. He always receives well wishes from the kindly man and his wife. And a fifty dollar bill.

The other birthday card has two cartoon dogs on the front. The larger dog is obviously the father of the smaller dog. They both hold fishing poles and walk towards a pond.

It's signed "Sheriff Steven" and includes a ten dollar bill.

A note inside, written in his precise script, "*Happy birthday Marvin. Let's go fishing soon. This is a promissory note and if you present it to me, I'll even clean all the fish. So, don't lose it, or you're outta luck. If you get to town today, come see me and we'll grab some pie at the diner.*"

Marvin grins at the card and note. He leaps up and sets both cards up on his desk, where he can see them every day. They're the only cards he'll receive.

His mother isn't reliable when it comes to holidays anymore. Burnt pancakes are the only gift she'll give him this year. Particularly after their latest bout.

Both sets of grandparents are dead as far as he knows. His parents had both been only children. Destiny determined long ago that he was to be isolated with regards to family. But he has other people he considers family.

Carey and Miss Jezzy always give him gifts in person, preferring not to send anything through the mail that Annette might intercept.

They've never said as much but he knows. Miss Jezzy's excuse that the mail delivery is unreliable due to sweet ole Mr. William's eyesight and that swampy road is quietly accepted by both of them.

Another handwritten note *"Dear Marvin, I hope these help you find happiness. Best wishes, Your Friend, Gabriel Williams."*

A slight smile as he carefully folds the note to preserve it. Grasping the archangel Michael necklace around his neck, he prays silently for the kind postal worker.

Opening his eyes again, he tucks the necklace into his t-shirt. Best to keep it there, close to his heart.

Dozens of cream colored envelopes inscribed with his name and address litter the bed. The return address is *"FISHER AND ASSOCIATES, 245 PARK AVE, NEW YORK, NEW YORK"*.

He opens the most recently dated envelope. A formal statement for his trust fund, started by his father, Maxwell Damon on the day of his birth, October 29, 1950.

Subsequent deposits over the years with the most recent being on October 29, 1966.

The line at the bottom of the document relates *"$500,000 due on October 29, 1968"*.

Marvin shakes his head, still unable to believe the jaw dropping amount that he has immediate access to.

This will change everything. And I can leave Mother with something, I won't just leave her high and dry in spite of everything that she's done. But our relationship is going to have to change dramatically.

Six more envelopes have various dates over the past three years. Return address is the same with the addition of *"MAX DAMON C/O FISHER AND ASSOCIATES"*.

His hand trembles, afraid of what might be inside. Taking a deep breath, he finally opens the oldest, dated October 29, 1965.

Dear Marvin, I hope you are doing well. I am getting in touch with you now that you're fifteen, thinking and hoping that you're old enough to begin to make decisions for yourself. Your mother…

Marvin stops reading and carefully folds the letter, placing it back in the envelope. Overwhelmed, he decides there is plenty of time to read these later.

A hopeful smile spreads across his face as he declares for the first time in eighteen years, "I have a father."

The manila envelope containing his birth certificate that he used at the DMV yesterday is under the open package. He retrieves it and removes the birth certificate, setting it aside without a glance.

Another document is in the envelope. A document that he had found during his laborious search through the morass of his mother's files in the attic.

He pulls it out and opens it slowly, re-reading it, still not believing his eyes.

It's a commitment form to the Psychiatric Center of California dated December 10, 1950.

Eighteen years ago.

Marvin reads aloud, voice cracking, "Annette Sinclair-Damon committed by husband, Maxwell Damon for rest and evaluation."

Marvin flips over on his back, dropping the document and putting his arm across his eyes, "Right after I was born."

A wave of dizziness slams into Marvin like a freight train, "Ahh."

He sits up, clutching his head, grimacing. The tidal wave leaves as abruptly as it came. And he hears something. That same voice?

Whispering…something.

Paranoid, he leaps up off of the bed and calls toward the closed bedroom door, "Is someone there?"

Silence.

He's alone, but he feels something. An energy, palpable, electric. A presence. The hair stands erect on the back of his neck and arms. He rushes over to check the bathroom, empty. His closet? Also empty.

Frantically, he looks around one more time. No one here. He sees the mirror across the room, singing to him like a siren, luring him to look inside for the answers he needs. To disappear into another world.

Not this time.

Slumping over to the window, he drops to his knees and drapes his arms across the windowsill, letting them reach out the window into the cool air. The October colors and breeze on his skin soothe him.

But he's still confused, "What's happening to me?"

Marvin closes his eyes and continues to take in the autumnal energy.

He pulls his angel necklace out of his shirt and clutches it, "Please help me."

Marvin's reflection observes him from his territory in the portal of the mirror. Deciding that Marvin is preoccupied, he seizes the opportunity and reaches through the glass.

Seeing that his arm passes through easily, a smile spreads across his face.

Marvin's smile.

He disappears from the mirror and reappears in the bedroom next to the dresser. Fully formed and corporeal, he wears the same clothes that Marvin does.

He is Marvin, but not really.

Mirror Marvin smiles and vanishes like a vapor through the closed bedroom door unnoticed as Marvin continues to lean against the window, eyes closed.

His eyes snap open at the sound of his mother's voice from downstairs, "I'm going out, Marvin!"

He turns to the sound of her voice, and his first instinct is to talk to her, tell her what he's found out and how it's been affecting him.

They've gotten through numerous trials over the years and she's his mother. He'll apologize and be open with her. No more games.

He'll give her another chance.

21

Annette marches out the front door, leaving it open, keys in hand.

Open doors are not an issue way out here in the sticks. And Marvin does love the fresh air, even on a cool day like this.

She heads to her car, sobered up thanks to a shower and some stale coffee that she found in a corner of her room. It tasted like motor oil but it worked. Her black ensemble this time closely resembles an Audrey Hepburn look.

She blinks away the bright autumn sun. Angry, she realizes she's forgotten her sunglasses.

Turning to head back in, she nearly runs into Marvin, "Oof, I didn't see you, Marvin."

Casual, he puts his hands in his pockets and leans against a porch pillar, "Should you be driving?"

He's not combative, at least.

She replies, "I'm fine now".

"You're sure?"

"Yes."

She wants to set things right, "Marvin, I regret our dispute earlier. I had been drinking and I wasn't myself. The telegram from my agency caught me completely off guard. Even though you're right about my career, I would have thought they could have shown a bit more respect. On a human level."

He replies, "I agree. The telegram was in poor taste."

Daring to hope that things can be repaired between them, she relaxes. Her plans will move forward much more easily if he's not agitated.

"Perhaps we can have a discussion about things later when I get back?"

He just stares so she walks toward her car again, feeling his eyes on her. Her sunglasses are forgotten.

He muses, "We have a lot to talk about. More than you know."

She turns smiling to find him directly in front of her, "We can discuss everything later, I promise."

The temptation to reach over to kiss his cheek is quashed by his stern expression. She quickens her step to reach the safety of her car.

I'm not afraid of Marvin? He's the kindest, gentlest boy in the world in spite of earlier events. Something is wrong. I'll handle it.

She smiles one last time as he stares straight through her.

Getting into the car, she starts it and heads down the driveway, watching Marvin in the rear view mirror.

He walks towards his workshop, hands in pockets. Shivering, she glances at her watch. Noon. How is it only noon?

Disgusted at the early hour, she focuses on the driveway, "I need a drink."

22

The sun sets behind the trees, lighting up their leaves, mimicking a blazing inferno engulfing the house.

Marvin gallops out the front door holding a long paper bag and another Yoo-Hoo bottle. He crosses the driveway towards his workshop. He has new bulbs for his fluorescent lights.

Both of the roll-up doors are down as usual but unlocked. Also, as usual. The only invaders he's ever had to deal with all have four legs. Possums and raccoons mostly. Once he found a groundhog. But it's been a persistent raccoon lately.

Marvin rolls up the left door and slowly enters the pitch dark building pulling the door down behind him. A sound. Rustling movement in the back corner. Raccoon must have gotten in again. Marvin sighs and flicks the lights on. They flicker, worse than before, but he'll take care of it right now.

Distracted by the annoying lights and focused on opening the bulb's packaging while balancing his bottle, he doesn't see Mirror Marvin in the farthest corner of the workshop, standing stock still.

Mirror Marvin, "Marvin."

Marvin starts and gapes at the intruder, shock settling on him like a cloak. His breathing is shallow as the lights finally give up the ghost, leaving him and the stranger in inky darkness. The light bulbs he holds and his bottle crash to the floor shattering in unison.

Marvin clutches his necklace in the pitch dark, "The Lord is my shepherd, I shall not want. He maketh me to lie down in green pastures. He leadeth me beside the still-"

The lights flicker halfway on.

Mirror Marvin, a foot away, stares directly into his eyes.

Placid, Mirror Marvin says, "Don't be afraid."

Marvin screams as the lights wink out.

PART 2

CALL ME HARVEY

23

Marvin screams in terror, Carey drives slowly and carefully up the isolated road on his way home.

The backseat is loaded with two grocery bags, several library books about law and court cases, the novel he was reading earlier and the pumpkin Marvin gave him.

Playing the radio on full blast, he sings along with "Judy in Disguise (With Glasses)".

The dirt road is hemmed in by thick woods on both sides. Carey takes great care as deer, rabbits and other creatures will dart into the road without warning.

Someone watches Carey, able to keep up with him on foot due to his cautious driving.

As Carey pulls into the driveway, the sun sets. Carey gets out of the car and grabs two bags of groceries from the back of the car, leaving the rest for another trip.

A twig snaps.

Carey stops and looks around but sees nothing. Hopefully it's not a bear, the chicken coop is shored up but a really aggressive bear could claw his way in.

He'll keep an eye out. He's had to scare a bear or two off over the years with his Gram's shotgun. Never aiming at them, he'd never do that.

He heads into the house and hears Miss Jezzy snoring before he gets all the way in the door. She snoozes in her recliner with Theodore at her side on the floor. They snore together like old companions.

Carey smiles, shakes his head and puts the grocery bags down on the kitchen table.

Reaching into his front pocket, he drops a wad of cash on the kitchen table. The cash from Marvin that morning.

Before retrieving the books and pumpkin from his car, he goes to the refrigerator for a cold soda pop. Or as Grams calls it, "Co-Cola."

He stops when he sees a picture held on the refrigerator with a magnet. He and Marvin, beaming great smiles, stand behind the farm stand, arms around each other.

It was taken about a year ago when Miss Jezzy decided that their great enterprise needed to be captured on film. One of the few times that she ventured out to the house.

Both boys wear white t-shirts with large yellow smiley faces on them. He takes the daisy magnet off the photo and holds it, studying the image.

He smiles.

The memory is interrupted when he hears his car door slam. He's confused until-

A loud SHATTERING of glass as a brick sails through the front window next to Miss Jezzy. She snaps awake, confused and groggy. Theodore barks and ambles up.

John Carter's voice is heard outside, "Come on out! Want another broken window?!"

He slurs his words.

Miss Jezzy leaps up, panic giving her more agility as Carey heads to the door.

She stops him with both hands on his shoulders and instructs him quietly, "Call Sheriff Steven."

The stomping of work boots thunders back and forth on the porch. Jezzy pulls a shotgun from the closet next to the front door and checks that it's loaded as Carey sprints to the wall phone, dialing frantically.

Someone answers and Carey screams, "Helen! Please send the Sheriff, we need help!"

She asks a question.

Carey breathes deeply, calming himself, "Carey Franklin, please hurry."

John splinters the front door with one kick and saunters in as Carey hangs up. He's wearing his eye patch and has cuts and bruises on his face from the jar that Marvin threw. He carries the pumpkin that had been in the back seat of Carey's car, along with a beer bottle.

Taking in the frightened woman and her grandson, he leers, "You forgot your pumpkin, faggot."

He hurls the bottle towards Carey and it shatters against the refrigerator where the photo had previously hung.

He staggers, drunk. He's often drunk. At eighteen, he's had a great deal of experience with dulling his constant pain. And this time the pain is physical. That old doctor took care of his eye, said he was lucky he didn't lose it.

John would have referred to him as condescending if he knew the meaning of a word like that.

Miss Jezzy lowers the gun since the boy is unarmed, "It's not his fault, John. It's your daddy's fault. He lost his way long ago. You can leave that place, I can help you."

A brief memory rushes through his haze. Miss Jezzy at their house after their mother died, patting their shaggy heads and giving them a smile and some homemade bread before their father ran her off.

But that was a long time ago. Things change.

SPLAT!

The pumpkin falls from John's arms as his hands go up to his face.

Screaming through his tears, "Why does everyone keep saying that!? It's too late!"

He lowers his hands and his lifeless eye falls on Miss Jezzy. He starts towards her.

"Stop it, John!"

Carey stands behind John, brandishing the crumb coated butcher's knife that was next to the pound cake. John freezes, sensing that Carey has the upper hand. Then he smiles because Carey only thinks he has the upper hand.

Roger Carter bolts in the kitchen from the dark hallway where he had been hidden after entering quiet as a mouse through the back door.

Miss Jezzy raises the shotgun at one boy, then the other, back and forth.

John screams at her, "Stop it old lady, we don't want you!"

Carey stands straight, confident, "The Sheriff is coming."

John turns on him, unsteady, "He won't make it in time."

Miss Jezzy is sick at heart to see the wreck of the young man before her. But she has to protect herself and Carey.

Having dealt with this sort of violence more than once in her life, she's more than prepared as she bellows, "I warned you before! You get on outta here!"

John laughs as he gestures at Carey standing petrified next to the phone, "Can't do that."

He seethes, pointing at Carey, spitting his words, "I got the shit beat outta me because of him! He has to pay!"

As Carey considers this, Roger pulls a knife out of his pocket and grabs Carey, holding the knife to his throat.

John turns to Carey and gestures to his eye patch, "You're gonna pay for this. Then your little clown boyfriend is next."

Miss Jezzy shoves John with the gun barrel, infuriating him. He grabs the gun barrel and pushes Miss Jezzy backwards, hard. She stumbles against her chair and drops the gun.

John turns back to Carey, slowly creeping towards him.

BOOM!

A warning shot from Miss Jezzy blasts out the kitchen window. The three boys freeze. Roger drops his knife and accidentally kicks it under the stove.

John had underestimated Miss Jezzy and her feistiness. Not again. He rushes her, screaming and grabs the shotgun. They fight over it until-

BOOM!

Silence. Smoke curls up from the barrel. Wide-eyed John is unhurt. Roger, near hysterics, puts his hands to his face, also unhurt.

CAREY FALLS.

Shot in the chest. Blood leaks onto the linoleum floor as Miss Jezzy grabs her chest. Her vision fades as her heart screams at her.

John and Roger scramble through the open front door, Roger hysterical, "No, no, no! This wasn't-".

John smacks him upside the head, hard.

John berates his brother, "Fucking moron! Stop!"

Roger, in disbelief, "No! We were gonna scare him, maybe cut him! Not this!"

John ignores him, "Too late for that. We have to burn the house, hide everything."

Roger screams, spitting in his face, "No! We need to run!"
John pulls a lighter from his pocket. He sets the front room drapes
on fire through the broken window. They catch very slowly as a
siren is heard in the distance.

Roger pleads, "BUT THEY MIGHT BE ALIVE!"

John is catatonic "No, no, they can't be."

Roger hears Theodore barking inside, near the flames. He grasps
his face with both hands.

"But the dog!"

John focuses again and smacks Roger, "It's done, it's over! Come
on!"

The boys race off into the woods behind the house.

24

Annette finishes a horrifying phone call, "Yes, Steven, I understand."

She listens then, "No, you don't need to come by, I'll-I'll handle it."

She hangs up and doubles over, hand to her mouth, sickened by the disgusting violence of what she's been told.

Steven was barely able to speak, he was so shaken up.

Not like him at all. He's tough as nails, one of the reasons she loves – means appreciates - him.

Annette opens the cupboard to remove a glass and fills it with water at the sink. As she makes her way to the couch to sit down, her mind reels.

Carey was so young, it's likely not his fault he turned out this way. Jezebel must have done something to encourage that sort of behavior. Unwittingly, I'm sure, she would hardly contradict her pious beliefs and risk his soul.

Something like this was bound to happen. Thankfully Marvin wasn't there.

This is exactly why I didn't want him to spend time with Carey. He's always been a target. Maybe if his mother had survived, he'd have turned out differently.

Although she was quite a fast piece of baggage, I'm sure a parade of men in and out of the house would have affected him. He was a sweet boy, though.

She takes a long sip of water and speaks out loud to her touchstone, Bobby Kennedy, "As tragic as this is, it does benefit me, doesn't it? Jezebel has always been a thorn in my side, to have her gone makes everything-"

Disturbed by barking of all things, she gets up and walks to the front window.

Marvin is slowly walking up the front steps followed by a sloppy-looking dog.

She's so distracted that she didn't even hear his truck.

Devastation is written all over his face and she tears up. She'll help him, perhaps this situation will serve to heal her relationship with him.

It would be good for something positive to come from this

horror.

She opens the front door for him, authentic tears falling from her eyes. Marvin and the dog come inside.

He doesn't make eye contact with her so she hesitates but decides to say something.

"Marvin, Steven, the Sheriff just called. I heard what happened. I'm so sorry."

He can barely speak, "Would you please get him a bowl of water?"

She quickly goes into the kitchen, retrieves a large bowl and begins to fill it at the sink.

Still unsure of what to say, "I may have said some things in the past but that doesn't mean I wanted-".

She turns to him.

Marvin holds his hand up to stop her from speaking. She takes the bowl and places it on the floor next to the dog. He laps up most of it quickly.

Marvin puts his hands in his pockets and stares for a moment before speaking, "You may have said some things? Some things? Some. Things."

She should have kept her mouth shut. This is not going to go well, "Marvin, I-"

He ticks off on his fingers, "Mentally deranged. Fairy. Pervert."

"Marvin-"

"And Miss Jezzy? Who came here every day for years because you're a pathetic, self absorbed drunk who couldn't care for her son. You always treated her like she was a servant, beneath you."

"Please, Marvin-"

"Let me tell you something. Carey and Jezzy are worth ten of you."

He gestures to the dog, "His name is Theodore. He's mine now. Be wonderful to him or you'll regret it."

Annette nods, terrified because she knows he's serious.

Marvin heads to the open front door, "I have to go to the hospital now."

He walks down the front steps and heads down the driveway, disappearing in the dark.

Theodore walks over to Annette and nudges her leg.

She regards him and smiles slightly, "Well, at least I have you for company, don't I?"

Theodore barks.

25

Pocono General Hospital reposes in a picturesque area, nestled deep in the valley between the soft sloping mountains.

The area for the small hospital was chosen specifically for its beauty.

When the first shovel was thrust in the soil at the groundbreaking, then Mayor Thomas declared, "Folks will heal a whole lot faster with this view outta their windows. I guaran-damn-tee it."

No one ever conducted extensive research to determine if the long dead mayor was correct. Folks have always been told that he died in this very hospital, gazing out the window at God's majesty, with a peaceful smile on his pallid face.

But the truth is that he died screaming, cursing and soiling himself as he withered away from a painful form of bone cancer.

But a story like that could hardly be printed in the hospital brochure or used for the numerous fundraising activities, so the Mayor's serene voyage on to his glory with the mountain backdrop is the agreed upon fable.

Marvin's truck squeals on the hospital blacktop, screeching to a stop. He throws it into park and leaps out simultaneously, sprinting to the entrance with lightning speed, ignoring Mayor Thomas' beloved view.

Steven makes tracks out of the hospital and meets Marvin, hoping to stop the boy from bursting in and causing a commotion.

Taller than the Sheriff and running at full speed, Marvin is difficult to stop but Steven is broad shouldered and stronger. His muscles strain through his uniform shirt as he restrains the wild-eyed boy.

"Marvin, stop. STOP!"

"I have to get-!"

"No, Marvin! Listen to me!"

He shoves Marvin back a step and holds up his hand when Marvin indicates his desire to dash around him.

God, please don't make me have to smack him.

Marvin disintegrates onto the concrete stoop and puts his head in his hands, "What happened?! Where are they?! I went-"

Steven lowers himself down on the step next to Marvin, "Miss Jezzy and Carey were attacked. Carey managed to call for help, but-"

He grabs Marvin's shoulder, forcing his head up, putting his hand under Marvin's chin.

With tears in his eyes, he relates the horrendous news, "Miss Jezzy passed away, she didn't make it. Carey is, well, they're working on him, but it doesn't look good, Son."

Rivers of tears run down his face as Marvin sneers at him. Steven realizes - *God he looks like Annette right now.*

Marvin spits his words, "Why didn't you get there sooner? Why didn't you save them? Isn't that your job?!"

Steven is bowled over, he's never seen Marvin this way, "I-I got there as fast as I could. Son, there was no way to stop it, it was too late."

Marvin wipes his face with his shirt, tears and snot smearing the yellow smiley face on his chest.

He stands and glares down at the Sheriff, "I'm not your son."

Marvin slumps into the hospital, leaving the devastated Steven McClane behind, staring after him.

26

Annette grandstands up the two wooden steps of the bungalow's porch.

She is heedful approaching the building.

Nestled deep in the forest, the pitch dark is thick as molasses. She paid extra attention when her headlights hit the bungalow so that she could plot out a path to the door.

Oh, how she misses New York City! No need to wander in the dark, risking life and limb to simply knock on someone's door.

She gazes into the lighted compact that she had at the ready and applies a touch of powder. She always wants to be camera ready, particularly now, preparing to see - *him.*

Dropping the compact away in her junk-filled handbag, she reaches out to knock on the door but hesitates. She closes her eyes and takes a deep breath.

She hasn't seen Max since Marvin was a baby. If there is a God, he's gotten fat and lost all but a wisp of that amazing mop of riotous, dark hair.

She knocks, more appropriately, she taps. After a few moments she knocks in her true Annette-style, nearly caving the door in. Steven always said that for a delicately built woman, she tended to bang on a door like an angry cop with a warrant.

"Max, open the door!"

A warm light blinks on and the door clicks.

No one locks doors out here, obviously he's been in the big city for far too long.

Max stands in the open doorway, backlit, pulling on a bathrobe over his pajama pants.

Dammit, he isn't fat or bald. He looks better than ever. I knew there was no God. He always did look good without a shirt. I wonder what he looks like without-

Annoyed, "For Christ's sake, Annette, it's late. What do you want?"

Not expecting a tear-filled reunion, nevertheless she's gobsmacked, "That's all you have to say to me? We haven't seen each other since-"

She adjusts her hair, her signature nervous gesture making a rare appearance.

He's piqued already, "I'm aware of the sequence of events. What do you want?"

He rubs his eyes. Those baby blues always melted her. Same thing with Steven and his eyes. It only now occurs to Annette that she definitely has "a type".

Well, to talk about Marvin, obviously. Something terrible has happened."

Max knows Annette too well to take this statement at face value. He once arrived at their New York City apartment early in the relationship to find her shrieking at the maid.

Noticing him, Annette stopped her diatribe long enough to announce that "something terrible has happened".

Rushing to her, concerned for the health and wellbeing of both his lover and the young housekeeper, he came to learn that the tragedy was, in fact, the purchase of chuck roast instead of sirloin by the soon-to-be unemployed young woman.

But this is different, her face is free from the righteous indignation that he grew so weary of for the few years of their relationship. She's serious this time.

Frightened for his son, he slips out onto the small porch and closes the door behind him. He doesn't want to disturb someone sleeping inside.

Naturally, Annette notices and her heart sinks for reasons unknown to her. Of course, he has some doxy in there. He couldn't travel out here to help her with their son without a woman along.

"What's wrong? Is Marvin hurt?" he implores.

She enjoys having this temporary power over him, having him hang on her words. And since Marvin isn't actually injured or ill, she feels no guilt overextending the moment.

She bites her lip and stares at her expensive Guy Laroche two-tone pumps. A splash of color in her mourning attire.

"Well, what is it?! Say something!"

Alright, alright.

"Marvin is fine. Well, not fine, he's devastated. Jezebel and her grandson, Marvin's friend, were attacked earlier. She's - she was killed, and the boy is quite badly hurt. Marvin is at the hospital now."

Max slumps against the closed door of the bungalow. "Oh no! Not Jezzy. Ah, God. She was still in touch with him?"

Angry about it, she replies coolly, "Yes, they were quite close. And her grandson was Marvin's best friend. They were together constantly. Inseparable."

Max runs both of his hands through his thick hair, Marvin's hair, "I'm gonna head over to the hospital, see him."

Annette considers, believing this might benefit Marvin, although it will be a shock. He certainly doesn't want *her* to come to the hospital to be with him.

She touches her ex-husband's arm, "I think that could be a good idea. He can be very quiet and difficult to communicate with when he's upset, so take it slow."

He puts his hand over hers, "I will."

He looks at her with that sheepish expression that always made it impossible to stay angry with him.

"I'm sorry I yelled."

Her momentary bliss at connecting with this man, the first man she ever loved, is cut off by the sound of a baby crying. A light switches on a moment later.

Max looks heavenward, face pinched, waiting for her reaction.

Annette scoffs, "Dear God. At your age? Pathetic. I should have known, the way you slunk out here to talk to me like a cheating scallywag."

"I'm not married to you anymore, sweetheart. I moved on a long time ago."

"Oh, I don't doubt it. Tell me, Max, how many children do you have littering the countryside? Might I have met one by accident?"

"Shut up, Annette!"

"One more question. When do you plan to abandon *that* baby?"

Before he can answer, a young woman appears next to him. With the uniquely feminine appraisal that one woman gives another, she takes in Annette from head to toe.

Placing her hand on her hip, she smiles and thinks to herself, *I'm younger, a LOT younger. But she's friggin' gorgeous. Looks like that broad from Streetcar.*

"Maxy, who's this?"

She gazes at Annette, cozy with her position at her husband's side.

Annette is unable to believe what she is beholding in this moment. She is dumbfounded at the marvel before her.

The young woman can't be more than twenty-three. She wears an expensive red peignoir and vocalizes like a gangster's moll from the 1930's. She wears a full face of makeup and her jet black bob is immaculately styled.

Annette smiles, knowing that the makeup was applied to impress her.

How long has she been listening?

She shakes her head.

Max turns on the young woman, "Go back to-"

Annette, ever the charmer and desperate to extend this awkward moment, thrusts her hand forward, smiling like the Cheshire cat.

"I'm Annette. And you are-?"

"Mary."

She chews and pops a gigantic wad of gum with open-mouthed enthusiasm.

My God, she's actually chewing gum. And it looks like she applied that makeup with a paint roller. Which is understandable, I can see those enormous pores from clear over here. And how many Judy Holliday films did she watch to cultivate that voice? Not enough, clearly.

POP! Goes the gum.

"Mary, my goodness. Aren't you simply…adorable. Is that your baby I hear?"

"Yeah."

POP!

Annette, wildly entertained, "Adorable and loquacious."

"Wha?"

POP!

And stupid. This is wonderful. Max can really pick them. And he bred with her, ugh, I hope the baby has his brains.

Max turns on Mary, "Will you please go check the baby."
POP!
"Oh. Ok, Maxy."
The outlandish idea of checking on her baby had never occurred to her. She walks away, chewing and popping her gum as Max sighs.

Annette leans in to watch her disappear into the bedroom, "Charming. When does she graduate high school?"

Max takes Annette by the shoulders, edging her back onto the porch.

He sighs again, "It's late and I have no interest in talking to you. I'll head over to the hospital and meet with Marvin. We need some time to talk about everything-but not tonight. Not after what he's been through. I'll just be there for comfort. We'll set up a time to talk later. Without you."

The last two words, a pronouncement, not open to negotiation.

Annette calculates. Then she spins and struts down the steps onto the gravel driveway, her shoes crunching.

"Well, maybe tomorrow? I'm going to New York for the day, a meeting with my agent, I'll likely stay the night. You could use the house. You can talk without me or your prom queen present."

Max yawns, "That sounds like a good idea."

God, he's handsome.

She twirls to face him again, smiling, "Of course, I'll need money for a hotel."

Max hangs his head and exhales as the baby's cries increase.

27

Marvin stands outside of the ICU room looking through the thick glass at his best friend.

Carey lies in bed, hooked up to numerous tubes and monitors. Marvin imagines the beeping and thrumming of the machinery even though he can hear nothing in the silent, deserted hallway.

Dr. Reeve speaks to a male orderly who proceeds to arrange Carey's pillows and bedding, tucking him tightly.

"Snug as a bug", Jezzy would have said.

The thought of Miss Jezzy brings a tear to Marvin's eye.

Dr. Reeve spies Marvin through the glass and acknowledges him with a nod before glancing at Carey's chart one last time. He exits the room and goes to Marvin's side, giving the boy a fatherly hug. Marvin barely hugs him back, caught off guard by the show of affection. Dr. Reeve has always been a handshake or pat on the back type of man.

The exhausted doctor shakes his head, "He's in a coma, can't believe he's even alive. Gunshot like that. That young man has a serious will to live. He had this in his hand."

He hands Marvin the picture that Carey had taken off the refrigerator. Marvin takes it, holding it like the most delicate porcelain.

Carey's blood stains the edge.

Dr. Reeve continues, "Miss Jezzy was my patient for many years. And my friend. A good woman, this is horrible. Steven got them both out of the house and got the fire out thankfully but it was too late. She's gone. She had you and Carey both listed as next of kin. She thought a great deal of you, Marvin."

"When will Carey wake up?"

"It's unlikely that Carey will ever wake up. But that's my medical opinion. I have to tell you that. Unofficially I'll tell you to continue to pray. I've seen God do some things that science can't explain."

"I understand."

"He would do well to be moved to New York City to one of the bigger hospitals. We do pretty well here with what we have but we simply can't provide him with the same level of care. A specialist would be beneficial for a case like this. But the cost-"

Marvin has a glimmer of hope, "I'll take care of the cost."

Dr. Reeve never anticipated this reaction to his suggestion, "Really?"

"Yes, I have - money coming to me."

"Very well. I'll make the arrangements. No guarantees, of course but his odds just went up. I'll send him on over to New York, good people over there. And I'll make a call right now. I know a doctor who will be very interested in Carey's case. He's equipped to handle this. See Miss Garcia in the office before you go. She'll help you with the paperwork and billing. You know her?"

The only daughter of his beloved carpentry mentor? Of course he does. Marvin nods and attempts a smile.

"I know you've had an ordeal tonight but I'd still like to see you in my office as soon as possible. Your mother came by in quite a state."

"Nothing new there."

"There are things you and I need to discuss now that you're an adult. And she doesn't need to be involved. Thank God for that at least."

Realizing his insult to Marvin's mother, "Sorry about that, Marvin. Been a long night."

Marvin's first real grin in hours, "I'm well aware of what a colossal pain in the ass my mother can be. At least now, we can talk about it."

Dr. Reeve chuckles, pats his arm and leaves him alone, watching Carey through the window. The male orderly exits the room and smiles at Marvin. His name tag, "Jackson". He has kind brown eyes and close cropped dark blond hair.

Marvin asks, "Can I go in?"

Jackson hesitates, looking around the empty hallway, "Alright, but just for a second. Just say you snuck in."

He winks at Marvin and heads off down the hallway and around a corner.

Marvin pushes the heavy door open and creeps in, as if he's afraid of waking Carey. But wouldn't that be a miracle!

If he woke up right now, sensing Marvin at his side. The imagined sounds of the equipment were spot on. Marvin has seen enough hospital scenes on Annette's soap operas to have known what to expect.

He stares down at Carey, afraid to take his hand.

I might give him germs or something, he's so fragile. And he doesn't know his grandmother is gone. He's going to be crushed.

He smiles and puts on his best, nonchalant voice, "You're gonna be fine, you know. I'll make sure. I mean, I can't run that farm stand by myself. You always said you were the brains and I was the braun. That's why we're such good partners."

His voice wavers as the tears finally fall, "I'm so sorry, Carey, I know this is my fault."

Pulling himself together he reminds Carey, "We'll be best friends and take care of each other forever."

A wave of dizziness envelopes him. Marvin clutches his pounding head, closing his eyes.

Loud heartbeat sounds.
Lullabye music.
A baby's cries abruptly cut off.
And that smell again!
Men's after shave.

As the dizziness subsides, Marvin steadies himself by putting his hand on the bed. He senses something and looks toward the glass separating him from the outside world.

He can see his reflection in the glass. But-

That's not his reflection.

He leaves Carey's side and goes to the door, keeping his eyes on the figure out in the hallway. He opens the heavy door and faces his doppelganger, unafraid this time.

Mirror Marvin looks at Carey, then back at Marvin.

He leans close, "Kill those bastards."

Marvin closes his eyes, inhales deeply and smiles as the door falls shut behind him.

Mirror Marvin hears something and vanishes as Marvin opens his eyes again.

A man walks around the corner and approaches tentatively. Tall, he has thick dark hair and blue eyes.

A brief glance tricks Marvin into thinking the Sheriff is back. But no. This man is different. He's well dressed - familiar? Not really

"Marvin?"

Marvin stares, dumbstruck, as his father greets him for the first time in almost eighteen years.

"Hello, Marvin."

28

Max takes in the sight of his son.

My son. I can't believe how grownup he is. He looks a lot like me. Except he has Annette's green eyes. And my mother's.

Neither of them speaks, no one wanting to go first.

Max finally breaks the ice, "I'm sorry to just show up like this, Marvin. Your mother told me what happened. That you said you were coming here."

There is a confused look on Marvin's face, barely perceptible as Max continues, "Miss Jezzy was a good woman, the best. She didn't deserve this. And Carey seems like a good young man."

"You don't know him."

Max smiles, "Well I knew Miss Jezzy. Her tolerance for bad behavior was incredibly low."

Marvin smiles, "Yes, it was."

Tears form again at the use of past tense for his beloved Miss Jezzy.

Max gestures to the end of the hallway, "Why don't we go outside? Get some fresh air."

Max sits on the stoop that Steven had occupied and motions for Marvin to join him. Marvin sits and hangs his head.

Max has questions, "Do you-"

Marvin interrupts, "Why are you here?"

Max realizes this won't be easy. "Your mother called me on your birthday. She's concerned about you."

"Where have you been all of these years?"

Max has been anticipating this question, "New York City. Directing on Broadway. I gave up on Hollywood several years ago."

Marvin finally looks at him, "But why would you abandon me?"

This was expected too. He and Annette both come from a world where the unexpected has to be anticipated and prepared for.

"It seemed the best thing for you at the time. I couldn't raise you, no court would give me custody over your mother. And I hired Miss Jezzy to care for you."

Marvin looks down at his lap again, "And then washed your hands of me."

Max's anger at Annette finally shows through, "Your mother made it impossible to negotiate any sort of visitation."

His hands curl into fists.

"Our divorce was extremely acrimonious. I thought that being around that type of hostility would harm you in the long run. I reached out when you turned fifteen. I thought you were old enough for me to explain myself. But you never replied. And I set aside trust money for you-"

Marvin matches his intensity, Max feels like he's looking at himself at that age, "I'd rather have had a father. All these years I've had to take care of *her*. I was the grown up. And I was alone in that house once Mother sent Miss Jezzy and Carey away."

Max hangs his head, "I'm sorry, Marvin. I can make it up to you. Give me a chance."

He reaches into his jacket pocket. He removes a pad and pen and scribbles on it.

He hands the paper to Marvin, "I rented a cabin for a few days. It's near your house. Here's the address and phone number."

Marvin tentatively takes it and nods.

After an awkward pause, Max offers, "Can I give you a ride home?"

He nods towards his 1966 Stingray, parked a few feet away.

Marvin shakes his head, getting up. Max watches him cross the parking lot and get into a red truck.

It's dark but the streetlight illuminates the driver's side window. The passenger side is pitch black.

Marvin sits still for a moment, staring out the windshield, then turns to his right and talks to himself briefly, before driving away, leaving his father alone again.

29

Marvin pulls into Miss Jezzy's driveway.

The house has scorch marks on the exterior wall outside the broken living room window. The pallor of death looms over the house.

Marvin sits in his truck, unwilling to get out, unwilling to see the damage, unwilling to put himself through even more pain. But he has to. He owes it to them. He stares at the truck door handle, unable to move it at first but finally he turns it and gets out.

He looks inside Carey's car as he passes it. Four law books litter the back seat. He opens the front door and reaches back to retrieve them. He carries the stack toward his truck and places them in the passenger seat.

Walking back to the house, the acrid smell of the burned fabric of the drapes assaults his nose.

Stepping up onto the porch, he notices that Miss Jezzy's flower vase is overturned. He sets it upright, arranging the Black-eyed Susans the way she would have liked. He'll replace the vase, this one is cracked now.

With a glance at the rocker, he heads inside.

There's minimal fire damage to the living room. At least the Sheriff got the fire out quickly. Remembering his outburst at him earlier, Marvin feels great regret. He took his anger out on the closest person to a father he's ever had.

Seeing his own biological father reminds him of how much Steven McClane has meant to him over the years. And to Carey as well. The three of them fish together frequently.

Carey always had the best luck when they fished along the Delaware River. The Sheriff said Carey's easy demeanor charmed the fish right out of the river and onto the bank.

But he knows that the Sheriff always had a special affection for Marvin, he hoped Marvin would call him "Dad" one day.

As Marvin got older and more aware of his mother's outrageous behavior, he realized that the Sheriff had dodged a figurative bullet in that department. He'll call him tomorrow and apologize.

He had wanted someone to blame when he lashed out earlier. But this couldn't have been prevented. Could it? Was this really his fault?

He's not going to pretend he doesn't know who did this. Would they have left Miss Jezzy and Carey alone if he hadn't thrown that jar?

John and Roger Carter have always been poor students and gotten into some trouble but this? Known to fistfight on occasion, neither boy could ever have been thought of as murderous.

The whole night feels like a dream until his eyes fall on Miss Jezzy's glasses near her chair before landing on the pool of thick coppery blood in the kitchen. The metallic smell hovers in the air. He can't believe that he's lost everything.

The remains of the pumpkin that he'd given Carey lay ruined on the floor.

Suddenly, he remembers, "Oh no. Poor Theodore." Assuming the worst and afraid of what he'll find, he heads back into the living room.

"He's fine."

A voice from deep down the dark hallway that Roger Carter loomed in just a few hours ago.

Mirror Marvin slowly appears and stands in the kitchen. Mirror Marvin. That's the name that Marvin has given him, since he's been elusive about his name. Not creative, but applicable.

Marvin finally asks, "Who are you really?"

Mirror Marvin pauses for a long moment, considering his answer, "A friend."

He points, "Look under the stove."

Marvin gets on his knees, careful to avoid the blood, and sees a flash of metal. He reaches under the stove and pulls out a pocketknife. The initials R.C. clumsily carved by hand into the wooden handle.

Marvin ponders as he considers the pristine blade, "I caused this. By hurting them."

"They just wanted an excuse. It would have happened eventually. You know that."

Marvin closes the knife and shakes it, "I should give this to the

Sheriff. Then they can both go to jail."

"Is that what you want? For them to go to jail?"

Marvin, staring at his new friend, staring at himself, "No."

Kneeling down next to Marvin, his mirror image asks, "What do you want?"

Marvin reaches into his pocket and removes the blood-stained photo. He unfolds it and holds it up for Mirror Marvin to see.

Mirror Marvin smiles at the image of the two best friends. The two boys in the photo didn't have a care in the world.

Marvin, stoic, "I want John and Roger dead."

Mirror Marvin's smile broadens as he nods.

30

Exhausted, Marvin trudges into his house from the back door into the kitchen, followed by Mirror Marvin.

Marvin assumes his counterpart can shut the door so he continues ahead of him. Mirror Marvin reaches for the doorknob with his face scrunched up, concentrating.

Unsure. He touches it! He shuts the door with great verve, spinning in a circle on his heels. He smiles, holding up his hand, wiggling his fingers in front of his face.

I'm getting stronger.

Marvin turns on him suddenly, intense but not angry, "Tell me who you really are. Stop being evasive. What's your name?"

Mirror Marvin puts his hands in his pockets, head down and walks over to the far end of the living room. He ponders while staring at the feature wall, head tilted with a lopsided grin.

He lingers on Jimmy Stewart and his shadow friend while he replies, "Call me Harvey."

He considers telling Marvin more but now isn't the time. He's not ready. An idea! Harvey reaches up and shifts the poster so that it's hanging unevenly. Hardly noticeable.

Marvin stares at the poster, confused about his new friend's motives in moving it. He keeps his distance from it, out of instinct. There's always been something about it that's not right.

A coldness.

It doesn't make sense. The movie was a comedy, really delightful. So why does he get a knot in his stomach every time he looks at that shadowy rabbit and the beloved actor?

Probably because it was Annette's big break and his birth ruined it for her. Well, he never asked to be born and he has a father now so she doesn't matter as much anymore.

Harvey glides over to stand between the portraits of the fallen Kennedy brothers. He sees his reflection in the glass of Bobby's photo, his own clear image next to the fallen man.

He's fixated, a thought occurring to him until he is distracted by Marvin's yawn.

He turns to Marvin, smiling, "You need some sleep, we'll talk tomorrow."

Sudden movement startles them both. Theodore waddles out from his nest in the corner of the dark room, bumping into a side table. Both boys sigh relief as Marvin falls to the floor, clutching the dog close to him, a living reminder of what he's lost tonight. Theodore covers Marvin's face with slobber, licking the tears.

Harvey glances into the corner and sees that Annette actually used her fur coat to create a bed for the decrepit old dog.

Harvey is surprised, "Huh".

Maybe she's not beyond hope. Then he remembers. His expression turns sour.

As Harvey considers Annette's uncharacteristic behavior, a car door slams outside and he vanishes into thin air. Theodore barks and wags his tail as Annette saunters in from the back door.

She carries a long, slim paper bag along with her handbag. Marvin knows what it contains without asking. She sets her things down and sits on the couch next to her son and the dog. Theodore, glad to see her, licks her hand. A genuine smile spreads across her face as she pats him and gestures to the corner.

She says to Marvin, "I had no idea where he would sleep. He didn't seem capable of handling the stairs."

It's nice not to have to perform for once. Authenticity feels invigorating, she might try it once in a while.

Her brief time caring for the dog had been pleasant. Initially she was horrified to see him treading up her driveway into her pristine home. Dogs can be so messy.

But when Marvin left for the hospital earlier she attempted to make him comfortable. She had genuine empathy for him, for losing his family so suddenly. And she regretted her handling of the situation with Marvin.

She doesn't possess any natural maternal instincts, she's had to work to understand the bond between mother and child. And she's failed more often than succeeded.

But caring for the old dog had awakened something in her, a part of her that Steven had always called her "hidden angel". He so wanted her to share that part of herself with everyone and her refusal to do it had only hastened the demise of their relationship.

She lightens Marvin's somber mood, "He ate a T-bone steak earlier so I'm afraid he has expensive tastes. So, I thought he may as well sleep on my fur coat. Because you're right, I have no use for it."

Without looking up, Marvin replies, "Thank you."

She actually reaches down and rumples Theodore's face with both hands before Marvin rises abruptly and guides the dog back to his bed. Already accustomed to his new life of luxury, Theodore climbs on the fur coat and curls up into a ball, falling asleep almost immediately.

Annette grins, "He's actually quite sweet. I rather enjoy him. I was never allowed a dog as a child."

Marvin faces her for a moment then heads upstairs, "Neither was I."

"Marvin?"

He stops but doesn't turn around.

She continues, "I'll be going to New York in the morning. Staying the night there. I have business. Will you be alright alone? Considering everything?"

"Yes."

He continues upstairs slowly, tired to the bone. Once he disappears, Annette retrieves her handbag and paper bag. Her back to the feature wall, she senses something.

Fear trickles down her spine as she shudders. Wheeling around, her eyes laser in on the HARVEY poster. She creeps toward it, it's slightly askew.

Did someone touch it? No, Marvin wouldn't touch it, he's always been rather - what do the kids say - *freaked out* by it.

As well he should be. Why does she keep the damn thing? A reminder of her power.

Overwhelmed with anxiety, she straightens the poster, then follows Marvin upstairs.

Time to dive into that paper bag.

31

As the morning sun peeks over the horizon, Annette strolls out the front door, suitcase in hand.

She's sober, having only dipped into the newest bottle of alcohol in her collection. She has to keep her head when she's driving. Particularly for such a distance.

Marvin always suggests she take the train into town but she can't tolerate the people who tend to ride the train. Always some varlet leering at her. There was a time when she was driven around New York City in a hired car, hoping never again to have to lower herself to getting behind the wheel. But those days are long gone. Her condition has changed.

She places the suitcase in her trunk (yet another task she used to delegate), slams it, and gets in the car. She checks her face in the rearview mirror, contemplating the enormity of this trip. Does she dare do this?

Speaking to her own determined likeness, "It's the only way."

After one last glance at the house, she heads down the driveway. Marvin watches her from his window on the second floor. After she turns onto the road, leaving a trail of dust in spite of her sluggish crawl, Marvin disappears from the window.

Marvin and Harvey both exit the house, heads together, planning, and cross to the workshop. Marvin gestures for Harvey to wait as he trots over to his truck.

Opening the passenger door, he leans in, opening the glove box. He removes the trust fund document and Annette's commitment form from his back pocket and places them inside. He shuts the glove box, locks it and puts the key under the floor mat.

He slams the door shut and runs over to Harvey, who puts his arm around him as they head to the workshop. When they reach the doors, they each raise a door in tandem and go inside.

Work to be done.

32

As the sun sets, Marvin leaves the house and walks to the workshop, taking in the cool fall air.

He's wearing his white t-shirt with large yellow smiley face, freshly laundered. Another chore he's always had to perform for himself since Miss Jezzy left them. He inhales the clean evening air, putting his hands in his pockets.

As he approaches the workshop, he stops and observes a squirrel on his chopping block. The small creature freezes when it sees Marvin but as Marvin creeps closer, the squirrel relaxes, oddly at ease.

It explores the ax that is stuck in the block.

Marvin shoos it away, picks up the ax, then calls after the animal, "Gotta be careful, this is sharp. Wouldn't want anybody to get hurt."

He swings the ax into the block with two hands, then opens the left door of his workshop. Disappearing into the blackness, he shuts it behind him.

He flips the light switch and the lights spasm, worse than before. The bulbs didn't get changed. So much has happened in such a short period of time, it just didn't get done. He stands pensively by the door, not noticing that the plague doctor mask is missing from its nail on the wall.

A sound of scuffling in the back of the room has him on alert. A raccoon? Possum? Last time it was Harvey.

He senses them before he sees them.

Roger and John stand up from where they were crouched behind a long wooden crate on Marvin's worktable. Both wear their leather jackets but the similarity ends there.

John is furious and vengeful. Roger is nervous and scared. Both are clear-eyed and sober which could be a problem. An unsteady drunk is easier to manage.

Marvin does a quick scan of the area behind them to see if they've chosen a weapon from his myriad of tools on the pegboard wall.

Everything seems to be in place, including the newest baseball bat on the lathe, nearly finished. Another project, this bat is meant for someone special.

John whispers, "Hey clown boy."

Marvin is silent, thinking. He's outnumbered but stands calm.

John again, "You gonna just stand there like a moron?"

Marvin tilts his head slightly, penetrating, patronizing. John steps out from behind the worktable, getting closer, followed by his pathetic, shaking brother.

John makes a finger gun and points it at Marvin, "You're dead."

Marvin remains still.

John creeps closer, gesturing at his eye patch, "First I'm taking your eye. Maybe both of them. I've got nothing to lose at this point."

Marvin has a hint of a smile. An idea!

He waves his hands in front of him like a magician. A great flourish, followed by placing his hands over his eyes for a moment. John and Roger are confused. This isn't what they expected. They freeze, regarding his odd behavior. Marvin quickly removes his hands and –

HIS EYES ARE GONE!

Only inky black, empty caverns remain. The brothers are terrified and rooted in place.

Roger squeaks, "It's a trick, it has to be!"

John, more angry than afraid, "How'd you do that, Marvin?"

Marvin puts his hands over his empty sockets again. When he removes them, his eyes are back to bright green. He does a Ta-Da motion like a magician, complete with a bow.

To Roger he replies, "It's not a trick."

Marvin pauses then sighs deeply, turning to John.

"And I'm not Marvin."

The baffled brothers are suddenly deafened by the sound of the floor fan. It sounds like a freight train in the enclosed space. They cover their ears as dust churns up from the floor creating a tan tornado cloud that envelopes the room.

Coughing and choking, they are blind and deaf. The fan turns off, the thrumming in their ears subsiding. The dust cloud remains, slow to settle.

HISS!

The momentary dead silence is interrupted by the propane gas being lit.

KNOCK!

The steamer pipes.

The empty lathe becomes visible as the dust clears but the boys don't notice it. Turning towards the sound of the pipe knocking, the coughing boys see the real Marvin wearing the plague doctor mask looming in front of them.

"The Monkees Theme" song blasts through the speaker system. Marvin's dig at John for criticizing his favorite band t-shirt two days ago.

Was it only two days ago? Feels like a lifetime.

The innocuous boy band's gleeful description of walking around and receiving strange looks from passersby fills the room. The Carter boys cover their ears again.

The sight of Marvin in the mask combined with the loud music terrifies the boys. They grope, half-blind, for the doors, hacking up dust and debris as they try to escape.

John's hand lands on the red handled ax hanging by the door. He grabs it and turns to protect himself but his idiot brother Roger slams into him with all his body weight and the ax clatters to the floor. John forgets about it and focuses on getting out of this hellhole.

As The Monkees croon about monkeying around, John and Roger both grab the door handle. Locked. They beat on it and yell for help. Freezing, they sense someone behind them.

Petrified, then turn.

Harvey stands with the brand new baseball bat resting on his shoulder, a huge smile on his face.

The music skips to a stop. The brothers are confused more than usual.

Marvin is unbothered by the dust, but how? It's not possible.

Roger pleads, "Hey, we were just messing around. Gonna maybe break something. That's all. We'll go away."

Harvey holds his hand up and cups his ear, pretending to listen intently, "All I heard was break something."

Both boys shake their heads and cling to each other, afraid for their pathetic lives.

Harvey considers them both for a second, twirling the bat with precision, then smiles again, "OK."

He swings the bat down and it wrecks John's right arm. The clean snap of a twig is followed by a shriek of pain. A satisfied expression spreads across Harvey's face.

He twirls the bat again and lays it across his shoulder as John falls to the ground, cradling his broken arm.

Horrified at the sight of his injured brother, Roger scampers on hands and knees behind the steamer. The intense heat radiates out, scalding him. Squealing, he finds his original hiding spot behind the worktable. He cowers, weeping silently, praying.

Harvey looms over the whimpering John. Marvin steps in next to him, still wearing the plague mask as the dust settles. John shakes his head, not comprehending what he's seeing.

It must be the pain. It has to be.

There can't be two Marvins.

The guy in the mask must just look a bit like - but Marvin removes the mask before John can convince himself of what he's seeing. It lays on top of his head.

John can't believe it, "What the fuck? How are-?"

A swing of the bat knocks him out before he can finish. Hearing the impact of the bat, a shriek from the back of the room causes Marvin and Harvey to turn in tandem. They stare at the worktable, then at each other. Nodding they head towards it.

Cornered, Roger attempts to scamper away crab-like, backwards. Harvey vanishes from Marvin's side and reappears behind Roger, who backs into him. He's questioning his own senses, just as his brother did a moment ago.

He just saw one of the Marvins disappear into thin air, that's not possible. But now he's right here, behind him.

Why did he listen to John?

How he'd begged his older brother to go to the Sheriff with him, to plead for mercy. Sheriff McClane had shown them both kindness over the years.

More often than not, he'd given them grief over their behavior, but always with a glimmer of empathy. Maybe they can still talk to him, and do the time required for their crime. Anything to get out of this hellhole.

Harvey towers over him, threatening with the bat as Marvin gets closer. Roger is trapped. Roger falls back on his butt against the back wall, afraid to receive the same shellacking with the bat that his brother got.

Harvey reads his mind and lays the bat down on the worktable, showing Roger his empty hands. Momentary relief floods Roger until Harvey and Marvin grab and lift him. When he sees where they are taking him, his guttural cries fill the workroom.

KNOCK. KNOCK. KNOCK.

The temperature gauge on the steamer registers three hundred fifty degrees. Roger digs his heels against the concrete floor but is no match for the two bigger boys.

This isn't real. They wouldn't really hurt me. They're just trying to scare me.

Roger cries out, "It was my brother! I didn't want to do it! It wasn't supposed to go that way! We were just gonna beat him up a little bit! Things got outta control!"

KNOCK.

Marvin spins Roger towards him, grabbing him by the collar, "You can't blame your brother for your actions. What about the time you threw rocks at Theodore? An old dog who couldn't run away from you. Or the time you tore up Miss Jezzy's garden, knowing that's how she makes money to live. The way you constantly terrorized Carey with your name-calling and threats. Your brother wasn't around for that. So, don't play innocent."

Marvin looks from Roger to the steamer to Harvey. It can't be opened while it's on.

"I can't open-".

Harvey holds both hands up, grinning, "It can't hurt me."

He leans close to Roger, "You, on the other hand. Oof."

Harvey opens the steamer with no worries. A cloud of steam escapes, covering him in fog but causing no harm. He waves it away.

Roger's terror gives way to acceptance as his bladder lets go, "I'm so sorry."

Marvin loosens his grip on the boy's collar and smooths his shirt. Roger smiles, hopeful. He's known Marvin his whole life, he's not the type to hurt anyone. He's seen him care for injured animals, help people. He's going to let him go.

Marvin leans close to Roger's face, "Bullshit."

He throws Roger into the steamer. Harvey shuts and clamps the lid with lightning speed. A brief agonized wail before…silence.

KNOCK. KNOCK. KNOCK.

Harvey studies Marvin, they've crossed a line now. The way that Marvin is staring at the steamer makes him wonder.

Is that a look of regret?

It's understandable, Marvin is a kind, loving soul. He's no murderer. He may have to talk to him, to remind him of what this is about.

It's not murder. It's justice.

Harvey puts his hand on Marvin's arm, reassuring. Marvin looks up at him, raises his chin and nods. They turn in unison and head toward the front of the shop.

John regains consciousness slowly. Ceiling lights flicker, casting horrifying shadows. And something creeps in as his vision clears. Miss Jezzy leans over him, her familiar gentle smile spreading across her face.

She shakes her head, "What you got yourself into, John Carter? You were a sweet little boy, you coulda made something of yourself. Why'd you do this to me? Why?"

Before he can respond, beg forgiveness, her dark face shrinks and rots in front of him.

Unable to move away from her, he watches wide-eyed in horror as the kindly old woman becomes unrecognizable, skin and muscles turning putrid and sliding off of her skull before she falls away to the floor out of sight.

Grateful that the hideous image is gone, he tries to sit up but a skeletal hand reaches over the side of the table, stopping him. The hand creeps towards his face.

He screams for his life.

He wakes up, heaving and shaking. He's lying in the wooden

crate on the worktable.

It was a dream. A horrible dream. Thank God.

Marvin leans over him. Harvey sits on the steamer, still unaffected by the intense heat.

Marvin nods to him, "Turn it off."

Harvey turns it off, the hiss of steam escaping, the knocking and groaning subsiding.

He opens the lid, looks inside, and pulls a disgusted face, "Yuck, you're gonna need a new steamer, Marvin. No amount of Comet is gonna get this out."

He shuts it again, then leans over John from the opposite side of the crate. John shakes his head, still trying to make sense of what he's seeing. Two Marvins?

Harvey reaches into John's pocket and retrieves his car keys. He makes a great show of dangling them in front of John and smiling. Then he tosses the keys to Marvin who puts them in his front pocket. Harvey walks away humming.

John tries to follow him with his eyes but his vision is limited by the crate. Marvin taps John's forehead to get his attention back. Turning back to Marvin he sees that he got some of his blood on his fingers.

Marvin holds his fingers up to his face, mesmerized by the bright red smear on his fingertips. It smells like copper, metal. He rubs his fingers together, transfixed by the texture of the fresh blood.

This image chills John, more so than anything that has happened so far. Marvin shakes his head, ending the distraction of the blood and wiping it on his smiley face shirt.

Focusing again on John, "Where is your stupid car?"

John mumbles, "Woods across the street, behind the speed limit sign," before passing out again.

Harvey watches Marvin from his place at the front of the shop, by the doors. Looking down, he notices the ax that John had tried to defend himself with. It's on the floor, kicked to one side.

Harvey gingerly picks it up by the blade with only two fingers and smiles, "Well, well, well. I love it when people make my job easier."

Setting it down against a corner wall, he opens the door and heads out into the black night.

<h1 style="text-align:center">33</h1>

Marvin drives his truck and Harvey rides shotgun.

They bump across the uneven yard towards the pumpkin patch. The crate that carries John is in the bed of the truck next to something wrapped in a tarp.

When Marvin crafted the crate earlier that day, he had a different name for it.

"It's a coffin," he stoically told Harvey.

He hopes in the depths of his soul that John has figured that out by now.

Marvin parks at the edge of the patch, careful not to crush any of his prized pumpkins. He likely won't be entering any contests this year. Too much else to do.

It's a shame too, he always wins at least one ribbon. But there's always next year, isn't there?

The harvest moon peeks out from behind some clouds, illuminating the yard. Harvey hops out of the truck, full of energy.

Marvin gets out more slowly, amazed at his counterpart's enthusiasm. They both grab the coffin and heave it out of the truck and over to the hole in the middle of the patch that awaits it. It's heavy but Marvin is up to the task. And Harvey matches Marvin's strength, outmatches him even.

Harvey glances down at the coffin and sees John's open eye looking through the space between the slats. He looks terrified.

Good.

John whimpers pitifully, "Marvin?"

The boys stop and set the coffin down next to the hole. A shovel stands in a pile of freshly dug dirt.

Harvey opens the hinged, squeaking lid then stands to the side to allow Marvin one last chance to face his enemy. Marvin leans down over John.

He can't find the words to say. Marvin gestures for him to say *something.*

John stutters, "I- please."

"Please what?"

"I know we were never really friends-"

Harvey guffaws, "That's the understatement of the damn year. You were a pain in Marvin's ass his whole life. Calling him names, making fun of him. Just because you were jealous because you knew you were nothing but a piece of shit."

John nods, tears mixing with the blood on his face, "You're right. I thought Marvin had everything and I had nothing. And Miss Jezzy-"

Marvin tenses at the mention of her name but Harvey places a calming hand on his shoulder.

John continues, "Miss Jezzy. She tried to help us but my dad wouldn't have her around. He hates colored people, taught us to hate them too. But she was a nice lady. She never gave up on us, even at the end."

Marvin's interest is piqued by this, "What are you talking about?"

He continues, "She said it wasn't too late, that she could help us. But she didn't know-"

Harvey chimes in, impatient, "Didn't know what?"

John looks him straight in the eye, "My dad came after me again. He started beating us both with his belt. I managed to shove him and he fell down the stairs. Broke his neck. He's dead."

Shrieking now, "I killed him! I didn't mean it! I didn't mean it!"

Concerned about Marvin's pensive expression, Harvey continues to question John, "So you thought you'd go on over to Miss Jezzy's and kill her and Carey too? Since you were on a roll?"

John rattles his head back and forth, hissing from the pain of the head wound, "No, no, nothing like that. I got drunk, real drunk and we just, well, you know."

Harvey folds his arms and glares down at him, "Well, what a charming story, John. Have to say I'm glad your dad's gone. Sounds like a real jackass. But that doesn't excuse your actions."

The faint sound of laughing children distracts them all. The noise drifts closer and closer. Harvey holds up a finger to Marvin, vanishes for a brief moment, then reappears with an enormous bag of assorted candy.

He shows it to Marvin with a sheepish shrug, "We owe old Mr. Grim at the corner market for this, I just stole it."

He rips the bag open, spilling several pieces on the ground then races toward the street, shouting as he goes, "Hi kids! Hang on, I'm coming! Sorry I'm late!"

The children know better than to come up the Damon's driveway. Every year "Mr. Marvin" (he's been Mr. Marvin for the past few years, primarily because of his height more than his age) sets up a table next to the road with candy and small pumpkins for the hordes of children that parade down the street.

Although Mrs. Damon has been known to provide small pieces of candy over the years, her desire to be left alone always seeps into her demeanor as she drops candy into the bags of the eager little neighbors with barely a smile.

Nonplussed by the arrival of the trick or treaters, Marvin grabs the shovel and crouches down behind the coffin, hidden by the hinged, open lid.

He places the blade of the shovel against John's neck to keep him quiet. Marvin and John hear Harvey greet the excited children. To them it sounds like there are four or five of them.

Marvin peeks around the lid and sees *himself* leaning down to speak to Jimmy Dobrovsky, a delightful little seven year-old who lives on the next street.

His father owns the butcher shop in town and is a wonderful trading partner for Marvin, providing him with steaks several days ago in exchange for work on his shutters.

Theodore is the latest happy recipient of the barter system that Marvin has cultivated with vendors throughout the area.

It's an out of body experience, watching Harvey stand in as him. But it seems right somehow. Something that Harvey should be doing, but he can't figure out why. He smiles.

Jimmy pipes up over the other children's banter, pointing towards the pumpkin patch, "What are you doing, Mr. Marvin?"

Marvin ducks down out of sight again. Johnny jumps up and down as he speaks, the sugar rush hitting him. The children's parents are nowhere to be seen.

There's no need to accompany the children, nothing bad ever happens around here in the land of unlocked doors and innocuous pumpkin patches.

Harvey laughs and replies, genuinely having a blast with the kids, "I'm burying a body. What else would I be doing on Halloween?"

He and the children all giggle.

John looks confused for a moment, then whispers to Marvin, "It's Halloween?"

Marvin reaches down and grabs a Tootsie Roll from the few candies dropped by Harvey. He tosses it into the box, hitting John in the face.

Marvin's muffled voice, "Trick or treat, asshole."

Another child gleefully asks, "Who is it?!"

Yet another jumper, candy has been going straight from the bags into their mouths tonight.

Harvey responds, "A really bad guy. So, we'll all be a lot better off without him!"

A chorus of children scream and yell, "Yea! No bad guys! Yea!" as they crinkle candy wrappers and giggle.

One child says, "Thank you!" and the others follow with a chorus of thank yous as their voices fade back the way they came, Marvin's house being the last on the street.

Harvey yells after them, "You're welcome. Now go have fun and be good or you'll end up in my pumpkin patch too."

The children yell back to him, "We will, Mr. Marvin!"

Harvey looks after them for a minute, awash in nostalgia for reasons known only to him. He runs back to the patch.

John asks, "How are there two of you?"

Marvin looks at Harvey and puts his hand on Harvey's shoulder, "This is my guardian angel."

Harvey bows low to John, stands, then salutes with a lopsided grin.

John pleads, "Please let me go, I'll leave town. You'll never hear from me ever again."

Marvin is curious, "You haven't even asked about your brother."

John hesitates, his lips moving.

Harvey gets close, his hand cupped to his ear, "What's that? You want to say something?"

John finally relents, "Where is he?"

Marvin gestures toward his truck as John yells, "Roger!"

Marvin puts the shovel back in John's face, "Quiet."

Harvey jogs to the truck, jovial, "I'll get Roger, he can't wait to see you."

Crickets chirp. Followed by the creak as Harvey leaps into the bed of the truck and the rustling of fabric. Harvey pulls the tarp out of the truck and drags it over to the coffin. He and Marvin each pick up a side and proceed to reunite the two brothers.

To call this hideous mass of gristle and bones "Roger" would be generous. Roger's eye sockets are empty, his eyeballs having melted away back into his skull and down his face in mucousy streams.

Third degree burns cover his entire body, his leather jacket and jeans are liquified into his skin, creating a hideous collage of colors and textures. Most of his exposed skin has slid off of his bones.

And the smell is - for the remainder of John's short life, he'll compare it to pork that's been boiled so long that the water has evaporated from the pot it sits in.

Roger's skeletal hand covers John's face but he's too incapacitated with fear to remove it. He can't muster the strength to scream at this point.

Marvin is calm, "It was quick. For him."

Harvey sits on the ground next to the coffin and leans over, resting his chin on his crossed arms, "You're not the brightest so I'll explain it to you. And I'll speak slowly. It. Won't. Be. Quick. For. You."

John cries as he sees what happened to his brother. And what will happen to him.

Marvin wavers a bit at John's outburst. Harvey has to think on his feet, it's too late to turn back now, they've come too far.

He puts his hand on Marvin's shoulder, turning him towards him. Harvey looks him in the eye and goes to the truck. "Daydream Believer" by the Monkees floats out of the open window of the truck over the misty patch. Davy Jones sings about sleepy Jean and a homecoming queen.

The last time Marvin heard this song it was-

34
Six Months Ago

$-\text{A}$ bright clear day, the sun bursting through the huge oak trees surrounding Miss Jezzy's house.

Unusually warm for April, Miss Jezzy lumbers out onto the porch balancing a tray containing three orange popsicles. She sets it on the folding table next to her rocker.

Shading her eyes and stretching her back, she searches the yard for her boys, "Come on now, 'fore they melt."

She listens but gets no answer. Used to their constant jokes and "silly nonsense" she descends the steps and puts her hands on her hips.

"Well, since y'all are gone, Imma eat all three!"

Uproarious laughter fills the air. Unable to find the source, but in good spirits, she shouts again, "Where y'all at? Gone back to the Maker?"

Marvin's voice, "Pretty close."

She follows the sound of his voice and finds both boys hanging on branches of the largest oak tree in her yard, limbs dangling. They hover twenty feet off the ground.

Miss Jezzy doesn't like heights, "Get on down here! You know better than that!"

The boys descend quick as squirrels as she continues, "Y'all 'bout scared me to damn death."

Jumping the last few feet, they run over and barrage her with hugs and kisses, begging forgiveness, until she smiles and waves them off.

Carey and Marvin run over to the porch, out of breath and each grab a popsicle. They yank the paper wrappers off and dig into them.

Miss Jezzy laughs and opens her popsicle more carefully as Theodore emerges from inside the house. She sits in her rocker and he lays down at her feet.

She pets him before snapping a piece of the popsicle off to feed it to him. He gulps it down enthusiastically.

Carey turns on the small radio under Miss Jezzy's table.

"Daydream Believer" by the Monkees wafts out. Marvin turns the volume all the way up as he leaps up and off the porch into the yard dancing.

Carey bursts into laughter and joins him. Miss Jezzy guffaws, slapping her knee, as her glasses slip down her nose.

Theodore barks happily.

Marvin imitates the dance that Davy Jones does on the Monkees television show as they blissfully enjoy yet another happy day together.

35

Remembering what he's lost, Marvin screams in agony, glaring down at John.

The condemned boy has given up, he mumbles incoherently to himself, eyes closed. Mesmerized again, Marvin kneels down and touches John's head wound.

The blood calls out to him. It has a message for him and when he sees the blood on his fingers he finally understands. He felt something special when he first saw John's blood but wasn't sure what it was, a stirring, a whispering memory.

He's always known in the depths of his soul but now he has total clarity as the message bubbles up from the abyss.

Harvey is unsure what Marvin is doing so he kneels down next to him, ready to provide the support system that Marvin has lacked his entire life.

Marvin shows him the blood on his fingers and Harvey nods, attempting to understand.

Marvin then puts his fingers up to his face and for one horrible moment, Harvey fears Marvin is going to consume the blood.

A Protestant, not a Catholic, he's not really gonna take communion that seriously, is he?

As Harvey prepares to stop him, he sees what Marvin's true intention is.

Marvin creates the Baby Marvin dots on his face. Two large dots on his cheeks and one on the end of his nose. Harvey smiles at him, finally understanding.

Marvin gets more blood from John's wound and looks to Harvey, eyebrows raised in query. Harvey, that lopsided grin on his face, nods consent.

Marvin creates the dots on Harvey's face as well, Harvey sitting still as a stone for the ritual.

Once Marvin has finished, he leans in close to John. He thumps his cheek to get his attention. John opens his eyes, petrified at the face he sees leering down at him in his final resting place.

Tears stream down Marvin's face, streaking the bloody dots.

He points at his face and declares to John, "THIS IS WHAT SUCCESS LOOKS LIKE!"

John's final words, "Fucking clown freak."

Harvey slams the lid shut and grabs the shovel.

He finishes digging the hole as Marvin does the Davy Jones dance in the pumpkin patch under the moonlight.

Muffled screams mix with the beloved tune from the radio.

36

The First Baptist Church of God's Glorious Mountains sits nestled in a peaceful valley.

The same valley that houses the hospital where critically injured Carey is currently being loaded into an ambulance destined for New York City.

The sun rises over the small whitewashed wooden building, but the church is empty today.

Parishioners are gathered in the cemetery attached to the church, surrounded by a white picket fence. A fence that Marvin has voluntarily kept intact over the past few years as most of the parishioners are well beyond fifty.

A serene and beautiful fall day, colored leaves drift down from a mammoth oak tree in the middle of the small graveyard. The oak tree reminds Marvin of the one in Miss Jezzy's yard, the one that he and Carey used to climb, much to her chagrin.

Several dozen white chairs face an exquisite cherry wood casket. Murmurs about the cost of the casket were heard upon the mourner's arrival.

Jezzy didn't have more than two nickels, where'd the money for that come from? God rest her soul, she's goin' out as she should, in glory.

Who paid for it? Marvin?! Are you sure? My goodness!

Miss Jezzy lies peacefully inside. Wearing her finest dark blue satin church dress, she appears merely to slumber, her dark skin contrasting against the white lace collar of her dress.

The chairs are filled with faces of all colors and varieties, sitting together to honor their departed friend. Dr. Reeve, Mrs. Bonilla, young Bobby, Postmaster and Mrs. Williams and Steven McLean are among the mourners.

Steven sits next to Marvin and wears a simple black suit. No uniform today. And no hat. Miss Jezzy always made fun of him for wearing a cowboy hat as part of his uniform.

"Steven, this ain't Tombstone and you ain't nobody's Wyatt Earp."

Steven watches Marvin closely, concerned for him.

Marvin sits solemnly in the front row, wearing a black suit and tie. He seems unaware of the Sheriff's presence although he had greeted Marvin with a handshake and hug upon arriving.

He sits with his arm on the back of Marvin's seat and hopes he can help with his grief.

Marvin feels isolated here at this church that he had never been allowed to attend. The place that he had hoped to make his new church home now that he's grown.

Without Jezzy and Carey, he feels that he has no place here after all. Marvin holds a bouquet of Black-eyed Susans from Miss Jezzy's garden with a yellow ribbon around them. He hangs his head, defeated and weary.

Pastor Agamemnon Higgins finishes his brief sermon. Fifty-six years old, he was a lifelong friend of Miss Jezzy, but he hides his grief in order to minister to his flock.

His dark weathered skin belongs to an older man but Pastor Higgins has earned his lines and wrinkles, having spent his early years working the fields of Georgia.

Known to talk quite a bit, Jezzy once said he'd "talk the ear offa the Lord God almighty Himself", he keeps his remarks simple.

Jezzy had a powerful soul and he's sure she'll be shaking her spiritual finger at him if he drones on too long.

His warm presence comforts the mourners as he perfectly balances his sermon between solemnity and celebration in spite of the horrible circumstances. The stalwart people in this congregation have faced losses that are inconceivable but their faith has taken them through the worst of them.

Pastor Higgins spreads his arms wide, "Now as we close, brothers and sisters, we continue to lift up our sister Jezebel's precious grandson, Carey, and keep him in our prayers. He is being moved to a more advanced hospital, no offense to our own kindly Dr Reeve."

Dr. Reeve smiles at the acknowledgement.

Pastor Higgins continues, "I also want to extend our hand in love to our brother in Christ, young Marvin."

Shocked, Marvin looks up, eyes swimming. Pastor Higgins steps toward Marvin, bending down and addressing him directly but loud enough for everyone to hear.

He takes Marvin's hand, "Miss Jezzy never suffered the burden of minding her own business as we all dearly know."

Soft laughter and a few 'Amens' from everyone and a smile from Marvin.

He continues, "She spoke of you, Marvin, often and with great affection. I know she ministered to you and that certain circumstances kept you from worshipping with us in the past. But you need to know that you have a home here with us you need it. You know some of the folks out here today. And the rest wanna get to know you. We're happy to add you to our family."

He stands and speaks to the crowd, "Amen?"

The crowd enthusiastically replies in unison, "Amen!"

Pastor Higgins smiles and raises his hands to Heaven, "Now go in peace and remember Miss Jezzy on this day. Love up on everybody you meet. And somebody better get me that piccalilli recipe."

Everyone stands amidst more soft laughter but they get quiet as they watch Marvin walk to the open casket and place the flowers on Miss Jezzy's chest.

He whispers, "Goodbye, Miss Jezzy."

Dr. Reeve strides up and puts his arm around Marvin as other congregants approach to give their final goodbyes to Miss Jezzy. They all greet Marvin with warm smiles and hugs. He knows many of these people and finds great comfort with them.

Steven stays seated as Marvin is surrounded.

A diminutive, stout black woman reaches up to straighten the much taller Marvin's tie. She has to rise on tip toe to reach him.

Another woman comments, "Watch out, Eunice is off fixing everybody."

Eunice turns sharply but smiles wide at the woman.

She faces Marvin again and brushes off his shoulders, "Nonsense, you don't need fixin', just adjustin'. Miss Jezzy'd be so proud of you. You're a good boy, Marvin. Takin' care of Carey like you are, you're sent by the good Lord himself. Now bend down here and give me a hug."

Marvin grins and gives Eunice a great hug, lifting her off the ground slightly to the delight of Eunice and the crowd. Pastor Higgins walks over to Marvin and puts his arm around him, guiding him to the church building. Everyone follows them.

Almost everyone.

Steven's gaze fixes on the horizon.

She'd have loved this day, she always enjoyed a beautiful sunrise.

He had spent innumerable early mornings on her front porch watching the sunrise, sipping her piping hot coffee. He always perched on the top step next to her rocker in spite of her repeated offers to sit on the porch swing.

"I always feel like I'm a kid when I'm with you, seems more appropriate to sit down here."

A scoff followed by a guttural laugh from her when he compared her thick coffee to boiled motor oil. She chided him that northerners wouldn't know good coffee if it bit 'em in the butt. That comment nearly choked him with laughter, the coffee threatening to spray out of his nose.

Tears had been threatening during the service but he kept them back, his desire to be a strong presence for Marvin overriding his own grief. He's also considered it unseemly to appear emotional in public, being the town's chief law enforcement officer.

He finally stands and approaches the casket. He shifts Marvin's flowers a touch, they were uneven and his methodical nature overtook him for a moment.

He gazes down at the small woman and remembers a particularly scorching-

37
1938

–August day.

Fourteen year-old Steven is on a quest. Cutting through the forest near Miss Jezzy's house, he spies her garden and the watermelons that are ripening in the blazing sun.

There are dozens of them and he only wants one. A small one, just enough to satiate him and his friends on their upcoming fishing trip.

Afraid to ask and be denied and also full of disdain for adult authority altogether he sneaks into the side yard, retrieving his pocketknife. Always kept razor sharp, because you never know when you'll need it, he flicks it open.

SQUEAK! SLAM!

The screen door hurricanes open, bashing the exterior door. Miss Jezzy darts out onto her porch at full speed.

"Steven McClane, Imma fixin' to call your daddy!"

Tempted to run, he stands from his crouched position, facing her. Thirty years later, he'll still wonder why he didn't take off into the woods.

Used to running off after committing his many minor indiscretions, *something* rooted him in place that fateful day.

He folds the pocketknife away, glumly facing her, "Please don't, Miss Jezzy. He'll smack me. I'm sorry."

The hangdog boy with the crystal blue eyes and mop of dark brown hair always melts Miss Jezzy's heart.

He's gonna break a lotta hearts when he's grown.

She shakes a finger at him, "Alright, but you better not do that again. Or Imma call the Sheriff on you too."

"No ma'am! Don't do that! He's mean as a snake. Nobody likes him."

A thought. Straight from God almighty himself. She puts her hands on her hips and smiles at him, "Then you should grow on up and replace him."

Saucer-eyed, the boy stumbles over his words, walking towards her. Hand on his chest, "Me? But, I'm a lousy student."

"Don't gotta be book smart to be Sheriff. We all see proof of that every day, with that bumbling, arrogant fool. You gotta have heart. And you have heart to beat the band, Steven. Now come on in here and get a cool drink. After that, you can sweep my porch and I'll give you a watermelon."

Steven leaps up onto her porch as she disappears into the house. Stopping for a moment, he looks skyward and ponders.

Then he breaks into a wide smile, "Sheriff Steven McClane."

38

"If it wasn't for you, I wouldn't be where I am," he smiles down at her.

"You gave me my come-to-Jesus moment. You did that for a lot of people. I don't want you to worry, I'll look after Marvin and Carey. I'll make sure they're OK and taken care of."

He wipes his eyes, "I'm so fucking angry. And you're about the only one who'd be able to help me get control of it. I'm gonna catch whoever did this. And I'm not gonna use my heart this time. They're getting a bullet in the head before they ever see a courtroom."

He pats Miss Jezzy's hand and heads away towards the church, straightening his shoulders.

A tall reedy man in coveralls with a shovel stands at a discreet distance. Homer lets the Sheriff pass through the open front door of the church before approaching the grave site. He reaches out to close the casket but a man's hand grasps his wrist.

Firm but not aggressive.

A quiet voice, familiar, "Give me a moment please."

Homer nods and walks away toward his resting place under a nearby tree. He must have missed one of the parishioners. Not like him though, he's learned to be very observant and respectful of situations like this.

No one wants to think about the aftermath of a lovely sunrise service like this one. No one wants to think about him or his job. But he had checked and been sure.

The Sheriff was the last person out here. Oh well. He sits and picks up the book he always keeps handy. Today it's *To Kill A Mockingbird*.

Harvey wears a black suit and dark sunglasses. He removes his sunglasses and looks down at Miss Jezzy, tears filling his eyes. He nods and smiles, putting his sunglasses back on.

After a quick glance around to make sure the grave digger is occupied, he vanishes like a vapor into thin air.

39

The phone rings.

Marvin dashes in from the back door. He needn't have hurried. Harvey is already home, having left the graveside before being accidentally seen by someone.

He picks the phone up, and waves Marvin off, "Hello."

Annette's voice booms from the receiver, "Marvin. Darling."

Harvey makes a nauseated face and hands the phone to Marvin. He grips it with two fingers, as if it's covered with filth. Marvin punches him in the arm playfully.

Harvey goes to the couch, leaping onto it on his back. His clothes change from the black suit into more casual attire in the split second he's midair. He lands, placing his hands behind his head. Marvin marvels at the transformation.

Harvey smiles.

"Hello, Mother."

"Hello precious pumpkin. I just wanted you to know that I'll be in New York for one more night. It's so early, I - where were you at this hour? I've called three times."

Gulping sounds and ice clinking against a glass cause Harvey to leap up.

How can he hear it?

He mimics a sloppy drunk by chugging an invisible beverage, his tongue hanging out, staggering and passing out face down on the couch.

Marvin tries not to laugh, grateful for the distraction, "Miss Jezzy's funeral. She always wanted her funeral at sunrise."

A long pause and rustling on the other end of the phone, "Oh dear. I'm sorry. Was it a lovely service?"

Marvin, back in a somber mood, "Yes. I have to go. I'll see you tomorrow."

"Alright, Marvin. I-"

He hangs up, then moves over to the couch. Harvey bounces upright to make room for him. Theodore wakes up and emerges from his mink bed in the corner. He waddles over to the boys.

They pet him.

Harvey says, "I just walked him, so he's OK for a while. I encouraged him to piss on Annette's rose bushes."

Marvin, "I saw you at the funeral today, in the distance. I hope no one else did."

"Don't worry about it, it's fine. I know how to avoid detection."

"You have to be careful, the Sheriff doesn't miss much."

"I told you, it's fine."

"It was a nice service, wasn't it? The pastor's message. And those people were so friendly to me. The only time I've ever felt part of something was with Miss Jezzy and Carey. With them gone, I thought my future would be lonely."

Harvey feigns great offense, his hand on his chest, "O Hamlet, thou hast cleft my heart in twain."

He dabs away fake tears with his shirt sleeve.

Marvin shoves him backward and sets him straight. "Except for you, dummy."

Harvey sits upright and nods as Marvin removes his suit coat and tie, tossing them over the back of the couch.

Good-natured distractions over, Marvin puts his face in his hands, "The way she died. All alone like that. It's-".

Marvin breaks down.

Harvey puts his arm around him, "No, Marvin. Listen, there's something I have to-"

A knock at the front door. Harvey vanishes.

Marvin pulls himself together and opens the door to find Steven.

How had he gotten to the door without either of them hearing his car drive up? Or him shutting his door? Gotta be more alert. The front curtains are open, if he'd looked in and seen Harvey...

Steven's dark suit is long gone, he's switched to a blue plaid shirt and jeans. Good thing Annette isn't here, she always said he looked like a lumberjack when he wore plaid and the Sheriff always hated it when she said that.

Did he wear it to spite her in case he ran into her? One can only hope.

"Hey, Marvin."

Marvin steps aside and Steven saunters in, hugging him and

tossing his keys on the small table next to the front door. An old habit that brings a smile to Marvin's face.

How many times has he seen this man lob his keys casually onto that table, as if he's arriving home instead of paying a visit?

Relief washes over Marvin. He realizes this isn't the type of visit that he feared it might be. He's known the Sheriff his whole life and knows he would be in uniform if he was here on business.

He would at least be sporting his badge. He always had it on when he brought Annette home after she'd gotten drunk in public.

Steven walks around the living room, observing the wall of photos and the Harvey poster, "Just wanted to check in on you. Wasn't sure if you realized I was sitting next to you at the funeral."

He rotates to face Marvin.

"I did realize, I'm sorry I didn't acknowledge you. I was-"

"Don't apologize, So-".

He stops himself before he refers to Marvin as "Son". It didn't go well the last time he used that moniker.

Marvin knows exactly what he's thinking, "I do owe you an apology but not for today. I spoke terribly to you at the hospital. I didn't know what I was saying, I needed to blame someone. I'd be happy if you'd call me 'Son'. It always made me happy to hear you say it. So, don't ever stop, OK?"

This brings an enormous smile to Steven's face that fades almost as fast as it appeared.

He stares at the wall again, unable to look at Marvin, "I broke every speed limit, trying to get to them in time. Cut one corner so fast, I owe somebody out on Fishpond Way a mailbox, gotta find out who the lucky recipient is sometime today."

He looks at Marvin over his shoulder, "Maybe help me install it?"

Marvin smiles. The Sheriff always has a way of making Marvin feel better no matter how dire the situation.

When Marvin was eight years old, he and the Sheriff were fishing at a pond within walking distance of Marvin's house when they were interrupted by screeching tires and an ominous THUD.

Rushing to the nearby road, Steven kept the boy behind him for safety. They discovered a fawn that had been struck by a car. The car was long gone and the animal lay on the side of the road, it's tiny white spotted body heaving.

In spite of his position behind the Sheriff, Marvin saw the animal and rushed to it, wanting to help.

He begged, "Bring him to Dr. Reeve, he can make it better!"

Steven had removed enough unfortunate animals from the road to know better.

He knelt down to Marvin, "He's not gonna make it, I need to put an end to his pain."

Marvin shrieked, "NO! He can go to the doctor. This is the baby I've been seeing in the yard at home, I recognize him! We have to help him!"

Steven got up, dusted his knees off and headed to his truck. He returned a moment later, gun in hand. Marvin wept, his head on his arms, his knees drawn up.

"Go, sit in the truck, Marvin." He checked the chamber of the revolver.

Marvin sprinted for the truck but turned one last time to face the Sheriff, tears streaming down his face, "I HATE YOU!"

Sitting in the truck, Marvin heard a BANG and felt a bump as the tiny creature was loaded into the bed of the truck.

As the Sheriff got in, he took Marvin's face in his hand, under his chin and looked him straight in the eye.

"Marvin, sometimes the only way to make things better is by doing something difficult, something hurtful and sometimes terrible. But you'll figure that out when you're grown."

The boy flung himself into Steven's arms and cried on his shoulder. And Steven McClane prayed harder than he's ever prayed in his life.

Dear God, please let that not be the fawn that he's so fond of. Please let that one be OK. If you do that for me, I'll make it up somehow. I'll make sure this boy is taken care of for the rest of his life.

The Sheriff and Marvin stare at each other from their respective places in Marvin's living room, not realizing that they are processing the same memory simultaneously.

They had buried the fawn in the woods behind Marvin's house, much to Annette's chagrin.

She had dashed out of the house complaining about blood, ticks, germs and numerous other imagined horrors that were going to be deadly to young Marvin.

In one of the only times that Marvin ever heard the Sheriff get angry at his mother, he pointed at her and yelled, "Shut up! Get in the house! I'm handling this!"

Emerging from the woods after the burial, which Marvin marked with a pile of smooth stones, they watched five deer scatter, including the baby that was seated in Marvin's heart.

Sheriff McClane had mouthed 'thank you' to the heavens unseen by Marvin. And he never forgot his oath to God.

Now facing the grown boy who had learned too soon about life and death, the Sheriff asks, "Did I ever tell you that Miss Jezzy is the reason that I'm a Sheriff?"

Marvin is agog, "No! How did that happen?"

Steven hesitates, "Let's just say that I was, what's the word, rambunctious as a kid and I may have been in the midst of a fruit burglary at the time."

Marvin puts his hands over his mouth, "Oh no, you didn't steal from her garden?!"

"Allegedly, allegedly. There was no jury trial. She suggested a different path for me and I took it."

He sighs, the happy memory gone, "And now I have to investigate her murder."

Marvin tension is perceptible to Steven but only because he's used to observing people. He chalks it up to the trauma of the recent event.

He has no idea what Marvin knows. What Marvin has done. Part of Marvin wants to tell him everything, even last night's rampage against the animals who committed the crime.

But he knows better. The Sheriff will uphold the law, no matter what the personal cost. And it would break the poor man's heart.

He continues, "Do you have any idea who could have done this? You knew them better than anybody."

Marvin opens his mouth to speak but stutters. He shuts his mouth, seeing Harvey appear behind the Sheriff crouched on the staircase, out of his view.

Harvey shakes his head "no".

Marvin replies to the man's question, "Not for sure. No."

Harvey vanishes again.

How did the Sheriff not realize someone was there? He doesn't miss anything. He's always had eyes in the back of his head.

Rolling his eyes at the Kennedy photos draped in black, the Sheriff continues, "Even a guess at this point would help, Son. I'm just investigating. If you have any idea at all, you can tell me."

Turning back to Marvin, "I'm not locking anybody up unless I have evidence that they committed a crime. So, you're not getting anybody in trouble."

Marvin feigns deep thought, "I don't know anyone who would do something like this. There's some trouble-makers around-"

Steven smiles, "The Carter miscreants? John and Roger?"

Marvin's hope that he wouldn't get to the brothers this quickly was dashed, but then again, they are really the only less-than-stellar citizens for miles around.

The Sheriff is a one- man-band of law enforcement in town, for that very reason. Everyone minds their business and stays out of trouble. He's chased off some "dope smoking hippies" a couple of times but the sporadic drunken brawl is his main concern.

And those have diminished precipitously since Annette started only drinking at home.

Marvin's mind labors, carefully choosing his words, "I doubt John and Roger would go this far. They're ones to yell and call names but that's about it."

Steven looks suspicious for the first time, concerned that Marvin might be hesitant about putting the finger on someone, "You're sure? Miss Jezzy complained about them more than once. Tore up her garden a couple times."

He reaches down to pet Theodore, curled up on the couch, "And didn't the younger boy hurt Theodore a couple years back?"

Marvin smiles inside, admiring the Sheriff's acting ability. He knows good and well that Roger Carter threw rocks at the dog, causing a wound that required Dr. Reeve's intervention.

In addition to having a mind like a steel trap, Steven would have memorized his files before coming here. Marvin suspects that he's having difficulty balancing his duties as a law enforcement officer with their relationship. And that is definitely to his benefit right now.

Unsure what to say, Marvin stammers a bit and sips water from a glass that's been sitting out all night. Again, he spies Harvey on the staircase. He's dressed like John Lennon on the cover of the Magical Mystery Tour album, complete with small round glasses.

He gestures "calm down, take a deep breath," leaning into the band's recent interest in Transcendental Meditation.

He sits in the yoga position, eyes closed, tips of the middle finger and thumb touching in the Shuni Mudra position.

The outrageous sight nearly sets Marvin off and he spits out a mouthful of water, trying not to choke on his laughter. He stares too long at Harvey this time.

Steven notices and turns to see what Marvin is looking at but there is nothing there.

"You OK, Marvin?"

"Yes, this water has been sitting out, must have dust or dirt in it or something. Oh gosh, I didn't offer you anything would you like-"

Steven waves off the offer but continues to stare at Marvin, "Are you sure about those boys? I had to brace John for going after Carey on the street the other day."

Marvin, more sure of himself, strengthened by Harvey's supporting presence, "I can't be sure about anything. They did do those things but this is a bit extreme, don't you think?"

Steven nods as Marvin continues, "And besides, they're cowards. I scared them off by throwing a jar of piccalilli at them last time."

Steven chuckles at this, "I heard about that. Good for you, Son. Well now, they aren't exactly the sharpest knives in the drawer either. And I suppose they would have come after you for throwing that jar, not Jezzy and Carey."

Marvin nods, "I agree."

The Sheriff heads toward the door, scoops up his keys as he turns back to Marvin, "I'm gonna head out to their place, talk to them anyway. Worst case, I put the fear of God into them and they behave for a while."

And find their father decomposing at the foot of their stairs. Dead as Marley, no doubt bloated and covered with flies. Which is exactly what he deserves but still-

Marvin can't decide if this would be good or bad for him. He wants to delay a search for the errant boys as long as possible. Maybe-

"I'm not sure you'll find them there, Sheriff. We're certainly not friends but I do know that their father is a drunk who uses them as punching bags. They were always bruised whenever I saw them. I heard they weren't staying with him anymore. That they had an aunt over in New Jersey?"

"I'm well aware of their father. I've been out there a time or two and tried to talk some sense into him. Some people can't handle their liquor. They get violent. Others just get broody like you-"

The unspoken words "your mother" hang in the air between them.

The Sheriff tosses his keys up and catches them, a routine sight that sets Marvin at ease. Again, he's being casual, not professional.

"You keep an eye out for them. They may come around to bother you since you hurt 'em. Plus, you messed up that shitty car of theirs. Ok?"

Marvin nods, "Of course."

Steven hugs Marvin and heads out the door, "Well, thanks Marvin. You take care of yourself. And listen, you and Carey were Jezzy's only family so you can go on over and take care of the house anytime if you want. It's yours now, until Carey wakes up. They moved him to the city today. Dr. Reeve actually had some hope when I talked to him. Carey's in my prayers."

He hands Marvin a business card, "This lawyer is handling Miss Jezzy's affairs. I've talked to him. Good egg, bit of a prig, but anyway. He expects to hear from you."

The Sheriff stares out the window towards the pumpkin patch.

The disturbed area is still a visible sore, they haven't been able to rearrange things yet. Marvin has an explanation prepared but it's not necessary.

Steven, "Pumpkins are looking really good. What's your secret?"

A huge smile of relief, "Fertilizer. Secret formula."

The Sheriff laughs as Marvin continues, pointing, "There's several already cut near the edge right there, feel free to grab one."

Steven reaches into his back pocket for his wallet, "Well thanks. I'm a little late but it's a tradition. Last couple days have been so-well, needless to say, I didn't get over here to buy one."

Marvin waves away the money.

He hands him a dollar bill anyway, "I have to pay you, Marvin. If I don't, next thing you know, some Nosy Nan will have us up on bribery charges. Trading pumpkins for favors. Everybody already knows you're my favorite person. Don't need to exacerbate the situation. World's a crazy place."

Marvin takes the dollar, "It sure is."

Steven claps him on the back and heads down the steps to his car, parked about fifty feet down the driveway. He passes it on his way to the patch.

Harvey reappears next to Marvin, behind the open door, out of sight. Still in his John Lennon finery.

Harvey fumes, "Golly gee Sheriff, would you like to go on over to my pumpkin patch? Don't mind the fresh dirt, dug a grave last night we did. Saved you and the taxpayers the cost of incarceration for two particularly nasty assholes."

Marvin, smiling at the departing figure of the Sheriff, enunciates through gritted teeth, "Shut up."

Harvey vanishes to the couch again, sitting next to Theodore as the phone rings again.

Harvey rolls his eyes, "It's like Macy's switchboard in here today."

Marvin watches the Sheriff choose a pumpkin from the edge of the patch. He heads back to his truck.

Harvey vanishes from the couch, reappearing next to the phone, "Hello?"

Marvin is laser focused on the Sheriff, oblivious to the phone. He knows he's pushing his luck.

It was a mistake to send him to the pumpkin patch.

What if he suspects something?

Fear of what Harvey would do to the most important person in his life rears its ugly head. Or is Harvey the most important person in his life now? Would he ever be in a position to choose between the two of them? What would he do if that horrible choice presented itself?

An impossible situation. A memory of Miss Jezzy's lesson about King Solomon worms its way to the forefront of Marvin's mind.

Miss Jezzy had proclaimed, "Solomon knew what to do, it was an impossible situation but he was wise. He'd asked the good Lord for wisdom above all else. Threatened to cut that little baby right in two. But knew he wouldn't have to. A lie to expose a bigger lie.

"So, it's alright to lie?" Five year-old Marvin was stunned.

"Well, if it's for a higher purpose, I'd have to say so. Just pray for wisdom, Marvin, always pray for wisdom. It'll help you with tough choices."

Harvey observes Marvin's pensive demeanor, hearing Max's voice on the phone, "Marvin, it's, uh, it's your dad."

Harvey holds the phone away from him again, another revolting voice from this damn phone. He grabs an apple from a bowl on the counter and heaves it at Marvin's back. Marvin turns angrily, arms outstretched, Harvey gestures at the phone.

Max's tinny voice again from the outstretched receiver, "Hello? Is someone there?"

Marvin waves at the Sheriff and heads toward the phone. Harvey stalls, conjuring up a phony greeting reminiscent of Annette's contrived delight at meeting Max's new wife.

Cheesy smile plastered in place, Harvey is much too loud, "Hello!"

He holds out the phone to Marvin again, shaking it back and forth, eager to rid himself of it.

Marvin mouths, 'Who is it?'

Harvey mouths back to him, 'Max'.

Marvin grabs the phone, shoving Harvey away.

Max finishes his sentence, "Wanted to know if you'd be willing to speak with me today. I could come by the house."

Both boys are relieved watching the Sheriff pull away.

Max again, "Marvin, are you there?"

Marvin recovers, "Yes, sorry. Ok. Yes, let's meet."

Max continues, "I know your mother went out of town, is she back? Because it would probably be best if-"

Marvin interrupts, "She's still gone. Come by any time after noon."

"Alright. Goodbye Marvin."

"Goodbye." Marvin hangs up.

Harvey shakes his head and walks away, gesticulating with a booming voice.

Marvin ignores him, staring out at the pumpkin patch as a satisfied grin spreads across his face.

Watching the dust settle from the Sheriff's truck, he realizes something. The Sheriff never once asked about his mother. He can't recall a single conversation in his life where the subject of his mother didn't come up, even tangentially.

"Good, he deserves better than her."

After Steven turns onto the road from Marvin's driveway, a call comes in on the radio.

Helen, calm but insistent. Not an emergency.

"Steven, pick up please."

He picks up with a sigh, "Helen, haven't I told you to call me 'Sheriff', in case somebody's listening?"

"Steven McClane, I changed your diapers when your Momma had to work late. Don't put on airs with me."

"Sorry, Helen, what's up?"

"Where are you?

"What's my 10-20 you mean?"

"I'm gonna hang up on you if you don't stop with your nonsense."

He shakes his head, "I'm headed back. What is it?"

"That woman has called here four times in the past half hour."

That woman.

Helen's less than loving appellation for Annette.

He exhales, not wanting to deal with her.

Not wanting to deal with her ever again as a matter of fact.

The thought is accompanied by a huge wave of relief. It's the first time he's considered booting Annette out of his life completely. Her absence from Miss Jezzy's funeral was the last straw.

He had always held onto the idea that they would find their way to each other "someday". Even if they didn't see each other for a year at a time.

But he's finished keeping his life on hold. He's learned in the past couple of days how short life really is.

Plus, she has no say over his relationship with Marvin anymore. Time to move on.

"If she calls again, tell her I said that unless she needs a law enforcement officer, she can go to hell."

"Steven! I can't say that to anybody. Even to her."

"OK, tell her that the line is reserved for emergencies and that if she continues to use it, she'll find herself sitting in a jail cell. I have a phone at home and she can reach me there. But also tell her I've changed my number."

"Well, my goodness, somebody got up on the right side of the bed. And it's about damn time."

He exclaims, "Helen, I can't tolerate such off-color language on official channels. I'm truly shocked at you."

She gives him a Bronx cheer, ending the transmission.

He laughs, smacks the steering wheel and speeds off ready to start his new life.

40

Max races out the front door of his bungalow hoping against hope that she's still asleep.

He almost makes it to his car.

Almost.

Mary sprints out after him, wearing her black peignoir this time. She has one in every color imaginable. Why does she need fifteen of them? He has no idea. He never ceases to be amazed by the footspeed of this strumpet he's forever tethered to.

Divorce is certainly an option but he's going to be in his baby son's life. He's not going to be cheated again. Mothers always have the advantage. So, he'll have to deal with Mary for the next eighteen years if he wants to be a real father.

Seeing how wonderful Marvin is gives him pause. Is it because I was absent? It can't be because Annette was a great mom. No way in hell. It must be because of Jezzy.

Whatever the reason, he's determined to make up for the horrendous past that Marvin has endured.

All of these thoughts race through his brain in the split second before the tart, barely older than his son, leaps down the two steps to the gravel path where his car is parked. The ostrich feathers around her robe and on her slippers make her look like a deranged bird soaring towards him, talons at the ready.

"Don't you leave me alone here! I can't take care of that baby by myself!"

Max cannot believe what he's hearing, "He's your baby. Of course you can take care of him!"

How did he get stuck with this dumb, gum-popping bitch?

Of course, he knows how. Damn his libido.

Mary clutches him like he's left her on the Titanic to go down with the ship,

"Why didn't you let me bring Estelle?"

POP!

He pushes her away, attempting to open the car door, "There was no time. And this place is too small to house her too. And you wanted to come on this trip with me for some reason."

She puts her full weight against the door, folding her arms, "Some reason? You're my husband, Maxy. You coming out here to see that woman and her son, of course I wanted to come protect what's mine. When we got together you said they wasn't gonna be a problem."

POP!

How he'd love to thrust his fist into her mewling gob and shove that gum down her fucking throat. For starters.

Max feels protective of Marvin being called "her son". He even uncharacteristically feels some sense of loyalty to Annette. A selfish bitch, but at least she wasn't stupid.

Mary is the least intelligent person he's ever met. And that's saying something since he spent many years in Hollywood. Some real dolts out there.

But Mary - she's in a category all her own. Inexperienced, unintelligent and dumb. She thought Pennsylvania was near Texas, bemoaning the extraordinarily long drive "down there".

Their "courtship" had been brief.

He woke up in his lavish New York City apartment hungover, horses thundering behind his eyes. Avoiding the bright sun beaming through the floor to ceiling windows overlooking Central Park, his eyes fell on the young woman sleeping next to him.

Who the hell is this? Oh wait, no—What the fuck? The cocktail waitress? Ah God. Great job, Max. She couldn't string two coherent words together.

Gently but firmly he tossed her out as soon as possible, assuming he would be rid of her. He would be sure never to patronize that particular club again.

But fate intervened when she showed up three months later, mascara running down her face, shrieking that he had gotten her pregnant.

That moment changed everything. He knew a phony performance when he saw one, he had been married to Annette after all. This girl wasn't lying. He was the father.

The only thought that cemented itself in his psyche was that it

would be a boy and that he could now do right by both him and
Marvin. He still harbored hope that Marvin would reach out to him
eventually.

So, he asked Mary to be his wife right there on the threshold of
the apartment. She hesitated, making sure it wasn't due to her
"unfortunate situation".

*She really is a moron. Of course, it was because of the baby, he'd only had
one real conversation with her. And that was a serious struggle. He found
himself limiting his vocabulary to words with only two syllables.*

But he convinced her otherwise. Claiming to have been pining
for her for the past weeks, he even managed a tear or two. She
bought it hook, line and sinker never questioning why he had not
simply visited her workplace again.

Yes - dumb.

Less than two years later, in the Poconos (nowhere near Texas),
he puts his finger in Mary's face, "Annette and Marvin are not a
problem, Mary. Marvin is grown now and I don't need to deal with
Annette, anyway. And I will have a relationship with him, I've told
you that. Seth will like having an older brother. And it's time I was
a father to Marvin."

Someone observes them from the woods, a few yards away.

Mary stomps her foot, hectoring him, "Well I thought we was
your priority."

POP!

Max paces, pushing his hands through his hair, his old habit to
contain his rage. Each grammatical error out of this fandangle's
mouth irritated him more than the last.

"Goddammit! I spend 24 hours a day with you! What more do
you want?!

The baby begins to cry as Mary pouts, "Well now you woke him
up. Great!"

POP!

Max grabs Mary by the back of her head and pulls her close, spit
flying in her face, "Get in there and take care of my son!"

He releases her, shoving her back. She folds her arms, wailing like
a bag of cats being thumped against a tree. Her two carat pear-
shaped diamond and matching tennis bracelet glisten in the

sunlight.

She stares at them and then him for a moment before running into the bungalow.

He looks after her, "Selfish bitch." Then he hops in his car and speeds away, spraying dust and gravel.

Harvey meanders from the woods, hands in pockets, having watched the scene.
He performs for his own amusement, gesturing to his audience of trees, "Welcome to Hollywood Squares."

He apes a roaring audience, clapping.

He mimics holding a note card and reading from it, "This one's for Paul Lynde. Paul, what washed up actor slash director favors the company of selfish bitches?"

He turns and does his best Paul Lynde impression, complete with ubiquitous laugh, "Peter, that would be Max Damon."

He throws his hands up and speaks in his regular voice, "Ding ding ding, circle gets the square."

Clapping his hands, he dances and spins around to the back of the bungalow.

> *"O, from this time forth*
> *My thoughts be bloody or be nothing worth!"*

41

Max sits on the couch in Marvin's living room, fidgeting, uncomfortable.

He hasn't put foot in this house since - well, since Marvin was a baby. It's unchanged except for the memorial section of the, *what the hell did she call it?*

Oh yeah, the fucking feature wall. His eyes fall on the Kennedy brothers. He gets up to take a closer look at RFK.

Marvin rattles glasses in the kitchen, preparing a beverage for them both. Max looks at Marvin, then back at RFK. Back and forth once more. Thinking.

He glances at the Harvey poster and remembers the hell that he went through after that movie. After her "big break". She blamed her pregnancy on him, claiming he had ruined her career and her life. He did everything he could for her, he thought moving into this huge house would be enough.

He got her to admit that New York City was no place to raise a family. And he promised that they would be close enough to "the city" (as New York City is referred to colloquially by the folks around here) to build up her career when the baby was old enough. But then-

He's brought back to the present by Marvin, "Here you are."

Marvin hands his father a glass of iced tea and sits in a chair across from the sofa with his own glass.

Max sits.

After an awkward silence, both sipping the tea, Max brightens, "Marvin, I don't know if your mother told you, but, I have a - you have a little brother."

Marvin's face lights up like a Christmas tree, "Really? How old is he?"

"He's six months old. His name is Seth."

Marvin says, "Seth. His name means anointed. God sent him to Adam and Eve to replace Abel after Cain murdered him."

He looks down at his lap, saddened, "Did you have him to replace me?"

Max sits forward on the couch, "Oh no, no. He was a surprise. Mary liked the name. I doubt she knows the meaning."

"Mary is your wife?"

Max flops back against the couch, gulping iced tea, "Yeah. All of this, the baby and everything was a shock."

He focuses on Marvin again, "I never planned to have another child. I wasn't a father to you so I had no right to be a father to anyone. But Seth has been a blessing. Every time I look at him, I see you and have regrets at how you were raised. I promise that Seth will have better. He'll be raised with love and stability."

Marvin nods, "I read the letters you sent me. Mr. Williams, the postal worker, had held them back because of Mother. But he finally gave them to me."

Dammit, he knew Annette was to blame for the delay in hearing from Marvin somehow. He should have hired a courier service to give them to Marvin by hand.

"I meant every word Marvin. I don't blame you if you don't want to have a relationship with me, I don't deserve you."

Marvin considers this, deciding to press on, "Why did you send my mother to an asylum after I was born?"

Max, stunned, nearly chokes on his tea, "You know about that?"

Marvin nods slowly.

Max wasn't expecting this, he needs to pivot. Show business is all about pivoting. Live shows interrupted by failing props or performers who drop a line. Films delayed by screaming, hysterics from puffed-up actors and actresses. He's dealt with his share of unpleasant surprises and always lands on his feet.

Annette was always a source of amazement to him. She could handle the most intense, ridiculous, outrageous hiccups to a schedule or performance. He doesn't have her preternatural skill, but he can manage.

"She's, uh, always been high-strung but, uh, she had, um, difficulties after you were born. She couldn't take care of you properly. She has a psychiatric condition that we weren't aware of. She heard voices, saw things that weren't there."

The world stops spinning on its axis.

Marvin sees Max's lips moving slowly, half-speed. He's paralyzed.

Processing what he just heard, he realizes the implications.

Harvey is real isn't he? He has to be. John and Roger saw him so this isn't like what my mother had. Right? I've touched him, he's pet Theodore. No, he's real.

A look of concern passes over Marvin's face as he reconstructs the past few days so Max leans toward him again.

"I got your mother the help she needed. She was diagnosed and put on medication."

"And this condition is genetic."

"Not necessarily."

"Dr. Reeve has been acting strange, wanting me to come in for an exam. Since I'm an adult now."

"He knows that it's possible that you suffer from the condition too. It's called schizophrenia. And it shows up in young adults."

Max smiles, sure of himself, "But I'm confident that you're fine."

Marvin doesn't comprehend Max's cocksureness but he'll play along, "You're right, I'm fine. Maybe I take after your side of the family. I do look like you after all."

Max's smile fades a bit. Quick glance at the wall of photos again. The phone rings.

Marvin trots over to answer, "Hello?"

Mary's grating voice emanates from the phone, with the accompanying gum pops.

"Can I speak to Max please? This is his wife."

Marvin holds the phone out to Max, "It's your wife. I'll just go upstairs to give you some privacy."

When Max grimly takes the phone, Marvin runs off. Max watches to make sure he's out of hearing range.

Whispered rage, "What the hell, Mary?! I've only been gone an hour!"

"That baby has been crying constantly. You have to come home."

Max puts his hand to his forehead, unbelieving, "Have you held him?"

Whining, "Yeah, but he doesn't like me as much as he likes Estelle. I don't know why."

Truly a mystery, Mary.

"I'll be back as soon as I can. I'm speaking to Marvin, it's going well. He's really a terrific kid."

She brightens, "That's nice. Did you ask about the trust fund yet?"

Max gets even quieter, "No Mary, I didn't. It's hardly appropriate right now."

"Well we need that money back, Maxy."

Mumbling to himself, "Because you've nearly bankrupted us."

She blathers on, "Marvin don't need that money, he's been OK all these years. He's what you call, uh, self -suspicious."

I can't believe I'm stuck with this ditz,.

"Self SUFFICIENT, Mary?"

"Yeah, whatever. Me and Seth need that money. We're your family now."

"I can't just ask him to give it all back already, Mary. We're only just getting to know each other."

"Well hurry up. And sure, let him keep a little something."

"You're too generous. It won't take much to convince him to give up most of that money. He's starting to bond with me and I was an actor for a while, remember?"

Mary huffs, "Yeah, but you was never that great. No Cary Grant. Get that money!"

"Goodbye, Mary!"

He hangs up hard. No, he was never Cary Grant, but he was still a decent actor. But directing was more his bailiwick.

But thank you for the reminder, you greedy halfwit.

He'd prefer not to have to direct his own son but he has no choice.

Marvin hovers in the upstairs hallway, listening on the extension. After he hears Max slam the phone down, he hangs up gently.

Devastated, he wipes tears from his eyes. He's not sure what he expected but it wasn't this. Why does everything come down to money with his parents?

Miss Jezzy was never like this. If only she were still here! He could rush over to her house and sit on the floor as she relaxed in her recliner and produced pearls of wisdom.

She had never once made him feel bad or question her feelings for him. Life just isn't fair sometimes. But at least he has Harvey, someone to help him through this terrible time.

He straightens up, reaching his full height, puts his shoulders back and shakes off his gloom. A glance in the hallway mirror. His eyes are bright green again.

He knew they had changed, he always does. He feels it when they do. Like someone else bubbles up inside him, looking out through his eyes.

But that person's eyes are gray. Looking toward the stairs, he grins. He heads downstairs, ready to put on a show.

After all, it's in his blood.

42

Harvey crouches outside the bedroom window of the bungalow, undetectable, sandwiched between two decorative hedges.

He watches Mary pace with the bellowing child. He positioned himself here because he suspected something.

Even in his unusual state of being, he possesses incredible intuition. Or maybe it's due to his state of being? Who knows?

Curiosity about Max Damon led him to this place today but his attention soon became diverted towards the woman he observes now.

A gut feeling? Does he even have a gut? He hasn't eaten since his arrival, but he feels no hunger. But then again, he can do things in the physical world.

Huh, might have a nosh later and see what happens.

Frustrated, Mary puts the crying baby in the crib, hands him the bottle already laying in there and stares daggers at him. Harvey has encountered two shitty mothers in his short time on this side of the - well, whatever divides the real world from the place he came from.

What are the odds? And both married to the same man? It feels like there's a yellow back novel in this scenario somewhere.

Mary walks (or stumbles?) past the modestly decorated double bed that she and Max share to the side table that is obviously hers. It's littered with fashion magazines, a huge box of chocolates, several bottles of pills and two empty cocktail glasses.

She steps on discarded garments from both her and Max as she makes her way to her oasis. Harvey is mesmerized.

What a fucking pig.

She weaves as she examines the prescription bottles, searching for the right one. Bringing the bottles up to her face and alternately holding them at arm's length, she attempts to read in her drunken haze.

Finally, she settles on one bottle and takes a tablet out. She tosses her magazines on the bed to clear a space and sets the pill on the table.

Confused Harvey watches as she uses her crystal tumbler to crush it into dust.

What in the hell?

Brushing the dusty remnants of the pill into her hand, she lumbers back over to the crib stepping on the same clothes as before.

Harvey recedes a bit to avoid detection but it's likely not necessary. She's hammered and wouldn't notice a pink elephant looking in the window.

Reaching into the crib, she removes the bottle of milk from the baby's hands, eliciting a new bout of screams. Clenching her fists, she screws up her face.

"Shut up!" Naturally this causes the poor baby to shriek louder.

She holds the bottle under her armpit, unscrewing the cap with one hand and emptying the pill dust from the other hand into it.

This is not her first time doing this, Harvey can tell. Smiling, she puts the cap back on, shakes it and hands the bottle back to Seth, who sucks on it greedily.

"That's a good baby, you be quiet now. Mommy needs rest."

Harvey restrains himself from leaping through the window and choking the life out of the abusive young woman. But it's not easy. He's discovered that he has quite a temper when provoked.

Mary goes back to the pill bottle that she had opened and removes her gum. She sticks it on the bedpost and pops two of the pills.

What a class act you are, Mary. Such a catch.

Closing her eyes, she waits for the pills to kick in. Once they do, she carries one of her empty tumblers out of the room. He hears her picking up the phone and dialing it.

Sure that she'll be occupied for a while, Harvey vanishes from his place outside the window and appears next to the crib.

He stares at the hungry baby for several seconds before reaching his hand in.

43

Mary slams down the phone, angry and humiliated yet again.

Maxy always does this. Treats me bad. He only cares about that baby. And now the money's runnin' out.

She rifles through the liquor bottles on the kitchen counter. Enough to populate a small bar, she finds most of them to be empty or close to it.

Flinging open and slamming the cabinets, she finally finds an unopened bottle of bourbon. She likes the feel of cracking the seal and opening a brand new bottle.

It reminds her of the night she met Max. Although that night it had been the most expensive champagne that her night club carried. He opened it like a pro.

She thought she'd caught a big fish when she ended up in bed with him that same night. Imagine her humiliation the next morning, when he woke up and practically shoved her out the door, barely dressed like a harlot.

Not one to be deterred, she'd kept looking for Mr. Right. A few weeks later, the chagrin of the shameful exit from Max Damon's apartment long dimmed, a new horror consumed her. She was pregnant with his baby.

Sure that he'd never believe her, she fell into despair. No doubt he thought she was a tramp and was sleeping with half the male population of Manhattan.

Well, she wasn't!

That was a terrible thing to assume. She'd only slept with about half the male population of the *upper east side*, an area that she coveted. And, as luck would have it, she hadn't been with anyone since their drunken romp.

So, she *knew* the baby was his.

To confront him, she arrived at his apartment with a performance at the ready, but when he opened the door, her true feelings and fears for her future leaked through. Leaked in the form of a tidal wave of tears that ruined her carefully applied makeup.

And the rest is history. Ignoble history, but history none the less.

She swigs from the newly opened bottle, there's no one to judge her out here in the sticks. After the initial satisfaction of shitting on norms, she grabs her tumbler and fills it nearly to the top. She does decide to use some ice to dilute it a bit. She's not an alcoholic after all.

Harvey hears Mary taking her anger out on the cabinet doors and emptying an ice tray into the sink. His hand is on the sleeping baby's belly. Being in contact with the little boy warms his heart.

Do I have a heart?

Harvey takes the contaminated milk bottle and puts it on the floor under the crib, out of the little fellow's reach. His gaze never leaves the baby.

Feeling an inexplicable fondness for him, he checks his breathing again. Seems normal. Not that he has any frame of reference. Harvey wonders how many women have put medication in baby bottles to "calm them".

These pills are meant for adults, there's no way to know what they would do to a baby. What if he died? The thought sets Harvey reeling. He shakes with rage, unsure what he should do.

He looks around the room, finally focusing on the guilty bottle of pills on the bedside table. His snarl turns into a sadistic grin, an expression never imagined on this, the face of peaceful Marvin Damon.

Mary wakes up in the living room, face down on the couch. She passed out on her way to the bedroom.

Must not have slept well last night. No wonder, it's too damn quiet out here.

She pulls herself up and stumbles through the open bedroom door with her cocktail, spilling a significant amount when she trips over her husband's shoe. She turns and kicks at it, missing the first time and nearly toppling backwards. The second attempt is more successful, she connects with the custom Italian loafer and sends it flying into the living room.

She lumbers over to the bed without so much as a glance at her sleeping baby. Propping herself up in bed, she begins to thumb through a fashion magazine. It's a useless endeavor, her vision blurred and doubled thanks to her booze habit.

She puts the magazine down, leans over to the side table and grabs the enormous box of handmade chocolate covered cherries. She pops one into her lipstick smeared mouth and downs it in a single bite.

An old lover once told her that she should be a model. He took close-up photos of her biting and sucking various erotic looking foods. The photos were quite good, even the ones where she was biting and sucking something else that would not bode well for a modeling career.

Not a legitimate modeling career anyway. The errant lover had made off with all of the pictures and, last she heard, had sold the reputation-killing ones to a magazine of ill repute. She never saw a dime.

Her desire to become an upstanding wife to a rich man was fostered by that unfortunate experience. Unbeknownst to her, future husband Max had seen the off-color photos never realizing that he would marry the enthusiastic set of ruby lips one day.

She's not magazine worthy right now. Her crimson lipstick is messed all over her mouth and teeth along with chocolate. She grimaces at the taste of the cherry.

They can't all be sweet. Maybe it's the bourbon affecting the taste.

The handcrafted cherries are not mass produced, each box is unique, just like the cherries themselves. She chooses another, then another, chasing them all with gulps of alcohol.

BANG!

The bedroom door shakes in its frame, slammed. Harvey steps out from behind it. Mary shrieks half-heartedly, frightened by the sound but woozy. She squints hard at him.

She yawns, "Who are you?"

Finally, recognizing her husband in this young man's face, "Oh, Marvin?"

Harvey doesn't move.

"How are you here? I just talked to Maxy, he's at your house."

Wondering how long she was passed out, she looks at the diamond watch on her left wrist. Dammit! Its face is swimming in front of her, making her feel nauseated.

Observing her, Harvey crosses his arms, leans against the back of the door and smiles.

Mary, concerned and confused, "I don't think you're supposed to be here, Marvin."

Harvey uncrosses his arms, puts his hands in his pockets and wanders over to the crib.

He pats Seth and smiles, "Had to meet my new brother. Seth, right? What a good sleeper he is. Dead to the world."

Mary starts to get up, but she collapses back onto the bed, dizzy, "Yeah, he's a good baby. Listen Marvin, I think we outta call Maxy. Ya got ya wires crossed or somethin'."

Harvey walks over and sits on the bed next to her, "No one got their wires crossed, Mary. Can I call you Mary? Mrs. Damon is so formal, isn't it? Makes you sound like an old lady."

Her nervousness evaporates as the conversation with the charming boy goes on. He stares at her as she shovels more cherries into her mouth with more alcohol.

She offers him a cherry and he waves it off, smiling and shaking his head. As she pops it into her mouth, he offers a handshake. She takes his hand.

"Nice to meet you. Call me Harvey."

44

Max hears Marvin's thumping tread on the stairs before he sees him playfully peek around the corner at him.

Max was prepared to put on a happy face but the sight of his son brings a genuine smile to his face.

Fuck that woman, I've got my son back. I'm not risking my relationship with him for some one night stand that ended up with her getting pregnant. I'll divorce her. Marvin can live with me and be with his brother. I'll get him away from Mary, she's a shitty mother. I have witnesses and I'll get the best lawyer money can buy. I'd do it right this time.

Max says, "I need to get back. Mary - struggles with the baby on her own. He can be fussy sometimes."

The lies come so easily. Maybe it's time to talk to that shrink again.

He continues, "Can you come by in a little while? Meet them both?"

Marvin nods quietly and offers a handshake. Max hugs him instead.

A tsunami of dizziness hits Marvin with the embrace.

Those sounds again. A baby crying then cut off. Music from a crib mobile, slow and distorted. That smell! MAX'S AFTERSHAVE! That's it! Why is this happening to me?

Marvin pulls away from Max abruptly, clutching his head.

Max is concerned, "Are you alright, Marvin?"

Marvin, quick on his feet and his father's son, lies, "Yes, sorry. I got dizzy. I haven't eaten since the funeral."

Max slouches, "I thought about coming but didn't want to make you uncomfortable thinking I was trying to insert myself where I didn't belong. It didn't occur to me that your mother wasn't there. I hate that you were there all alone."

He really means it.

Marvin is happy to know this at least. Unbeknownst to both of his parents, he is a human lie detector.

He replies, "I wasn't alone, loads of people turned out. And Sheriff McClane was there for me."

He hopes the words "because you weren't" are implied.

Max thinks, "McClane? Steven McClane?"

Marvin nods.

Max continues, "I knew him, he was two years behind me in school. Everybody said he looked like my little brother."

Marvin realizes that there is a strong resemblance between the two men.

He had never seen photos of his father, only been told that he looked like him but with green eyes instead of Max's blue.

He's also been mistaken for Steven's son on several occasions when they went a town or two over to hunt or fish.

When he was about ten or eleven, he vaguely remembers one particularly friendly black woman who ran a roadside stand selling blueberries.

Stopping to buy several quarts of the fruit, they had chatted with the vivacious young mother and her brood.

Before they left she remarked, "I never seen a boy lookin' more like his father than you do, little one. Good thing he's a handsome fella."

She winked at them both as they bid her goodbye. They had laughed about it in the truck on the way home but Marvin secretly wished that it was true.

The only thing he wanted more than siblings was a father. Looking at Steven McClane on that ride home, he realized he had one.

He had never faltered in his love or care for Marvin. Even as Steven's relationship with his mother had its ups and downs, his relationship with Marvin was solid. Steven had set Annette straight the final time they had argued.

Annette had threatened, "If you and I aren't together, you can be sure you won't be seeing Marvin anymore."

Grabbing her by both shoulders, he had gotten right up in her face, "Don't you threaten me, sweetheart. I'm gonna be in that boy's life. I love him. A helluva lot more than I love you. He needs me. Get used to it."

This was followed by him grabbing his keys from the small table next to the door, tossing them up and catching them, then slamming the door on his way out.

Marvin had witnessed this scene from the perch on the staircase where Harvey had hidden.

Even at thirteen, he understood that the only stable force in his life had just walked out the door. But he knew he'd be back.

Marvin decides to test his father's ego. "He's been great all these years. We spend lots of time together. He's been a father to me."

Max notices that Marvin didn't say ,"He's been *like* a father to me".

The absence of that one, tiny word changes everything. Knowing he should be grateful, he nevertheless feels jealous of this man who was his substitute. But no more.

He'll get Marvin away from here, from his mother. And from the stand-in father. He can sell his apartment and buy them a small house in upstate New York, clearly Marvin has thrived in the country.

His career has been on hold for a year or so since the nightmare that is Mary entered his life, but he can pick up where he left off. He, Marvin and Seth will build a terrific life together. But a few things have to be done first.

Max notices Marvin's pallor and touches his face, "Why don't you sit down and I'll get you something from the kitchen?"

Touched by the sentiment Marvin smiles, "No, no. It's fine. I promise to get something after you leave."

Max nods assent and heads to the front door with a final glance towards the Harvey poster.

Annette can stay in this house and rot.

He turns and nods before leaving. Marvin stands at the window and watches as his father gets into his expensive sports car and takes off down the driveway.

The tears finally fall, performance over.

45

Mary struggles to get up again but Harvey shoves her back hard, her head smacking the headboard next to her abandoned gum.

THWACK!

Mary pleads, "The baby."

He can't believe it. She actually mentioned the *baby?*

Harvey scoffs, "Oh please."

He mocks her gum chewing and flapper accent, "The baby. My baby."

He backhands her across the face, his anger rising as he thinks about the baby at her mercy.

He continues, "The *baby* will sleep for hours thanks to you and your pills."

Her eyes widen at the accusation, *How does he know about that?*

Harvey grabs a bottle off the bedside table, "What do you need pills for anyway?"

He reads the bottle, "Oh, anxiety. Charming."

He drops it back on the table and grabs three more of the bottles, reading them, "Sleep. Sleep? Why do you need this? A boozehound like you can't help but pass out. What's this one? Pain? What pain?"

She speaks in her calmest voice, frightened but hoping to regain control, "I get back pain."

"Back pain. From laying around all day? Certainly not from hard labor."

He grabs the anxiety pills again and leans close to her, "What the hell do you have to be anxious about? Other than the police finding out you've been drugging that poor baby."

Mary gets some of her strength back, "Hey, wait a minute. He don't sleep too good, the doctor said I could-".

Harvey strikes her again then stands and paces, running his hands through his hair, talking to himself, "What doctor? Dr. Feelgood? This is unbelievable! Why does Max keep screwing selfish whores who won't care for their children?"

He sits down again, grabbing her chin and turning her head

towards the crib, "Do you have any idea what a blessing a baby is? What a miracle?"

Mary tries once more to get up, but Harvey grabs her by both shoulders and shoves her down, pinning her there, "I won't let that baby suffer like Marvin has!"

Mary is petrified, she had no idea Max's son was crazy, "Oh my God, listen, Marvin-"

Harvey takes a deep breath and backs off. He raises his hands up and smiles, putting Mary more at ease.

He considers, then speaks, very calmly, "One more time, Dear."

She attempts to smile but suddenly he wraps his hands around her throat.

"I'M NOT MARVIN!"

He squeezes as she flails, eyes like saucers. Her limbs thrash.

Just as abruptly, he releases her and tries to pull himself together. He sits on the edge of the bed, rocking back and forth as he holds his head in his hands.

"I'm sorry, I didn't mean to lose my temper. So-" He stands and paces as Mary coughs, unsure what to do.

He nods and smiles at her, "You still have to die."

The terror returns to Mary's eyes as he stands and carefully takes the half empty pill bottle off the table. She watches carefully. He turns to her and winks. She smiles as his figure doubles in her eyes. She's so drowsy.

He continues, "So, here's my problem. No steamer or big wooden boxes around here. I had to make do."

He shakes the bottle, "Apropos, don't you think, Mary?"

When he sees her confusion, he says slowly, "That means appropriate or suitable, OK?"

She yawns again as she is hit with a dizzy spell. Realization dawns on her.

HE DRUGGED THE CHERRIES!

Harvey watches the truth settles in, "Congratulations, you're not as dumb as I thought. It was enough to get started but, sadly, not to finish the job."

Mary crawls away from him, trying to get to the other side of the bed but he grabs a handful of her hair, and drags her back. He holds the bottle up to her mouth, twisting her ear to make her open up.

He chuckles, "Saw Miss Jezzy use this trick on Theodore. Who knew it would work on people?"

Already weakening, Mary opens and chokes down a few pills. Harvey holds the glass to her mouth and forces her to drink. Choking and gagging, a few manage to go down as she sputters some out on the bed.

Harvey pats her head, "Good girl."

Barely conscious, Mary finally looks over at Seth's crib and whispers something. Harvey can't hear so he leans close and gestures for her to speak.

She says, "What about my baby? I did my best."

Harvey sits back, genuinely moved by her entreaty, "Maybe you did. I have no idea what you've been through in your life. How you've been treated. Maybe this was the absolute best you could do."

He smooths her hair and smiles down at her as she pleads with her eyes.

He cuts her throat swiftly with Roger Carter's pocketknife.

"But I fucking doubt it."

Blood spurts from the deep gash in her neck; he drops the knife on the floor, watching the life drain away from her onto the quilt and pillows strewn around the bed.

When she is still, he walks over to the crib and looks in at the sleeping baby. Noticing he still has the pill bottle he puts it in his pocket.

You never know when you might need something like this. I do like to be prepared.

He sees Mary's purse on the dresser and digs through it. He looks back at the corpse, blood flooding down her décolletage onto her expensive peignoir.

"You don't mind, do you?"

He cups his hand to his ear and waits for a response.

After a few seconds, he responds, "Groovy."

He pulls out a wad of cash that could choke a horse and shoves it in his pocket.

He spies an ornately carved wooden jewelry box. He opens it to find several very expensive and gaudy pieces.

Who the hell travels out to the country and brings all of this shit?

He pulls out a pair of teardrop shaped sapphire earrings, at least three carats each. Holding them up to his ears, he smiles and poses in front of the mirror. They go in his pocket too.

"I should have brought a suitcase. I didn't realize there was gonna be a clearance sale."

Turning to her again, "You really should advertise better."

He cups his hand to his ear again, "What did you say, dear? These earrings aren't my style? Oh, that's OK. I wasn't planning to wear them. I'm not - like that. Honestly, you people from New York just assume the worst about everyone, don't you? I'm just saving them for a rainy day. But thank you for your input. Always appreciated."

He blows her bloody corpse a kiss.

He checks on the baby again, smiling and patting his back, "It's almost over."

46

Thunder booms as Marvin stares at the empty driveway, the dust from his father's car settling.

Tears roll down his cheeks and drop on his t-shirt. Staring out at the beautiful fall colors, he follows the path of a bright red leaf as it drifts down onto the porch.

Fall has always been his favorite time of year. A time of preparation, getting things ready for the long winter sleep. He's always loved planning and adhering to timetables.

Ever since his premature thrust into adulthood at age thirteen, he has been dedicated to his future. Barely a teen, he had realized that his mother never really took care of them, they had been living off of some mystery money for all these years.

More than the money that his father had probably provided after the divorce.

A check had arrived every month addressed to his mother. He had always accompanied his mother to the bank to deposit it. But the last time he was allowed inside the bank with her (he was nine at the time) the new bank clerk's jaw had gone slack when she saw the check for some reason.

She had looked from the check to Annette, to Marvin, back to the check again. When it appeared that this cycle would continue, Annette finally intervened in her own special way.

"Would it be too much trouble to have my check deposited before the second coming? Honestly, I have more to do than to stand here while you gawk like a simpleton."

Snapped back to reality, the young clerk apologized, "I'm sorry, I've just never seen a check from - one of them - before."

"I can assure you that you won't be seeing checks from anybody if you don't deposit this in the next two seconds. This is outrageous. I know the bank president. I doubt Mr. Sullivan would be happy to hear that he's hired an ogling nitwit!"

The young girl finished the transaction with lightning speed and handed the receipt to Annette who snatched it from her. This was the last time Marvin was permitted to come inside the bank,

Annette explaining that it would be more "fun" for him to wait on the sidewalk.

But Marvin had seen those envelopes from Hyannis Port, Massachusetts every month for as long as he could remember. He called the town Hyena Port one time only to have Annette chastise him for snooping in her mail.

Bribed with a large slice of chocolate cake at the diner later that week, she suggested he let her handle the mail from then on.

He had woken up on his birthday with indescribable joy, ready to embark on a new adventure, a future on his own.

He had planned to continue a relationship with his mother, but not to live with her. But now, after the past few days, he knows that isn't possible.

Marvin is devastated at how stupid he was to think that he could have a relationship with his father. His entire life has fallen apart in only a few days. He's lost everything.

Neither of his parents really love him. Other things always come first. Fame, recognition and most of all - money.

Wiping his face, he decides and states, "I'll move to New York City for a while, until Carey is better. Then we can find somewhere to go and start over. I'll build my business, become a success and my parents can both go to hell."

Harvey appears out of thin air in Marvin's truck. He sits in the passenger seat and opens the glove box. Marvin squints to see what he's putting in there. Cash and, wait, what? Jewelry?

What in the world has he been doing?

He's been gone a while, Marvin has missed his comforting presence. Harvey shuts the glove box with a smile and sees Marvin standing at the window. He waves until he notices Marvin's somber expression.

He opens the door and walks up the front steps approaching the window where Marvin watches him. They stare at each other for a moment, Harvey finally putting his hand up on the glass.

Marvin puts his hand up as well feeling the connection in spite of the cold barrier between them. There had always been something between them, keeping them apart. But not anymore.

Another tear rolls down Marvin's cheek. Harvey turns and stares at the empty driveway, imagining what could have happened with Max. Wrath clouds his eyes.

Harvey vanishes and appears next to Marvin in the house. Thunder, closer, rattles the window. The deluge begins. The wind gets stronger, sending a swirling flurry of leaves toward the house.

Harvey wipes a tear from Marvin's face, "What happened?"

Marvin speaks in a monotone, "It's all been a lie. Max just wants the trust fund back. He didn't come here because he loves me. He probably agreed to split it with Annette when she called him. I don't know anymore. Nothing makes sense to me."

Thunder crashes again, on top of them, flickering the lights.

A quick glance outside before grasping Marvin's shoulders, Harvey states, "It's time you knew the truth."

He points at the far wall in the living room as the lights flicker again. Marvin's gaze follows and falls on –

THE HARVEY POSTER!

Marvin stands staring up at it.

How did I get here? I don't remember walking over.

He reaches toward it, touching the frame.

Has he ever touched it? Wait! He did, once. It was years ago and he was curious. When Annette had seen him touch it, she had gone ballistic, screaming in hysterics that he was not to touch her things.

He pulls his hand away now, like he's been burned. He looks at his hand and expects to see blistering but he is uninjured. His hand shakes violently, his whole body shuddering uncontrollably. There's always been something off about this poster.

How could such a sweet, funny movie poster feel so evil?

Thunder shakes the house again, lightning illuminating Marvin's tear streaked face. Harvey turns Marvin towards him and places his hands on either side of Marvin's head.

Harvey closes his eyes and focuses his energy. Marvin inhales sharply as his eyes go wide and he shudders violently again.

He remembers-

47
November 15, 1950

-Hazy distortions alternate with blackness.

Moving images, blurred. Lullaby music overhead, slowed down, distorted. Crying next to him. Wooden slats surround him and as he looks up he sees the mobile turning lazily. Animals and small round mirrors float above him.

His face, multiplied six times. And - another.

A scent, faint but getting stronger. Floral, spice. His mother. She looks down at him, stone-faced. Beautiful, even when she's not smiling. She never smiles.

The red velvet pillow that she rests him on when she feeds him his bottle. In her hands. Crying distracts her from him. She looks to his side and sneers. She reaches the pillow in. Muffled crying. Crying stops.

She stands straight again, gazing at him, considering. She shakes away the hesitation, leans toward him with the pillow. Overwhelmed with the smell of her.

Thunderous sounds approach, shaking the room.

BANG!

Door slams into the wall. His mother yanked back out of his sight.

His father screaming at her, "Annette, my God! What are you doing?"

He leans in next to him, hysterical, "NO! NO! You killed him!"

His crazed father grabs him up roughly and holds him close. Musky smell, spicy. His smell. He feels his father's heart racing, his heavy breathing.

His mother from the floor, "Max, I-"

As Max swings around to strike Annette, Marvin sees his identical twin brother's lifeless body in the crib.

48

Marvin's primal screams drown out the thunder as he shatters the poster glass with both fists.

He rips the frame down and throws it onto the floor. Glass sprays both boys and the frame splinters into pieces.

Harvey watches as Marvin picks up the large manila envelope taped behind the poster.

Out of breath, he looks at Harvey. Harvey nods and Marvin opens it.

Two official documents.

BIRTH CERTIFICATE:

Harvey Robert Damon.

Born: October 29,1950.

Sex of child: Male.

Single, twin, triplet, other: *Twin*.

Number in order of birth: First.

Sobbing uncontrollably, Marvin leans on the man he now knows is his twin brother.

Harvey holds him, patting his back, "You've always known. You just weren't ready to remember. I've been with you, you just couldn't see me. It's why you've constantly felt so alone. You weren't supposed to be. You and I were supposed to be together."

Marvin looks at the birth certificate again, wiping his face, "I had it in my hand. *My* birth certificate. It said *twin* right on it and I didn't notice it! That's why she hid it so well and was hysterical to see me with it!"

Marvin focuses on Harvey, really seeing him for the first time,

"You're a ghost."

Harvey nods and smiles, "Something like that. Listen, everything is going to be alright. Truth opens doors, Marvin. When you started to learn the truth on your birthday, I just had to walk through. The more you learned, the stronger I got. Annette and Max took everything from us. They have to pay."

"I've already decided, I'm - we're going to leave town. Never see them again."

Harvey points out, "There's no death certificate. I didn't even get that much respect from them. She murdered me and he covered it up. Come with me."

Harvey takes Marvin by the hand and leads him out the front door into the slanting rain and driving winds. Both get soaked but Marvin is unphased by the weather.

Harvey leads Marvin off the porch and to the south side of the house, the side where Marvin's bedroom window is. Marvin looks up and sees his window, he remembers looking out and wondering if he was losing his mind only a few days ago.

Harvey points at the red rose bushes that line the side of the house, the late blooming flowers pelted by rain, losing their ruby petals in the wind.

"He buried the body there, then planted these stupid flowers to cover my unmarked grave. And she actually keeps them in a vase in the house. Religiously. To remind herself that she has the ultimate power. That she won."

Marvin falls to his knees and digs wildly with his hands, unhinged.

Harvey drops down and stops him, "No, Marvin. Leave him alone. Now isn't the time."

Marvin, overwrought, "Him? But it's you. I have to save you, you can't breathe under there. It's dark and lonely!"

Harvey holds Marvin's mucky hands and shakes him, trying to get him under control. He forces Marvin to look directly into his eyes. This has the desired effect. Marvin's breathing regulates and he stops shaking.

Once Marvin fully regains his composure, they stand up together and trudge back into the house through the onslaught.

After entering the house, Harvey vanishes and reappears instantaneously. He's dry again, holding a blanket out for Marvin. Marvin's teeth chatter, the damp cold seeping into his soul. He accepts the blanket with a barely perceptible nod.

Determined and sure of himself, Marvin states, "We have to finish this."

"Yeah, we do."

Marvin lowers himself to the floor next to the remnants of the poster, draped in the blanket. He adjusts it, realizing that it's the blanket Annette keeps folded at the end of her bed. Yet another item that Marvin was forbidden to touch.

Fitting that her murdered son should comfort his surviving brother with it.

It was handmade in Europe specifically for her. A gift, supposedly.

From whom?

He doesn't know.

For what occasion?

He doesn't know.

The mysteries and lies surrounding his mother no longer concern him.

Grabbing a jagged piece of glass, Marvin slices his left palm, creating an ugly slash. Scarlet drips onto the polished wooden floor. He takes his right finger, dips it in the blood and creates the Baby Marvin dots on his cheeks and nose.

He doesn't need a mirror, he never has. He became a pro at creating his persona when he was just four years old.

Masks slide on so easily, then right back off again.

Marvin applies the fated dots to his dead brother as well.

PART 3

"THIS IS WHAT SUCCESS LOOKS LIKE"

49

*H*arvey was there when the national sensation known as Baby Marvin was birthed in that audition room.

Marvin, in his unjaded innocence, had seen him in the corner waving at him. It had surprised Harvey at the time. Marvin had never seen him before. He decided to keep to himself from then on, observing Marvin from a distance, keeping an eye on him until he was ready to make himself known.

He would be that voice in Marvin's mind keeping him out of trouble. He would be another guardian angel.

He doesn't remember dying. He's thankful for that. Imagine the horror of seeing your own mother's face as she ends your young life. He saw his death for the first time when he opened Marvin's mind to the memory.

He hated to do it, but Marvin deserves to know who he is and what happened. And, it furthered Harvey's ambition to set things right.

His loyalty to Marvin is not something that any living person could understand. The protective nature is obviously not genetic, he's not sure where it comes from. Harvey believes in God, in the afterlife and in destiny.

He was there at Miss Jezzy's knee with Carey and Marvin, unseen, but listening to the Bible stories.

Never full of enough hubris to compare himself to Christ, he does understand the complexity of dying and being reborn. It creates a new reality, one in which the blessed reborn is stronger than before. All things considered he does believe himself to be blessed.

Dying so early, he avoided the inevitable life of misery with Annette that Marvin has suffered.

He intuitively knows that he could have moved on to peace, or Heaven, or infinity; whichever of these realities are awaiting those who have moved beyond this mortal coil.

He read Hamlet with Marvin, wishing he was able to turn pages or pick up the discarded book when Marvin wasn't using it. He found other ways to read his favorite play and memorized it long ago.

He watched Richard Burton perform the role on Broadway in 1964 and was mesmerized. The lessons he hadn't learned from Miss Jezzy's informal catechisms, he had learned from the Bard:

To what base uses we may return, Horatio!
Why may not imagination trace the noble dust of
Alexander
till he find it stopping a bunghole?

*And his personal favorite, the one he would have had inscribed on his
gravestone, had he lived a normal life and death:*

If thou didst ever hold me in thy heart,
Absent thee from felicity awhile,
And in this harsh world draw thy breath in pain,
To tell my story.

He knows the day will come when Marvin will leave this life.

He'll be there, holding his hand, helping him make the wondrous journey from this life to the next.

And when Marvin takes his last breath, he'll vanish one final time to join him in eternity.

50

Max squeals his car up to the bungalow, just ahead of the downpour.

He hops, grabbing a bag of groceries from the passenger seat before darting up to the front porch. Grabbing his keys from his front pocket, he accidentally elbows the front door and it drifts open.

Can't believe it's not locked considering how paranoid she is. Living in a big city does that to you. Probably drunk again. I should have brought the baby with me, she's incapable of caring for him. Well, things are about to change for the better.

Crossing the threshold with the bag, he's momentarily confused by the dead silence. There's always a racket going on. The baby laughing, crying, cooing. Mary playing the radio or yelling at him.

And of course, the endless drone of the television. She keeps it on even when she's not watching it.

He welcomes the quiet reprieve. The bedroom door is closed and something is stuck to it. He walks over, still holding the grocery bag and finds a note.

Sleep on the couch.

He tries the door, it's locked. Sighing he heads into the kitchen to put the bag down. He studies the note again. The handwriting is puzzling. Doesn't look like her writing.

Angry at his over-thinking of the situation, he crumples it and throws it on the floor.

I was right. Drunk and incoherent.

He sniffs, noticing the blanket and pillow folded on the couch.

As the downpour begins, Max stares out into the ebony night, contemplating his life.

Everything is going to improve now.

He smiles at the thought and grabs the phone. Dead. Dammit. He wanted to call Marvin to tell him not to come out in this torrent.

Unpacking the groceries, he sees headlights illuminate the wall over the couch. He goes to the window, still holding a can of tomato sauce in his left hand. A bright green car is creeping up the short driveway.

Who could this be? It's not Marvin, he has a red pickup truck. But who else would come out here in this weather?

His own urban paranoia surfaces and he reaches out to lock the door.

The car stops, some distance from the porch and the driver gets out. It's pitch dark by now but he can see that it's a tall man with a slim build. Is there someone else in the passenger seat?

He sees movement and a shadow. Lightning flashes and floods the car with light. The passenger seat is empty after all.

And it *is* Marvin, Max glimpsed him briefly when the lightning put on its show. Marvin walks very slowly, dragging something behind him.

Max throws the door open, happy to see his son but then he stumbles back, horrified.

Marvin edges up onto the covered porch, head down, soaking wet. He raises his head, red running down his face, he looks like he's been crying blood.

Max's focus moves to his son's eyes. Lifeless, the green gone, replaced with gunmetal gray. And something underneath.

DEATH.

Max shifts his gaze to see what Marvin is dragging. It's an ax.

Max, unsure, "Marvin, I hoped you'd reconsider coming out in this storm. I tried to call but the phone was dead. And it looks like you were almost here anyway."

Marvin stares at him, dead-eyed, dripping wet.

The hair on the back of Max's neck goes up as his stomach knots up. This isn't the same boy he spent time with a couple of hours ago.

"You're soaked, let me get you a towel."

He turns towards the kitchen but –

HE SEES MARVIN IN FRONT OF HIM in the house?!

And he's dry, with Baby Marvin dots on his face?! Smiling.

How?

Terrified and confused, Max turns back to the porch. Marvin is still there glaring at him. He swivels his head back and forth, afraid he's losing his mind.

Angry Marvin on the porch, smiling Marvin in the house.

Again and again, he shifts between the two.

He finally closes his eyes, overwhelmed, moaning. He doesn't even realize he's still holding the can of tomato sauce until he feels someone take it from him.

The world spins.

Petrified, he opens his eyes once more.

Indoor Marvin's face is right in front of him, "Hello, Dad."

The can of sauce bounces up and down in his hand before it smashes into Max's temple.

Pain.

Blackness.

51

Max's head swims as he opens his eyes.

Blurriness gives way to a foggy haze. He brushes the side of his head that hurts. A lump is forming. The pain brings him back to full consciousness.

He's sitting up on the couch. Marvin, soaked and disheveled, and Harvey, dry and pristine, stand over him. The realization of what he's seeing finally settles on him.

"Harvey?"

Harvey nods slightly, a half grin on his face.

"How? It's not possible. Harvey? Harvey died. He-"

Marvin shakes his head, "Died?"

Harvey furiously paces, still holding the can of sauce, "Died? Died? Really?"

He plops down on the couch next to Max and puts his arm around him, pulling him close.

"I was murdered by my mother and you covered it up! You put her in a country club asylum for-."

He repeatedly snaps his fingers, searching for the words but can't find them.

He asks Marvin, "What the hell was it?"

Marvin, deadpan, "Rest and evaluation."

Harvey, leaping up, "That's it! Rest and evaluation. For murdering an innocent baby."

He tosses the can back and forth between his hands.

Leaning down close to Max again, "Tell me. Whose idea was it to shove every trace of my pitiful, short existence behind that *Harvey* poster?"

"Your mother must have done that when she got released. I left shortly after that. After I made sure that Marvin was taken care of."

Harvey, bemused, "You're such a swell guy, Max."

Max tries to explain, "I-"

Harvey interrupts, "You buried me in the yard next to the house like I was garbage. No marker. Nothing."

Marvin, robotic, "Just some rose bushes."

More furious pacing from Harvey wandering around the entire room, "Oh, the rose bushes!"

He flings the can of sauce into a table lamp, shattering it into a thousand pieces. Max holds his arms up to protect himself from the flying chips.

Harvey picks the can back up and aims it at the front window, but Marvin pipes up, "That's enough."

Harvey stops, obeying his brother, but he continues to mumble under his breath in a wild variety of voices and accents, "Rose bushes. Rose bushes."

Max weeps, his face in his hands, "You don't understand. I didn't know what to do. She had killed you and was about to kill Marvin."

Harvey rushes Max, the can hovering over Max's head, "So you planted rose bushes! Very nice rose bushes! Love the rose bushes!"

Marvin places his hand on Harvey's arm, "That's enough."

Harvey lowers his arm and looks Marvin in the eye. He nods his head, pats Marvin's arm and wanders away toward the kitchen. He opens cupboards and searches through them.

But he won't be silent, "My father compounded with my mother under the Dragon's tail, and my nativity was under-"

Marvin, again, "Enough."

Harvey nods his assent.

Marvin faces Max, remembers, then faces Harvey again, "King Lear?"

A nod and hand clap from Harvey.

Max sees an opportunity. Both boys are calm. He wants to connect with Marvin, who is more coherent, if not detached. Harvey is too volatile to deal with.

He pleads with Marvin, "My sons. My boys. I was so happy when you were born. I couldn't wait to tell everyone that God had gifted me with two sons."

Harvey picks up a glass half-filled with bourbon. Sniffing it, he makes a disgusted face and talks to himself again, "Yuck. People drink this stuff?"

He focuses on Max as he pours the drink out onto the counter, "Let's dispense with the talk of God, shall we? You and our mother haven't exactly walked Christ's path now have you?"

Max tries to connect with Marvin again, "Annette had a tough time carrying you both."

Harvey finds a bunch of grapes in the grocery bag and grins. He pulls one off and eats it. He's mesmerized by the taste of food. He throws the rest one at a time at Max as he speaks.

"And then moving here from New York was another strain but I wanted to raise you here in the country, where I grew up."

More grapes pelt Max. Marvin is irritated by his brother's behavior but doesn't intervene. He knows that Harvey has almost two decades of pent-up rage roiling inside of him. He needs a release.

Max ignores Harvey and stays focused on Marvin, "We had barely moved in when she had you. You were born right there in the house I had bought for us. We were a family."

After flinging the last grape, Harvey vanishes from the kitchen and appears next to Max again but speaks to Marvin, "Far out. A family. Except for one little detail. Annette never wanted children,"

He nudges Max, "Right?"

Max nods sadly, "I agreed to that and married her anyway. I knew I'd convince her to have children eventually."

Harvey laughs, "Because you're such a charmer, right Dad?"

Max continues, "She seemed happy when she got pregnant but she had issues after you were born. She developed-"

Harvey warns, "Don't say it."

Max looks directly at Harvey, "I will say it. She developed schizophrenia."

Harvey hops up, speaking directly to Marvin, feigning shock, "Can you believe that? Mere moments after giving birth to two children she never wanted, she developed a mental illness. That's crazy."

Marvin looks at him sideways, still speaking in a monotone, "Did you do that on purpose?"

Harvey realizes his ironic use of the word crazy, "No. Guess I'm just unintentionally good at communicating. The dead guy is a wordsmith. And also, hilarious. Yet another irony."

Max looks at Harvey, "So you *are* dead?"

Harvey folds his arms and retorts, "Well, I wasn't vacationing in

Europe all these years."

"How are you here? And able to be like a-"

"Living person?" Harvey asks.

Max nods, curious.

"Well, I'm not entirely sure."

Harvey looks to Marvin, "But I suspect it has to do with a bond that can't be broken, a bond bigger than life and death. When Marvin needed me, I was able to come through for him."

Max entreats as he tries to rise, "Marvin-"

Harvey shoves him back down, "Let's stay on the subject please. Annette never had any mental illness. She's just a selfish, disgusting bitch. She never wanted children. Not your children anyway. After all, you're not a Kennedy. She'd have popped out a dozen for dear old Bobby. She was afraid having kids with a nobody like you would interfere with her imaginary career. And you knew it. You knew she was lying about-"

Harvey performs grand arms gestures and puts on a high-pitched voice, "Hearing voices! Seeing things!"

Marvin speaks, "You both made it up to keep her from going to jail. That's why you were so sure I was fine, there's no condition to inherit."

The baby cries from the bedroom. Max jumps up, concerned about his baby son.

"My wife. My son. Please."

Harvey, calmer, "Your wife? Speaking of selfish, disgusting bitches."

"Now just a minute."

"Oh please, save the chivalrous bullshit for somebody else. Did you know she's been drugging our brother?"

Marvin and Max both express shock, their faces identical as Marvin begins to waver.

Max cries, "What?!"

Harvey paces again, using the entire space as a good actor would, "I dropped by here earlier today. He was crying and she ground up one of her pills. By the way, what is it with you and broads on medication? Honestly. Anyway, she put the pill in his bottle and fed it to him and he's been out for hours."

Max collapses on the couch, "I didn't know. I'll get the baby away from her. I'll do for him what I wasn't able to do for you. I'm sorry I let Annette dictate everything."

"You left Marvin with Annette. A woman who murdered me in cold blood. You took off and you never looked back. Why should we trust you to do anything?"

"I, I hired Miss Jezzy to help with Marvin back then. For stability. I knew she'd take care of him. I had to leave. Annette was-"

He looks to Marvin, "You know how she is. You would have been more miserable if I'd been around and we had fought over you all the time."

Thunder booms again, right on top of them, the worst of the storm is here.

The mention of Miss Jezzy's name brings Marvin to full attention, "Miss Jezzy and Carey were the only decent things in my life. Now they're gone."

He looks at Harvey and smiles, "But I have my brother back. I have to focus on that. He's my family. Always has been, I just didn't know it."

Max implores, "I'm your family too, Marvin. I want to be with you, with both of you."

Marvin stares daggers, "And the money? My trust fund? You want it back, right?"

Max wilts, "At first I, yes, I was going to ask for some of it back. Mary has spent more than you can imagine over the past year or so. So, I was going to ask for some of it back. But when we met and I saw you, I forgot all about it. I decided to leave Mary and take Seth away from her. And now that I know about the pills, it will be easier. You can come and live with me and Seth. We'll all move far away. From Annette, from everything."

He faces Harvey, "And Harvey, I still don't know how you're here but now we can be a family if you'll forgive me. I'll do whatever it takes."

Harvey can't believe what he's hearing, "Just like that?"

"Yes."

Harvey, decisive, "I appreciate that, *Dad*, but it's unnecessary.

Mary's dead. I killed her earlier."

Max falls back onto the couch and processes what he's been told.

He finally replies, "The baby's OK?"

Harvey, "He's nifty. I'd never hurt my brother."

Max bursts out laughing, clutching his sides, tears rolling down his cheeks. Marvin and Harvey gawk at him, then at each other, perplexed.

Max notices their confusion, "Don't you understand? This solves everything. The four of us can start over now."

Max stands and paces, mirroring what his dead son did a moment ago, "We'll have to get rid of the body, dump it somewhere. I'll say she ran off."

Harvey is surprised at Max's thought process, "Not necessary. We're framing a couple of ne'er do wells for the crime. We drove over in their car."

Max, constructing a scene, "Good. Good. You've thought this through. Guess directing is in your blood."

Harvey mimes looking through his hands like a director framing up an image, "It sure is, Dad."

Max rubs his hands together, "Terrific!"

He gazes up at his twin sons, tears sparkling in his eyes, "You're finally going to have a dad. And we-"

Marvin, the drying sanguine mess on his face splitting into an evil comic book villain's grin, "I already have one."

SWISH!

Marvin takes Max's head off with the ax. His one-handed swing removing it in a clean swipe while Max was mid-sentence.

Max's headless corpse falls over onto the couch leaking blood, twitching for a moment, then becoming still.

His head comes to rest on the floor at Marvin's feet, the expression one of unfulfilled happiness.

Marvin attacks his father's lifeless body, hacking it over and over with the ax. Blood drenches the couch.

He yells, "It's too late, it's too late, it's too late," with each stroke of the blade.

The walls are spattered, the couch is a ruin and Marvin's *Keep on Truckin* t-shirt is soaked.

Some blood also douses Harvey, annoying him.

He stops Marvin mid-swing, "Enough."

Harvey reaches down and picks up Max's head by the thick, dark hair and speaks to it directly, "Don't worry, I'll plant some rose bushes."

He tosses the head onto the couch. It lands face-up next to the mincemeat that was his upper body. Harvey reaches into Max's pocket, retrieving his wallet. He removes a wad of cash and stuffs it in his own pocket before he vanishes.

Marvin hears the car trunk opening and closing but continues to stare at the pulpy mass that used to be his father. His biological father, that is.

His real father is currently pouring over photos and documents in his small office in town, praying to find some resolution to the hideous crime committed upon Miss Jezzy and Carey.

He rises to stretch his aching back, thinking that this crime is the worst problem he's going to be handling. He doesn't yet know about the crumpled body of the child abuser who lays at the bottom of a rickety staircase in the "low" part of town.

Nor does he suspect he'll be greeted with a gruesome scene at a cottage rental near Marvin's house.

Harvey reappears from the car with the red handled ax, Marvin's spare from the wood shop. He holds it carefully by the blade, smears Max's blood on it then drops it on the floor.

"Oh John, you've been a very bad boy. Look what you did."

To Marvin, "Remind me to thank him for putting his prints on this ax."

He snaps his fingers, remembering, "Oh wait, I can't."

Marvin, still stoic, "What about the wife?"

Harvey runs toward the bedroom, vanishing through the door. He unlocks the door from the inside and pokes his head out, immaculate and clean once again.

The baby has stopped crying and coos, soothing himself. Harvey glances over at the baby then back at Marvin.

He feels a bond with the baby and worries about Marvin's state of mind. Harvey's the stable one right now.

In spite of his erratic behavior and outbursts, he has complete control over his actions.

"What about the baby?"

They planned to kill Max from the time Marvin put the blood on their faces next to the ruin of the poster. It was entertaining to see their father actually discuss a future with them though. As if his crimes were all forgiven in a matter of moments.

The real corker was his reaction to becoming a widower so suddenly. Neither of the boys could have imagined that. Having spent time with Mary, Harvey understands the man's gleeful attitude.

Marvin lays his ax against the front door and heads towards the bedroom, "I'm coming."

Harvey stands by the crib, patting the baby. Little Seth looks up at him with a smile and Harvey feels a connection, not unlike the one he shares with Marvin. He'd let Marvin take the lead on everything so far because Marvin has been the victim in more ways than Harvey has.

Harvey was murdered, no doubt he is a victim, but it was one incident. A decidedly huge incident nonetheless. Marvin has been victimized over and over since then.

Marvin comes into the room, stopping and taking in the scene. Mary, cloudy-eyed and lifeless sits propped up in bed, Roger's bloody knife on the floor.

Marvin feels nothing when he sees her. She might as well have been one of the mannequins in the store windows he was always fascinated with as a child.

Marvin turns to the crib. Max's blood drips down from his hair onto his ruined shirt. His shoes make a SQUISH sound as he treads over, leaving crimson footprints on the discarded clothes littering the messy room.

Harvey observes him as he approaches.

Squish, squish, squish.

Harvey is prepared for anything. Marvin has been hurt more than anyone has a right to be. And it's made him unstable for the moment. He'll need to take care of him until he can set himself right again.

Harvey finally understands why Marvin applied the dots on his face. They tether him to innocence, to the defining time of his life. Without them, he might have lost himself completely. But the dots are a life raft in this temporary sea of tumult that they are both navigating.

He's happy that Marvin has his touchstone. And he'll be here too. He's protected Marvin his whole life, been that whispered warning in his head, that gentle guiding hand that has kept him from harm.

Don't cross the street yet. Careful, that's hot. Slow down on this uneven path.

They are two halves of a whole, when one is weak, the other is strong. It's a routine yin and yang that neither of them has to think about. It just happens naturally.

In fact-

Harvey thinks to himself, *"Can you hear me, Marvin?"*

Marvin stops at the crib and switches his focus from one brother to another. From Seth to Harvey. He nods in the affirmative, his lips upturned for the first time since their arrival at the bungalow.

Harvey nods back as Marvin picks up a small homemade quilt and leans over into the crib.

52

Heads popping up, the seven deer wander into the three acre pumpkin patch, cautious but comfortable in this familiar yard.

The center of the patch is disturbed, a shovel standing sentinel. The metal handle reflects the waning full moon that fights to shine through the receding storm clouds.

The deer avoid this strange area around the shovel, their instincts guiding them away from it. Something inexplicable happened here.

They freeze. They wait. Sounds approach.

They tend to ignore breaks in the quiet in this place but now they reconsider. Not the usual hubbub they are so comfortable with. These sounds confuse them, putting them on alert.

A giggling baby. A man's labored breathing. Something heavy dragging and scraping along the gravel driveway.

They recognize Marvin from a distance, they know him. But something is - he's changed since they saw him last.

Always accompanied by glowing waves of gentleness, seen only to them, he's become - *DEATH*.

They scatter into the woods.

Looking over Marvin's left shoulder, six month old Seth gleefully coos and giggles, wrapped in his blanket. His father's blood streaks his face, transferred by Marvin.

Harvey walks several feet behind them, shaking a teddy bear at the baby eliciting the laughter. He has a bag slung over his shoulder bulging with baby items and he carries a suitcase.

He had told Marvin that he would carry the baby but Marvin insisted on doing it. Harvey had decided not to mention the fact that this would create a huge mess because Marvin had a singular focus.

"I'm saving him."

Shoving the partially open front door of the house with his shoulder, Marvin leaves a red streak behind.

Gripping the bloody ax, he walks inside leaving the door open behind him. Harvey follows and clicks it closed.

Bleary Marvin takes in the dim living room with his gray-green eyes. He is unrecognizable amidst the gore on his face and in his dark, wavy hair and on his white *Keep on Truckin* t-shirt.

He sets Seth down on the floor with great care, leaving a bloody handprint on the back of the light blue footed pajamas the child wears.

The six month-old little boy is nonplussed by the horrifying situation, he sits up on his own and continues to be delighted by everything he sees.

THUMP!

Startled, but lacking the energy (or will) to fight, relief washes over Marvin when he realizes the old bloodhound, Theodore, has slumped off of the lavish sofa onto the floor.

He had been dozing comfortably against a tufted pillow. He alternates between the sofa and his fur coat bed.

The curious dog waddles over to investigate the strange little creature on the floor.

The baby reaches his podgy hands out toward the animal and squeals with joy as Theodore licks the blood from his face.

The remnants of the movie poster, Jimmy Stewart smiling up at the shadow of a huge rabbit, greet Marvin. Harvey's birth and death certificates are strewn among the glass shards.

Realizing he's still holding the ax, Marvin stares at it in disbelief.

"I did it," Marvin whispers.

Standing by the front door, giving his brother some space, Harvey puts the luggage down and folds his arms.

"We did it," Harvey corrects him as he looks around the room.

Remembering, he retrieves his birth certificate from the floor. He folds it and places it in his back pocket as he stares at the Robert Kennedy photo.

Marvin asks, "Did we miss anything?"

"No. Roger's knife, an ax with John's prints on it, their puke green car at the cabin. Max's expensive car is missing and all that money he brought with him. And some of Mary's jewelry. The fire I set will probably destroy all of the evidence but you never know, hence the ax and knife. It looks like those dopes went over there to rob them on their way out of town and then decided not to leave any witnesses. After all, they have nothing to lose at this point.

They'll be suspected of Miss Jezzy's murder soon enough."

"And they took the baby?

"Yes, but apparently even those two cretins had second thoughts about killing a baby. They'll leave him on Miss Jezzy's doorstep in a couple of days. An anonymous call to the Sheriff and he'll be scooped up right away. You're next of kin and an adult now so you can take the baby. I'll handle the whole thing. He'll be perfectly safe."

"Where's Da - Max's car?"

"I drove it into the river. Nearly killed me to do it, I would have loved to have kept it. It was a beauty."

He laughs, "Nearly killed me. A pun. Interesting. I'm really getting the hang of conversation. Oh, and I dumped that steamer of yours too. No saving it, I'm afraid."

Marvin drops the ax on the kitchen counter and wipes his bloody hand on his pants, "I-".

He hangs his head.

Harvey bounds over and puts his hands on Marvin's shoulders.

"Hey, listen. You've been through a lot, Marvin. Just take your time. Don't worry. I've thought of everything."

The giggling and chatter of the happy baby catches their attention. Marvin smiles and shakes his head, "He's a cute little guy. I wasn't sure if we should-"

Harvey cuts him off, "He is innocent and innocence is sacred. He's our brother and we'll raise him. The right way. You can raise him as your son. Folks will go along with it, people appreciate you and will gush over your sacrifice. That would be for the best, I think. And I'll be Uncle Harvey."

"I was raised with lies. I don't want to do that to him."

"Well, let's cross that bridge when we come to it, alright?"

Marvin nods and looks away, deep in thought. Harvey senses what's on his mind.

"Before we, well earlier, I mean, there was something I wanted to tell you about Miss Jezzy."

At the sound of her name, Marvin looks at his brother, hopeful.

Harvey gets close to him. "I have to show you something. Like before. Is that OK?"

Marvin nods slowly and closes his eyes, bracing himself. Harvey clasps the sides of Marvin's head.

The energy jolts Marvin's eyes open.

He sucks in his breath, but-

53

-This memory is clearer than the last one.

Almost a normal person's view of things. He shares Harvey's thoughts and feelings as he looks through his eyes.

He *is* Harvey in this memory.

He's stampeding up the porch steps to Miss Jezzy's house as John and Roger disappear into the woods. Flames slowly spread in the living room. He can smell the burning chintz drapes.

The front door is open, thank God! He's unable to manage things in this physical reality right now.

Sprinting into the house, Miss Jezzy is lying on the floor. Attempting to get up, she falls back again. She mumbles for Carey but gets no response. Carey lies still, his brown skin deathly pale.

Harvey kneels next to Miss Jezzy as the flames spread to her recliner. Drifting in and out of consciousness, she grimaces with pain. He tries to touch her but can't. He stares at his useless hands, flexing them in front of his face as he cries out in anguish.

Hearing his torment, Miss Jezzy opens her eyes and focuses on him. Near death, she is on a plane of existence between worlds and she knows who is kneeling next to her, crying.

When the realization hits her, she smiles, no longer in pain. She reaches for him but is too weak.

"Harvey."

Not a question, a statement.

Harvey's shock gives way to happiness at being recognized, "Yes, Miss Jezzy, I'm here."

"Carey, is he-"

Harvey, agonized, lies with a smile, "He's gonna be fine, the ambulance is here."

She smiles, then remembers, "Marvin, my Marvin-"

"I'll take care of Marvin. I promise. I'll take care of both of them."

She dies, a satisfied smile on her face as a mournful howl distracts Harvey. He turns to see a confused Theodore wandering around the recliner as it succumbs to the flames.

He hears sirens in the distance but can't wait for help.

He prays with all his might, then, "Theodore, come on boy, let's go."

He calls and clucks his tongue until he gets the dog's attention. Theodore wags his tail and follows him out the front door.

Not wanting to deal with the Sheriff, he lures the dog into the woods, "Come on, let's go home."

Marvin's vision of Harvey's experience shifts to the forest right beside his house.

Marvin sees himself happily getting into his truck to go to Miss Jezzy's house. They were going to carve the pumpkin and spend time together.

Harvey waits patiently in the woods until oblivious Marvin has driven off. He walks the long driveway up to the house followed by the dog as the phone inside is heard ringing through the open windows.

54

Harvey releases Marvin from his grasp as Marvin collapses in tears.

Harvey kneels down next to him.

Marvin sobs, "She didn't die alone."

"No, she didn't. Find peace with that. And I have a feeling she's around, keeping an eye on us."

"Is she like you?"

Harvey ponders, "No. Even though she died - that way, she's at peace. So, don't start looking for her to come out of the mirror."

"How did she know about you?"

"A question for the ages. I was prepared to *be* you, to give her comfort. But it wasn't necessary."

"She'd be disappointed in me. In the things I've done. She was a good, forgiving Christian woman."

"She was also smart enough to know who doesn't deserve forgiveness. I think she would have swung that ax herself if she could have. And remember, even Jesus flipped the moneychanger's tables. Remember she always liked that story?"

Seth topples over and gets fussy.

Harvey suggests, "Go clean up, I'll watch him."

Marvin rises to head upstairs, but his eyes fall on the ax on the counter.

Can he ever use it again for the purpose it was intended for? Can he be normal again?

Harvey pipes up again, "Don't worry about that."

He chatters to Seth, "We'll clean it up, won't we, buddy? Yes, we will. Yes, we will."

He grabs the baby and gives him kisses and nuzzles his neck amidst baby giggles.

After Marvin has made his way upstairs, Harvey grabs a dish towel and runs some warm water over it, all while balancing Seth like a seasoned parent.

He squeezes out the excess water and wipes the blood from Seth's face, managing to keep the perturbed baby smiling in between gentle strokes.

He drops the bloody towel in the sink and declares, "One last task to perform, Seth."

Glancing up the stairs, "This will be the most difficult for Marvin but it has to be done."

Seth pats Harvey's face, putting his hands in his brother's mouth and in his hair. A palpable bond.

Harvey clutches Seth's tiny hand in his own, kisses it and muses in an English accent, "Though this be madness, yet there is method in't."

He sighs and holds the baby close.

55

Dusk is falling, the last rays of the sun giving the living room an orange glow.

It fades as the seconds tick by. Noise at the back door. Moments later it flies open, Annette struggling to enter the house.

Overwhelmed with shopping bags, she lurches in, wearing a new black dress and matching beret. Her green eyes sparkle like emeralds.

As the room gets darker, Annette drops her multitude of bags and flips the light switch. Nothing happens. Exclaiming, annoyed Annette tries it several times to no avail.

With a huge sigh, she is suddenly aware that something feels - wrong. She gives the room a once over with her eyes. Everything seems in order but-

The Harvey poster is gone!

Panic-stricken, Annette falls back against the door, fumbling for the knob behind her, ready to run away. The pounding of feet coming down the stairs strikes terror into her heart. Everything slows down for her.

THUD. THUD. THUD.

He knows. He knows. I have to go.

Her hand convulses on the doorknob, unable to turn it. She's scared witless and won't face the uncooperative door, won't have her back to-

Ready to collapse, her fear subsides when Marvin joyfully trots into the room, holding an oil lamp.

"Hello Mother! How was your trip?"

She falters, cautious, "Fine."

He stops, cocking his head to one side, "Are you alright? You seem anxious."

"I-I just had a rather harrowing drive."

She can't help it, her eyes fall on the enormous gaping space on the wall. Marvin notices.

"Oh. I have some bad news. Your poster fell off of the wall during that pounding storm last night. I cleaned up the broken glass, cut my hand on it."

He holds up the bandage but she's unconcerned about his injury. Her eyes remain on the bright rectangle surrounded by floral patterns faded by years of light exposure.

"I put the poster in your room so you can decide what to do with it. I know someone who can get some new glass for it in town. Mr. Peters. You know him, right?"

Of course she does. He undresses her with his disgusting milky eyes whenever he passes her in public. She hates him. But then again, she hates everyone.

Marvin's smile finally puts her at ease so she replies, "Yes I know him. Thank you for taking care of it. It must have been some storm."

"I'm sorry, I know what that poster means to you. Thankfully it's not ruined. Just the glass and frame. But the contents are completely fine."

Did she notice something behind his eyes just now? No, she's being paranoid.

He would never behave normally if-

Everything is fine so she attempts to steady her voice, "Oh, alright. Thank you."

Smiling, he heads to the drink cart and pours her a bumper of scotch. Annette is flabbergasted, is he going to drink-

"Here, you've had a long trip. It's not for me to decide whether or not you drink."

He hands her the glass.

She takes it with a fluttering hand, grateful that he's not drinking but stunned that he offered her alcohol.

He hates that she drinks. He's made that quite clear over the years. Something is off about him.

That niggling voice of doom won't leave her alone.

"You're a grown woman after all. Responsible for your own decisions. Right?"

She downs the drink in one unladylike gulp, scowling for a moment at the glass.

Marvin smiles again.

Feeling better, she kisses his cheek and gushes, "I bought you something in New York, you'll love it."

Marvin hands her the lamp as she grabs her suitcase, leaving the bags behind and heads upstairs, leaving her son in the dark.

"Of course, I will."

His smile vanishes as soon as she is out of sight. He stares straight ahead, pulls the bandage off of his uninjured hand and puts both hands in his pockets, his smile gleaming as the room goes dark.

56

Annette is surprised to see that her bedroom door is closed.

Did she close it before she left? She doesn't think so. Oh, it doesn't matter, she's happy. All of her concerns were for nothing.

The next time Marvin is out of the house, she's going to destroy those documents. She's thought about doing it over the years but always hesitated.

That poster is the constant reminder of her deep rage at being forced to be a mother. The birth and death certificates of her oldest twin - *was he the oldest? Oh, who can remember.*

Their presence acknowledges her strength of character. She's always decided who and what she is.

Not prepared to end her pregnancy in a dank, unsanitary hovel in New York City, she waited.

She wasn't going to risk her life to get rid of the unwanted parasite, she would do it later when she was safe and sound.

Harvey had been fussy since birth. It's why he was the first to be smothered. Max had held him and walked him up and down the house trying to soothe him. But the constant noise! And the suggestion that she nurse him to calm him?

Was Max out of his ever-loving mind?

The feeling of holding that pillow over the shrieking little demon brought Annette the same joy that she had felt when audiences clapped and cheered for her back "in the day".

Max's intervention to save Marvin was a blessing after all. Going to the psychiatric facility in California was a much needed vacation.

She acted the grieving mother when required but secretly relished the attention and pity. And she was able to spend a great deal of time outdoors in the temperate climate. She'd convince Max to move out here when she returned to that jerkwater town. Or back to New York.

That rose-tinted vision of her future was not to be. Expecting to be welcomed home with open arms, she was met with a gloomy man, dark circles under his eyes. He was thinner and uninterested in the return of his wife.

He held Marvin to his chest, protecting him from the shrew on the threshold of their home.

Seeing Marvin elicited an unusual response from Annette.

Was she glad to see him? Is that possible?

She decided then and there that she would be a mother to Marvin, the mother that he deserved. She certainly felt more capable of that than nurturing twins for heaven's sake!

And another thought crept into her mind. With parents as stunning as Marvin's, he was bound to be an exceptional looking child. There might be an opportunity in that for her.

But there was one problem and he was staring down at her with his bleary blue eyes. She had assured Max that she was sorry for what had happened and that she intended to make up for everything.

She would be a good mother and also a loving wife. He had laughed at that last remark. Informing her that he would be divorcing her and taking Marvin, he had shut the door in her face.

Her threshold light bulb moment and the plans that followed were slipping away. Not to be deterred, she barged into the house and informed Max that he could have his divorce but that she was keeping Marvin.

And that Max would be out of Marvin's life for good. She further communicated that she had records of his numerous affairs in a safe deposit box. Letters, receipts, pictures.

Now what sort of example would that be for Marvin?

She also had documents that illustrated the creative accounting practices over the years that would land him in jail.

Disheartened, Max handed her the baby and slunk out of the room. Before he left, he informed her that she wouldn't get a dime from him.

She replied that the house was plenty compensation. And after all, she had her check from Massachusetts every month.

Standing at her bedroom door with her eighteen year old son

downstairs, she sighs and smiles at the fond memories of her previous life.

And this next chapter will be-

Wait, what is that sound? Is that music?

Oh, it's probably something Marvin is playing on that record player of his. He always leaves it running when he's not in his room.

She opens her bedroom door and gasps. The suitcase thuds to the floor as she leans against the doorframe, desperately trying to hold onto the oil lamp with trembling hands.

Dozens of white candles are lit throughout the room. The eerie glow bends and tilts, distorting things. Everything is hazy for a moment, then clear again.

The farthest corner of the room next to her closet remains dark but she sees something there. Something large. She doesn't keep anything in that corner, her eyes must be playing tricks. She is tired and a little light-headed.

She drank that scotch much too fast. Thinking it's a table of some sort, she creeps towards it. The music gets louder as she gets closer. Lullaby music.

Strange.

Did Marvin make something for her in that wood shop of his? How thoughtful, he really is a wonderful boy. It's a shame that she's been forced to take the upper hand with him.

Nothing as drastic as with Harvey, but still-

Eyes adjusting to the dark corner, she sees a crib. Marvin and Harvey's old crib. And their mobile, turning slowly, the melody sounding hollow. The animals and mirrors remind her of the last time she was in this position.

Before she-

Max had gotten rid of the mobile after the - unpleasantness. He must have just shoved it up in the attic because she's sure this is it, not a replica. He said the sound made him sick to his stomach and bought Marvin a new one.

Her perspective vacillates between nebulousness and vivid sharpness. She's tired, she needs a good night's sleep. She sets the lamp down on the table behind her chaise and turns it off.

The candles provide enough light. But why has Marvin set up his old crib? The skin pricks up on the back of her neck as she gets closer, a musty smell gradually invading her nostrils.

Dizziness overtakes her, she grasps the side of the white wooden crib. Gaining her balance again, she looks inside. Marvin's old blanket, blue with little lambs on it.

A wave of nostalgia hits her when she sees it. Forgetting everything else, she gently lifts the blanket out of the crib wondering if it still has his scent on it.

Then she screams. For an eternity she screams, burying her face in the blanket to block out the hideous offering in the crib.

The scotch is affecting her senses.

This isn't real, it can't be!

Chest heaving, unable to draw a breath, she lowers the blanket and peers over it at what lies in the crib.

A tiny skeleton rests on her red murder pillow, the head turned towards her. Black, empty eye sockets bore accusation into her soul.

She can't scream any more, her body is frozen in horror. He knows.

How does he know?

Annette Sinclair-Damon looks away from the son she murdered almost eighteen years ago. Next to him are two documents. She doesn't need to pick them up to know what they are.

A birth certificate and a death certificate.

Shock takes over again and her body convulses. Her vision blurs and doubles, worse than before. She drops the blanket back into the crib, only partially covering the ghastly thing in the center.

Is it crying?

Turning away from the crib, she sees Baby Marvin's face smiling down from the far wall, fading in and out.

He's laughing at her. He can't be.

She stumbles towards the picture, holding her hand out in front of her, greedily grabbing anything that will help to steady her.

She created Baby Marvin! First she created Marvin, then turned him into Baby Marvin. All of it was her doing! Having to do the work of two parents thanks to Marvin's contemptible father.

Wait! Max!

Max will help her. She'll call Max. He's helped her before. And she'll make sure he gets that trust fund back. Well, some of it. She'll need quite a bit for the fees for - her scheme.

Strategizing, always strategizing. Baby Marvin's very existence is due to her planning. Her hard work! Toting him to that audition, all the way in New York City.

Movement in the mirror over her dresser. Her gaze is drawn to it. She sees her younger self in it, her back to the mirror, shuffling through her handbag in slow motion, then drawing the red dots on his four year-old face as he sits on the counter next to the sink.

The scene plays in black and white except the dots. Red. Blood red. Like the blood she has on her hands.

NO!

Four year-old Marvin looks from young Annette to her, sneering at her from the mirror. His voice is the voice of eighteen year-old Marvin.

Pointing at his face he snarls, "This is my brother's blood."

Young Annette turns toward the mirror with delight, her skirt swirling around her legs.

She holds a dead baby in her arms. Rotted, crawling with worms, flies circling his tiny head.

Harvey, the six foot tall rabbit from the film, comes into the mirror restroom and takes the bundle from young Annette. But this Harvey has blood dripping from his razor sharp teeth and his four inch long claws.

If this had been Jimmy Stewart's vision, the film would have been entirely different. Harvey faces her, holding the decaying bundle out towards her.

Four year-old Marvin shifts and morphs into eighteen year- old Marvin as young Annette crumbles to dust.

Grown Marvin hops off of the counter and, never losing eye contact with her, walks toward her from the opposite side of the mirror. Lurches really, as if his legs don't work properly. A horrible black and white image with red dots blazing against his gray skin.

This isn't real!

Annette is frozen, unable to even cover her eyes.

Marvin stops as he reaches the mirror, continuing to gawk at her with his dead eyes. In her haze, she had wandered over to the dresser and now she finds herself only two feet away from her son's hideous, distorted image.

Hypnotized by the red dots, she reaches out and calls hoarsely, "Marvin."

His hands thrust through the mirror and grasp for her throat. Slate tentacles that intend to throttle her, to send her to join her dead son.

Annette retreats, praying for the first time in decades that this hideous image of her son is bound to this mirror world that her imagination has created.

It is her imagination, isn't it?

Determining at that moment that she has consumed her last drop of alcohol, she stands straight, shoulders back and faces the image. His arms retreat back to his side of the mirror.

It's OK, it's OK. It's not real.

The image breaks into a fiendish grin and Marvin crawls through the mirror! Knocking over her bottle of perfume and her other beauty concoctions, he never loses eye contact with her, the grin frozen on his face.

Arms grasping the edges of her dresser, he flips up and over and lands on his feet in front of her. With a bow and ta-da motion with his hands, he regards her.

She croaks, "You're not real."

His breath, putrid and earthy like a freshly dug grave, assaults her, "Oh, aren't I?"

Resigned to whatever portion this being has in mind for her, she closes her eyes.

His fetid breath again, closer, "This is what success looks like."

Feeling him retreat, she dares to open her eyes.

The dismal figure heads home, to the mirror repeating his maxim, "This is what success looks like. This is what success looks like…"

He reaches her dresser, climbs up and passes through the mirror feet first landing with a THUD on the floor of that bathroom she had pulled him into fourteen years ago.

Harvey the gory rabbit waits for him with the noxious bundle. As the mirror world fades, he walks to the bathroom door and passes through on his way to the audition room that changed his young life forever.

The rabbit follows him.

She's hungover, that must be it. But she's never suffered visions before, hallucinations. She pretended to have had them to avoid paying the price for infanticide years ago but this, this is real. She needs to call Max.

As she heads toward the bedroom door to get to the phone in the hallway, it finally occurs to her. Something was in the drink Marvin gave her!

She whirls around, staying upright by some miracle, to find herself staring at the crib again. Her skin pricks up, worse than before. Someone is behind her.

Petrified that the cackling black and white effigy of her son has made his way into the room again, she freezes. Unmolested by the similitude, she turns, apprehensive.

Marvin comes into focus. He's in color, not the person she saw before.

"Marvin?"

Her vision doubles.

Two Marvins? What was in that drink?

The two of them are talking to each other but she can't make out what they're saying.

She's falling.

She totters backwards and is caught and carried to the bed. One of the Marvins lays her carefully in place and sits next to her. He's so distorted. And her head is throbbing now.

She grips her face as she hears crying. A baby is crying. Not like before, this is louder, more real. Not a newborn cry.

It's Marvin, she should go to him.

But no, it can't be. Marvin is grown, isn't he?

She starts to rise, putting her hands against his chest, but Marvin pushes her back down with his bandaged hand.

"Don't try to get up."

"The baby," she mumbles, "I have to go to the baby."

The other Marvin, who is standing, leaves the room and the crying stops after a few moments.

Marvin helps her to lie back down with her head on her pillow, some blood leaking from his bandage onto her hands. With the little strength she has left, she clutches his arms, transferring the blood back to him.

"What's going on?"

Marvin pulls his angel necklace out from under his shirt collar, "Justice."

Annette nods then collapses into blackness.

57

Marvin waits on the couch with Baby Seth and Theodore.

Seth feeds Theodore pieces of beef, laughing every time the happy dog slobbers on his hand. Marvin, cleaned up and re-bandaged, pats the little boy's head.

The power is back on, light fills the space. A simple switch of the main breaker that he had shut off earlier. Marvin glances at the kitchen wall clock. Midnight.

Harvey appears out of thin air, without the face dots. Reaching into his back pocket, he hands Marvin a ticket stub.

"I almost forgot. If anyone asks, you loved *Night of the Living Dead*."

From another pocket, he draws a small white box, offering it to Marvin, "Milk Dud?"

Marvin is curious, "You've been disappearing a lot since yesterday."

Harvey sits next to Theodore, who reaches down to lick his hand.

He nods, "I'm sorry I've been in and out. Had to impersonate you. You've been quite the gad about town the past couple of days. The Cider Festival, the movies. You helped old man Jordan change his tire too. Very public, very visible and very far away around the time when certain people met their untimely deaths. My method of travel has certain benefits."

Marvin eats his candy, gazing at the box, "Mother used to buy these when we went to the movies."

Uh oh, Harvey thinks. *You can't waver now, Marvin.*

He understands the complexity of emotions but things have gone too far to turn back now.

He reaches over and puts his arm on Marvin's shoulder.

"To say you loved her doesn't make you disloyal to me. Every single memory you two have isn't terrible or tragic. I understand that. But when you weigh those against her crimes, justice must be served."

Marvin brightens, "We can just leave her here alone. We can go anywhere we want after Carey gets better. We have money."

Harvey walks over to the spot on the wall where the poster used to hang. Staring at the wallpaper, he pulls a document out of his back pocket. His trump card. He didn't want to have to use it, but Marvin is having doubts.

With his back to Marvin, "She's been out and about a lot the last couple of weeks. Doesn't that seem odd to you? She rarely leaves the house. Except to get her fake medicine every few months."

Marvin acknowledges this, "Yes, I had noticed. But I didn't really think anything of it."

Harvey turns, holding up the document, "She's been planning for her future, Marvin."

He hands it to Marvin. Marvin reads it in disbelief as Seth grabs for it. Harvey takes the baby before he rips it.

Marvin folds it up, puts it in his pocket, his green eyes changed again.

He squares his shoulders, "Let's finish this."

Harvey smiles as the baby giggles.

58

Annette regains consciousness, staring up at her ceiling.

It was a dream. It's all been a horrendous dream. Groggy, she's unsure what happened. She must have been terribly hungover. She remembers her vow to herself.

She's done with booze. Steven was always trying to get her to stop drinking, but she refused. And Marvin has always hated it.

A fresh start would be welcome right now. She's due for one.

She only has to deal with Marvin and then she can decide what the future holds for her. Her relationship with her son will change dramatically, he'll balk and fuss, but eventually he'll come around and they can pick up the pieces.

And Steven, he's been on her mind constantly since that day in town when he lit her cigarette. She misses him, it's time to start over with him as well. She's finally coming into her own.

But that dream was so real! She stares at the ceiling, still afraid to look anywhere else. But she has to make sure it was all part of her vivid imagination.

Glancing around the room she finds - nothing. Her room is back to normal and her suitcase is even unpacked and put away.

What a horrible nightmare!

It was so real. She thought she saw - no, it was just a dream.

Thank you, God. My new life may even include some time for religion. Since God helped me, that is. Life is about negotiation, give and take, after all.

Marvin appears in the doorway, setting something on the floor out in the hall before entering, "Hello, Mother."

He goes to her dresser, picking up her lipstick.

REVENGE RED.

He proceeds to carefully draw the Baby Marvin dots on his cheeks and nose. When he's finished he turns to her with a smile and a ta-da motion accompanied by a deep bow.

Just like that thing in the mirror.

After her disturbing nightmare, this sight is unwelcome.

She puts on a cheerful demeanor, "Marvin, dear, why are you wearing those dots?"

"I was feeling nostalgic."

He picks up a full tumbler of scotch that was already prepared on the dresser. He offers it to her. She's taken aback again. She can't believe he's offering her another drink. Her mouth feels like it's full of cotton so she takes the glass and downs the drink.
Just this last one.

"New York was a disaster. I could not get a meeting with my agent."

He knows she's lying, "Your former agent?"

She sneers briefly, not needing the reminder, "Yes. And frankly, I missed you and this house."

"Ah, this house."

He sits next to her on the bed, "So much has happened here in this house."

He smiles at her, "So many memories."

She touches his chin, thanking God again that everything is normal. That dreadful dream is long gone.

"I came home early. I'm sorry I fell asleep earlier, it was a monstrous drive."

She yawns, tries to sit up but can't. Her body is leaden.

"Don't get up."

Annette has trouble focusing on Marvin. He sits very still, that smile plastered on his face. But his eyes, the smile doesn't reach them.

What's - her vision doubles, she sees two Marvins again and a baby? The Marvin sitting next to her gets up and takes the baby from the second Marvin who sits in his place.

The baby looks just like Marvin but it can't be, he's right here. He's also going out the door. What's happening to me?

"Marvin, please," she can't move, her limbs betraying her.

Marvin reaches into his back pocket, drawing out a document, "You were never going to let me leave here, were you?"

Annette's eyes widen. She wants to speak but it's difficult. The cotton remains in her mouth.

Marvin lasers in on the document while he speaks, not wanting to look at her vile face, "All of these errands you've been going on lately. You've been busy. You've been planning to get me sent away, like you were all those years ago. So, you could keep my trust fund for yourself."

He holds the document up for her to see.

COMMITMENT FORM:
PSYCHIATRIC CENTER OF
NEW YORK
Dated November 1, 1968.
Marvin John Damon to be committed by mother,
Annette Sinclair-Damon for evaluation.
Re: Symptoms of schizophrenia.

Annette, speechless, implores Marvin with her eyes. He feels nothing for her.

A small smile, remembering, "I told Miss Jezzy that we all had good and evil in us, turns out I was wrong. You only have evil inside of you. You have always had your demons, Mother, I leave you to them."

Marvin heads to the hallway as Annette is hit with a smell. Something slightly sweet and pungent.

Marvin stops at the door. Bracing himself against the frame, he turns to her, "By the way, I hate this damn house."

She passes out again, hearing the phone ring in the distance.

59

Marvin sprints down the stairs into the living room.

Seth is sleeping in his crib, Harvey is nowhere around. It's fine, Marvin expected this.

He picks up the ringing phone, holds it to his ear for several seconds then hangs up again.

His attention is drawn to one of Annette's hat boxes in the middle of the coffee table.

Reverently, he opens it to find his brother's tiny skeleton laying on a blue satin pillow, the red pillow having been discarded in the fireplace.

Annette's polka dot sun hat lays cast aside on the floor.

Marvin kneels, clutching his Archangel Michael pendant, "Yea, though I walk through the valley of the shadow of death, I will fear no evil; for thou art with me; thy rod and thy staff they comfort me. Surely goodness and mercy shall follow me all the days of my life: and I will dwell in the house of the Lord forever."

He places the lid back on the box, then notices that Harvey is behind him, head bowed in prayer.

Marvin asks, "Is it done?"

Harvey nods, "I went to the hospital in New York, checked on Carey, he's still in a coma. I spoke to the doctor and a couple of nurses. Then I made my fake phone call home to Mother. Thanks for picking up. I acted suitably upset for the people watching and raced out. I would have made quite an actor. Is everything ready?"

Marvin nods, "Just the baby, the crib and-"

He points to the hatbox.

Harvey picks it up gently, "I think I'd like to be with Miss Jezzy, can we dig out a spot next to her? Since the ground is freshly disturbed, no one should notice."

Marvin pats his brother's shoulder, "Absolutely. We can do that. She'd like to have you with her."

Harvey gives Marvin the box, "You pack up Seth, I'll take care of the rest."

Harvey snaps his fingers and the Baby Marvin dots appear on his face once again.

Then he picks up Annette's hat and puts it on.

"How do I look?"

Marvin tilts his head and gets close, "Looks better on me."

Harvey feigns great insult as the brothers laugh together.

It's almost over.

60

Annette starts awake again, her mind reeling.

That horrible pungent smell is overwhelming. And music again. "Will You Still Love Me Tomorrow?" by Ben E. King.

Looking to her right, she sees Marvin's record player in the corner.

How lovely of him to set that up for me? He really is a sweet boy, I'll miss him.

She smiles, turning her head to her left, seeing Steven sitting on the side of her bed.

Oh, thank the maker!

He's wearing one of his hideous plaid bumpkin shirts but she doesn't even care. She'll buy him a closet full of them now that they're starting over.

He smiles and those dimples make an appearance. The first thing she noticed about him, that smile. Or was it his bright sapphire eyes?

After the whirlwind year of parades, photo shoots and personal appearances with the president, Annette and Marvin had returned to their normal life.

Much to Annette's chagrin. How she had loved the attention that she garnered!

Your son is adorable. What a sweet little boy? He's lucky to have such a supportive mother. You're so beautiful, have I seen you in the pictures?

Steven had just been elected Sheriff after having served as a deputy in the next town over for several years. Marvin had begged her to get lunch at the tacky diner that Steven loves so much. Sitting in that booth with Marvin, she had gotten butterflies in her stomach when she first saw him swagger in.

Absolutely gorgeous.

Both had the same thought pop into their minds when their eyes met. He had taken off his cowboy hat and sidled up to their table.

Noticing Marvin, he had bent down and spoken to him. And the baffling part was, he hadn't mentioned "Baby Marvin". He treated him just like a normal little boy.

He pretended to pull a quarter out of Marvin's ear, causing a roar of laughter and the two became fast friends.

Looking back, she wonders if Steven ever did love her, really love her. She knows he wanted her, but that was just sex.

The way he smiled at Marvin was always so genuine, so heart-felt. His smiles at her as the years went by became more and more - charitable?

But now, as he sits next to her, his smile is the one she remembers the best.

She'll tell him everything, "Steven, I-"

Steven is *gone*.

Marvin sits next to her on the bed where Steven was a moment ago. He was never there. Why is she so confused about everything?

He's wearing those dots. Why? It's strange. Maybe he does have mental problems? That would make my life a great deal easier, wouldn't it? If I didn't have to lie. Dr. Reeve will certainly come around when he hears about this.

She smiles at her son, unable to move well, her body still feeling like it's in quicksand.

Marvin's holding something in his hand, her good sunhat. Why in the world-? It's the wrong time of year for that particular hat.

He shows it to her, "Needed a box. A nice one. To bury the baby properly. Knew you wouldn't mind."

Confusion. Dread. The skeleton was real! A million thoughts go through Annette's mind. She has no idea what's real and what's a dream anymore.

How can she manage Marvin right now? He's calm, which is good. It's also bad, he must be furious at her.

Peace overwhelms her. Why didn't she think of it before? Of course. If her mind weren't so muddy it would have occurred to her sooner.

"I'm so sorry you found that, him, Marvin. I never wanted you to find out. I thought it would be better for you to never know, to never have to feel that loss."

He just stares at her, rapt.

"Marvin, your father, well - I'm sorry to say this but he has quite a temper. After you twins were born, he was quite overwhelmed and drank heavily. Miss Jezzy had delivered you both, if only she hadn't tragically died-"

"Been murdered."

"Oh yes, of course. I'm so sorry. But she could have verified what I'm telling you. He'll deny it of course, he never did take responsibility for anything."

"So, Max killed the baby?"

"Yes. It was an accident, of course. He dropped him and he died. I'm devastated that you've had to learn all of this. He put me away, tried to blame me for it! But I wasn't in that, place, very long, they could see I was fine."

"Then what are those pills for?"

Caught in a lie, always calculating, "I had to agree to take them so they'd let me go. Just a formality. And Max was gone when I got home. Miss Jezzy had taken care of you."

"Ah. So, Miss Jezzy knew Max killed the baby?"

"Yes, sadly, she did. She buried him for me. I had roses put there later as a marker. No one knew I had given birth to twins so no one realized anything had gone wrong. I grieved alone."

Is this bitch actually welling up with tears?

"Except for Miss Jezzy," he quips.

"That's right."

"Who helped cover up a murder, the false commitment of an innocent woman and is conveniently dead and unable to confirm any of this."

"Yes."

Downstairs, Marvin checks his watch, dialing the phone.

Steven answers, mumbling, half asleep, "Hello."

Huffing and puffing, Marvin blubbers, "It's Marvin."

On full alert, "What's wrong, Marvin?!"

Marvin wails "I'm, I didn't know what else to do. I'm in New York to visit Carey and just spoke to my mother. She has been drinking heavily and I'm not sure how much you know but she spent time in an asylum years ago. She's supposed to take her pills, she hasn't been. She's been throwing them out. I'm afraid of what may happen."

The Sheriff, gently, "Marvin. Marvin, calm down. I can go by and check on her right after-"

Marvin performs harder, crying, "She's been so depressed since I turned 18. She's barricaded herself in her room and said she's gonna burn the house down. Please hurry!"

Harvey leaps up from his spot on Annette's bed, flinging her sunhat into the far corner of the room,
"Yep, that sounds just like Miss Jezzy. Scheming, conniving - oh wait, no, that's you."

She stares at the finger pointed at her, then at him again. She's felt uneasy around him for the last few days. His finger. From the hand with the cut on the palm, she still has blood on her arm from him earlier. A bad cut. But the bandage is gone.

How?

And Marvin has worn that stupid angel necklace constantly since he got it, tucked into his shirt, only a bare hint of the chain showing at the edges. But nothing there now.

He's breaking into a smile, "You're figuring it out, aren't you?"

He lunges at her and grasps the sides of her head with a snarl. Her head flies back against the pillow.

A bright flash behind her eyes:

She's leaving the house after the document argument, mostly sober. Heading to her car she hears a voice say, "I know."

She turns to see Marvin on the porch but there's something else. Something she noticed but didn't process at the time. Behind him and on the second floor, nearly out of view, obscured by the sunlight on the window. Barely there. It's Marvin! At his bedroom window. His arm reaching out and grasping a leaf.

Another flash

She hangs up the phone, processing the horrible crime at Miss Jezzy's house.

While she's pondering, she sees Marvin coming up the driveway with the dog. But something else, at the end of the driveway, past Marvin and the dog, dust kicked up from - from what?

And the door is open, it was closed before she came in to answer the phone. She's sure of it. Marvin must have left it open on his way to Jezzy's house. He left and his truck kicked up dust on his way out and down the road.

During the confrontation on the porch and in the house after the murder, Marvin wasn't wearing the necklace. And the things he said, he wasn't himself.

Dawning terror and disbelief, "Harvey!"

Releasing her head from his death grip, Harvey points at the Baby Marvin dots, raging tears cutting rivulets down his face.

"THIS IS WHAT SUCCESS LOOKS LIKE!"

CLICK! HISS!

A flame from her lighter. Standing up, he tosses it on the floor.

WHOOSH!

The gasoline catches instantly, the room exploding into flames.

Annette screams.

Harvey strolls, not a care in the world, untouched by the flames to her bedroom door where her chaise awaits, dragged out of place earlier.

He props it fully in front of the locked door, blocking it from anyone wishing to break in.

He looks back at her one last time and vanishes through the closed door as flames spread toward her on the gasoline soaked floor.

61

Marvin's truck slowly rumbles down the winding driveway kicking up the familiar dust cloud.

The house mushrooms into flames, every window blowing out simultaneously. The flames consume everything quickly, lighting up the night.

Theodore sleeps in the comfort of Annette's fur coat in the bed of the truck next to Baby Seth's bags. The disassembled crib lies under him. A stack of Monkees records. The sweater from Miss Jezzy.

A large pumpkin and a baseball bat. The books from Carey's car. The portraits of Robert and John Kennedy, minus the black fabric. The framed note from Mr. Garcia. Marvin's copy of "Hamlet". Marvin's birthday cards.

And the Baby Marvin poster from his room.

Marvin drives and Harvey holds Seth. Neither have the dots on their faces.

They never will again.

The hat box sits on the seat between them. Harvey reaches into his back pocket retrieving his birth certificate. He opens the glove box and places it in with the cash and earrings.

Marvin notices the cash as Harvey pulls out the trust document and looks at it.

"Five hundred thousand dollars. You're rich, Marvin."

"We're rich."

"There's more. Something else I found out during my investigations. Hey, maybe I should be a cop instead of an actor. What do you think? I could be a deputy to Sheriff McClane."

Marvin just shakes his head, always amused by his brother.

"Ok, anyway, I found out why Annette is - oh, I guess, *was* - obsessed with the Kennedys."

"That's no mystery. She knew the brothers growing up. Her mother worked for them. She had a crush on Bobby."

"It's more than that, Marvin. When I saw the photo of Bobby Kennedy up close, my own face reflected in the glass next to his, I wondered about the resemblance I saw."

Horror dawns on Marvin, "Oh, don't tell me-"

"No no no, it's not that. Sadly, we are indeed the spawn of the late, not-so-great Max Damon. It's our mother. She wasn't in love with the brothers. They're *her* brothers."

Marvin is speechless.

"Annette Sinclair-Damon, the high and mighty, was a bastard. Ignored as trash by her real father, Bobby has been sending her a check every month to help her. I think he genuinely cared about her. But, that gravy train ended when he was killed. Not enough to get rich on, but it helped keep you from being on the streets. Combined, of course, with your income as a jack-of-all-trades."

Marvin and Harvey laugh then announce together, "We're Kennedys."

Marvin reaches for the radio, "How about some music?"

"I Can See For Miles" by The Who. Roger Daltrey belts out about deceit, tricks and lies. Harvey laughs, turning it up.

Theodore barks, wagging his tail as they roll along the rural road, a siren blaring in the distance.

PART 4

THIS IS WHAT HAPPENED TO BABY MARVIN

62

1974

A Georgian Colonial house rests where the former Victorian house was incinerated.

A vision of symmetry with elements from the classical architecture of Rome and Greece, it invites visitors while also oozing formality. Red brick dominates with pristine white shutters surrounding the windows.

A small covered entryway's white pillars lead to a black front door. The door is open, as usual. Marvin stands on the small porch, waving as a white panel truck trundles down the familiar, long driveway.

Twenty four year-old Marvin, a satisfied grin on his face, stares after the truck. His own four year-old face, in cartoon form, is painted on the sides of the truck:

BABY MARVIN'S FINE FURNITURE

The black scripted words swirl around the jubilant face with the signature red face dots.

Marvin sports an expensive gray suit with blood red tie. He's an entrepreneur, an established, successful businessman.

The transition from a thirteen year-old boy desperate to pay his mother's bills to a well-heeled executive millionaire was easier than he thought it would be.

Recently recognized by TIME magazine as the richest man under twenty-five in the entire country, his business is booming.

Marvin trots down the front steps and across the drive to the place where he and Harvey meted out justice to John and Roger Carter six years ago.

The brothers are together for eternity, rotting under his pumpkin patch. He kept the patch for sentimental reasons. Not the romanticism of having disposed of the human garbage that took

Miss Jezzy from him.

No, that would be antithetical to the life he's built for himself. A life based on love and optimism. It's sentimental because the first business he ever had was selling pumpkins at his farm stand.

And now he's created an empire from that as well.

The workshop is long gone, having succumbed to the inferno that consumed the house when Annette "killed herself".

She's Annette now, not Mother. And she killed herself.

What a tragedy.

He's accepted the pats on the back, the sympathy, the hugs with no sense of guilt. He deserved sympathy for what he was put through, for what she was about to do to him. That commitment form she had for him was the coup de grace for anyone who harbored any affection for Annette.

Of course, he felt obliged to share it with people, Steven most of all.

Marvin doesn't call him Sheriff anymore, or Steven. He's Dad. He always was but it took Annette's hastily planned funeral to finally set it in stone.

Dozens of people had shown up to support Marvin. If he hadn't attended, only Pastor Higgins would have been present to bury the universally disliked woman.

Yes, Marvin buried his mother in the cemetery of the "colored church". Belief that the love, joy and goodness of the people surrounding her might seep into her soul from the dark earth she rests in was the driving force behind that decision.

He prays for her soul, hoping that her actions were the result of some terrible event from her past and not because she was evil. She's far away from Miss Jezzy and Harvey though, no need to tempt fate.

The Sheriff had awakened to a surprise a few mornings after Annette's untimely death.

A muffled voice on the phone led him to Miss Jezzy's vacant house. He had discovered a six month-old baby with eyes that were a specific green color that he recognized.

Fortunately, Marvin happened to arrive at that exact moment in his truck, back from New York for one of his visits to check on Carey.

Ostensibly to gather some of Carey's belongings, he had seen the child, exclaiming that it was his brother, son of his father. He'd seen his picture when he visited with his father the other day.

But he hadn't heard back from him. Which surprised him since Max had expressed a deep desire to connect with him in the future.

Concerned for the welfare of Max and Mary Damon, Steven had sped out to the address that Marvin provided. Marvin watched the remarkably untraumatized kidnap victim at Steven's home, where he was currently living.

Marvin felt terrible that Steven would have to come upon such a gruesome scene but it couldn't be avoided. A call a short time later informed Marvin of the bad news.

Upon arriving back at his house, Steven had announced that he'd be glad to take care of the baby but Marvin let him know that he would be taking on the responsibility himself.

"I owe it to my father."

Steven had teared up when Marvin added, "But he will need a grandpa."

Steven became a full-time father and grandfather after deciding to leave the Sheriff's department. He closed the files on Miss Jezzy, Max and Mary after discovering the car, ax and knife at the bungalow.

He put out a bulletin on the Carter boys and Max's car but doubted they'd ever hear from them again. After finding someone to replace him, he'd turned in his badge and taken up wearing plaid shirts every day.

Marvin revealed that he had found his twin brother and Steven was surprised but then again, he wouldn't put anything past Marvin's mother. His feelings for her had withered considerably when she missed Miss Jezzy's funeral but they died altogether when he found out about her plans to put Marvin away.

For him, it was the world's shortest grieving period. It was like a switch finally flipped in his brain and he was done.

On the rare occasions when he does refer to her, she is "Marvin's mother".

He's been dating a very kind woman who teaches history at the high school. She also favors plaid shirts on her days off when they all go fishing.

Marvin couldn't be happier.

Marvin strides up to the new structure that sits a bit further out from the woods than his beloved workshop had once stood.

One story, lined with windows, taking advantage of the natural light. He waves in at his brother. Harvey, wearing a beret, puts his paintbrushes down and motions him in.

There was a moment six years ago when the twins panicked. After they had left Annette behind. In the high-priced New York City hotel that night, they had looked at each other and read each other's minds.

Is this it? Is Harvey going away again? Back to wherever he came from? Is his mission done?

Although proven to be quite real, corporeal and "human", both feared that his appearance in Marvin's world was somehow temporary.

A well-timed visit from beyond to help him right the wrongs inflicted on him. Would he disappear as quickly as he appeared? His human remains had been carefully laid in an unmarked grave next to Miss Jezzy and prayed over.

Both afraid to go to sleep at night, they fought to stay awake, to take shifts in case - but nothing happened.

Each morning Marvin woke up abruptly, leaping up to make sure his brother was still there. The snoring made it clear that he needn't have worried.

"There are more things in Heaven and Earth, Horatio, than are dreamt of in your philosophy," Harvey always opines.

The discovery, a few months later, that Harvey had a heartbeat cemented his existence as permanent.

Marvin finds his brother working on his latest masterpiece. This art studio was a gift for Harvey's birthday last year. Everything that an up and coming painter could want or need.

Marvin gazes around the room at the myriad of canvasses lined up against the back door. Still more hang on wooden posts that line the center of the room.

All are signed simply, *Harvey ∞.*

Most of the paintings are landscapes but Harvey has delved into the world of portraits recently. He's working on one of Seth. Marvin glances at it with a critical eye then gives him a thumbs up.

"But I prefer your landscapes," he muses.

"Always a critic." Harvey shifts his beret insolently.

"And that hat continues to be ridiculous."

"Beret, you Neanderthal. And I continue to wear it as I, myself, my very existence in fact, is ridiculous."

Pointing at a fall mountainscape, "Sold that one to Mrs. Williams. Gonna run it by later. I'll take Seth, she loves seeing him. And her chocolate chip cookies are out of sight."

Marvin remembers that day the beloved postman had changed his life forever.

He feels tremendous gratitude for the strength of character that Mr. Gabriel Williams showed that day.

His mother's threats were not to be underestimated. He knows that now more than ever. If Mr. Williams had truly known the depths of her malevolence, he would never have shared those letters with Marvin. He would have destroyed them.

And, as a consequence, Marvin would likely have ended up in an asylum and Annette would have become richer than Midas.

Marvin had known that day that it would be the last time he saw Mr. Williams. He hoped against hope that he was wrong but he's come to understand that his feelings are never wrong.

Mr. Williams died peacefully in his sleep on the first day of his long awaited retirement. Upon hearing the news in New York, Marvin rushed back to his hometown to comfort Mrs. Williams and to pay off her mortgage.

A year later he also gifted her with the dream dining room table discussed with her husband on that fateful day of Marvin's life. He continued to look after her, to make sure that she had everything she needed as she and her late husband never had children.

She eventually shared with Marvin the intuition that her husband had about him, about "the gift" or "the sight" as her people called it.

Marvin guessed that this is why he was able to bring Harvey into the real world. Of course, Harvey was pushing from the other side so it was bound to happen.

Marvin doesn't see spirits, his "gift" is more psychic and it comes quietly and gently. Just a feeling here and there about something. Unfortunately, it's usually about the passing of someone he cares about.

Harvey and Seth stayed in New York when Marvin visited Mrs. Williams and the times he took on the various tasks and procedures that followed the deaths of his "beloved" parents.

He also managed to put in that rail for Mr. Jacobson's porch. But they didn't stay in New York for long.

Harvey is no longer a secret. If you ask anyone around town, they have quite a tale to tell. Miss Eunice will flat talk your ear off about it.

That sweet boy, Marvin, well - his awful mother and runaway father took his twin brother when they were born and adopted him off! Can you imagine? They were simply too lazy to raise two children. Well, you know what a terrible mother she was, imagine if she had two children.

Anyway, Marvin found the adoption documents in the attic one day and I guess that's just one more reason that nasty woman had to kill herself. Not that I am glad she's dead, far from it. As a Christian woman, I would never wish harm on anybody. I pray for souls like hers.

But I honestly think Marvin is better off. And his brother! Oh my goodness! What a doll Harvey is! Looks just like Marvin, although I can tell them apart because he has a slightly different demeanor.

Nobody else can, but I can. I don't know where he's been all these years, he doesn't talk about it, but I'm so happy the two of them are together.

Well, it's the three of them actually. Marvin's taken to care for that little baby after his daddy and mama got killed. It's his brother but he's fixin' to raise him like a son.

That's the best choice, if you ask me, a child needs stability and Marvin can give him that.

The house isn't the only thing that's changed. The rose bushes are gone, replaced with Black-eyed Susans. Expensive, sprawling playground equipment occupies space near the pumpkin patch. The pumpkins are bigger and brighter than ever.

A homemade scarecrow is propped in the middle of the patch, right over - the source of the proprietary and very effective fertilizer.

Marvin and Harvey both head back to the house.

But only after Marvin pulls the beret off of Harvey's head and flings it into his studio before they cross the driveway. Both stop briefly next to the steps leading up to the house.

An Italian marble gravestone stands gleaming in the bright sun.

THEODORE
Beloved friend and companion
1955-1972.

An intricate carving of Theodore also decorates the stone. Both men pat the marker and make their way up to the house. Marvin plucks a dog biscuit from his pocket, laying it on top of the stone.

Marvin's psychic gift was present when he petted Theodore two years ago and knew he was going to die that night. He knew it like he'd never known anything else, it hit him like a ton of bricks.

Already living the life of Riley, Theodore's last night was especially wonderful. He had enjoyed a particularly fine cut of steak for dinner (cut into small pieces due to his difficulty chewing) and reclined on the couch with Marvin, Harvey and Seth to watch Lee Marvin (Marvin's namesake) and Rodney Dangerfield on the Johnny Carson show.

Marvin held back his tears as he felt the animal's life slip away while Johnny guffawed at his guests.

63

Seth Damon colors in his favorite coloring book.

He lies on the wooden floor, carefully choosing each crayon with a scrunching of the brow under his dark wavy hair and squinting of his green eyes. His tongue will occasionally make an appearance if he's particularly absorbed in his difficult decision-making process.

The six year-old occupies a room that approximates the place where Marvin's old room was in the former house. Bright blue walls are covered in Seth's own drawings, and some sketches from his Uncle Harvey. Seth's current favorite animal seems to be tigers based on his recent drawings.

Hearing footsteps on the stairs he pops up, ready to greet his father and uncle. He wears the Archangel Michael necklace that helped his daddy through the toughest time of his life.

He once told Seth it was for protection and good luck. Seth once asked if Archangel Michael was a woman and was told that he wasn't.

"Why do you ask?" Daddy said.

Seth just shrugged. He supposes the ghostly old woman he sees all the time must not be him then. So, he has two protectors. Really he has three.

The night Theodore died, Seth had slept through it. Daddy had let him stay up very late for some reason and told him the next morning. Seth had cried for hours until the dog appeared next to him on his bed and laid down. He sleeps with Seth every night.

Harvey swoops in first, grabbing the boy and tossing him in the air. Marvin follows, much more sedate and gestures for a handoff. Harvey hands the laughing boy to Marvin and sits on the bed, admiring the latest creation on the floor.

Marvin sets the boy down and adjusts his suspenders. He wears them with a striped t-shirt and shorts. Marvin grabs a comb from the dresser and works to tame the waves.

"Daddy, what if they don't like me?"

Marvin crosses his eyes and puts his tongue out making the boy laugh.

Harvey pipes up, "Don't be silly. Everyone loves you."

To Marvin, inquiring, "And maybe we don't have to go to the audition? We just had one last week."

In a rare display of anger at his twin brother, Marvin's eyes darken slightly, "Seth likes doing it."

Harvey holds his hands up in surrender as Marvin's eyes, brilliant emeralds again, fall on the familiar faded poster on the wall next to Seth's dresser.

<u>SAFE</u> <u>DRIVING</u> <u>DAY</u>
<u>1954</u>
<u>PRESIDENT</u> <u>EISENHOWER</u>
<u>WELCOMES</u>
<u>BABY</u> <u>MARVIN</u>

Memories flood over him, all good, all special. He's learned to categorize his memories and he only allows the appropriate ones to surface from the deep well of his emotions.

He truly wants Seth to have experiences like he had as a young child.

Seth smiles and glances into the mirror over his dresser. He scrutinizes his reflection. His reflection isn't happy about the audition. His reflection has a cross expression on his face.

"It's OK," Seth thinks and closes his eyes. *"It makes Daddy happy and he loves us!"*

Opening his eyes, he peeks at the mirror again. His friend is gone, for now.

All is well.

Seth smiles and hugs his father.

64

Miss Jezzy's house has been restored into a gorgeous cottage.

Obviously lived in, there are still Black-eyed Susans bobbing in the yard along with the breeze. The garden has been expanded into the previously empty lot next door along with a large chicken coop. A dozen happy hens scratch and chat together in the grass.

A new model Mustang sits gleaming in the driveway.

The old rocking chair sits on the front porch. MISS JEZZY scrawled on it by then 12 year-old Marvin.

Two other chairs are set up on the porch, a television interview is unfolding. Marvin, in another expensively tailored suit (this one cerulean) sits alongside Diane Clayton.

The young, arrogant bigot from the farm stand has grown up. Fresh from New York City, the budding journalist learned a great deal about life and the people who populate it when she fled the nest and her parents' somewhat stilted worldview. This all came as a great surprise to everyone, including Diane.

Marvin and Diane are chatting, laughing and generally enjoying each other's company. She still has a special glint in her eye when she looks at Marvin, who has grown even more into his looks.

And Marvin has taken notice of her as well, her entire being lifted from that quicksand of nastiness that she had been trapped in. Always a beauty, she's become ethereal.

Marvin had never considered a romantic relationship before he was free of Annette. Too busy in his teens and early twenties, he's rethinking his life as he gazes at the beautiful girl in front of him.

We've all changed so much. And Seth needs a mother. And she would be good for me too. And maybe Seth could have a little brother. Children shouldn't be alone.

Hank, the director, fusses around the cameras. Tall, blonde and good looking, he favors Troy Donahue but there's a layer of slime that covers his essence once you get past the smile and dimples.

Although only a local news channel director, he carries himself like he's Francis Ford Coppola.

Always with one eye on Diane, he pushes and shoves the crew

and generally behaves like a high school bully.

Marvin notices. He notices everything. He has experience with bullies. It didn't end well. For them. But this jackass and his behavior don't rise to the level of pumpkin fodder.

Hank claps his hands and gets everyone's attention. They know the drill, all falling into place. Brief silence then Hank holds up three fingers. Two. One.

He points at Diane.

"Good morning Pennsylvania. I'm here with a young man you may not quite recognize," she smiles directly to the camera.

To Marvin, beaming at him, "Although I have to say, I can see that little boy in your face. But without the red dots."

Both laugh as she continues, "But I have to admit to our viewers that I would recognize you anyway, having grown up with you."

To camera again, "Have you guessed yet?"

She reaches behind her and holds up a small poster of Marvin with President Eisenhower, "Baby Marvin, the face of President Eisenhower's Safe Driving Day. It's been 20 years. Tell us what you've been up to."

Marvin speaks to Diane, as they rehearsed. It's her job to involve the audience, not his, "Quite a lot actually. I own a furniture company-"

She cuts in, "Baby Marvin's Fine Furniture. I have a few pieces myself. Beautiful. Now, why did you want to have this chat here and not at one of your factories or your home?"

Marvin stands and puts his hand out to her as she rises. Electricity between them as he grips her hands. They walk the few steps to the rocker almost forgetting their true purpose here today.

"I wanted to show you the very first piece that I ever made."

Laughing, "I was 12 so it's not perfect."

Diane gets close and runs her palm over the top.

"Well I think it's wonderful. And I know it was a gift for someone very special who's no longer with us."

Her first hint of regret at her past behavior flashes across her face but passes quickly. She's a professional.

"Miss Jezzy helped raise me. I offered to make her a better version of this chair when I got older but she wouldn't have it."

He does his best Miss Jezzy impression, including the finger shake, "Go on and leave my chair alone!"

They both chuckle briefly but then a wave of sadness crosses Marvin's face.

Diane sees it and grasps his arm, "But she lives on in a way, doesn't she?"

"Yes, I named my rocking chair line after her."

Having saved the moment, Diane leads Marvin back to the chairs.

"What else have you been up to?"

"Well, I also founded Precious Pumpkin foods. Our pumpkin pie mix is our best seller."

She reaches forward and touches his knee, "It's wonderful, I always use it at Thanksgiving. I was curious though and I have to ask."

She doesn't want to ask him about this but Hank gets in her eyeline and scowls at her. Marvin senses how much she hates this man.

"I know you met President Nixon when he was Vice-President all those years ago. What do you think about the Watergate scandal?"

Marvin was prepared for a question about the latest political fireball, "President Nixon was a very kind, nice man when I met him and I leave it at that."

He turns to face the camera, "Judging people takes you to very dark places."

"Well, that's a very healthy attitude. Where does that come from?"

Marvin sits forward, his eyes boring into the camera, "All that I am I owe to my parents. They are fully responsible for the man you see before you."

"Such a tragedy, losing them both so close together. You must miss them a great deal."

"I think of them every day."

"But there was a silver lining for you in the midst of that tragedy. You found out you had a twin brother."

"Yes, it was a great shock. I found his adoption papers in the attic. I'm sure my mother was waiting for the right time to tell me. Honesty was so important to her. So I've spent the last few years getting to know him and also raising my son."

He points out towards the cameras to Seth, cowering against someone's leg, a dark hand on his shoulder, comforting him.

Diane lights up like the fourth of July when she sees him, "Oh there he is, come on over sweetheart."

Seth buries his face in Carey's leg but he leans down and jostles him, smiling, "Go on now, be a big boy and go see Daddy."

As Seth rushes into his father's outstretched arms, a look passes between Diane and Carey.

A look that communicates the regret and shame of long gone trespasses and the forgiveness that follows.

Both smile at each other.

Carey's recovery from the gunshot wound to the chest was described as miraculous and divine.

After laying in a coma for six months, he had awoken to Harvey reading sections of a law book to him. He was droning on about torts and lawsuits when Carey's eyes opened.

His voice, unused for so long, was gravelly, "Marvin?"

Harvey flashed a great smile, "Not quite."

After calling Marvin to notify him of the wondrous news, he had explained everything to Carey.

Well, not everything.

When Marvin entered the hospital room several hours later, his best friend was getting to know Harvey. He had known his grandmother was dead, no one needed to tell him.

She had been a constant presence in his room as he slept in his coma. She had talked to him, told him not to grieve. She'd made sure that Carey understood that the only direction to travel was forward.

After Harvey left the room, vanishing back to the Poconos from the empty hallway, Marvin had sat with Carey. Carey had been able to digest all the news that Marvin had for him.

Looking out the window at the New York skyline, "How can I

ever thank you, Marvin?"

"Come back home, get your law degree and help me raise Seth.

A tearful smile and nod were all the confirmation needed.

Carey watches as Diane focuses back on the camera, "Well, thank you Marvin for stopping in to chat for a minute. Viewers were very interested in you."

Direct to camera with a smile, "So to answer your question, dear viewers, *this* is what happened to Baby Marvin."

"Thanks so much, Diane."

"Cut!" The voice of the director is more high pitched than expected.

Marvin leans in to Diane, "Stay for lunch?"

She brightens, "Of course, thank you."

Momentarily distracted after cutting, the director rushes to Diane, "Listen, hot stuff, you need to lay off the eye shadow. You look like a prostitute."

Diane stands, and with moist eyes asks Marvin, "Can I just use your bathroom? And I need to make a call if that's OK."

Already on his feet after the ugly remark, Marvin takes her hands in his, "Take your time, I'm not going anywhere."

Seth peeks around at her, bringing a smile to her face. She squares her shoulders, not bothering to look at Hank and walks into the house.

Hank turns on a dime and slaps Marvin's arm in a friendly gesture. Marvin's eyes go gray, regarding the charmer.

Hank looks around, "Thanks, Pal. Appreciate it. Great idea doing it here. Nice location."

He leans down, hands on his knees, and focuses on Seth, "Come here, little guy."

Seth hears his special friend's voice in his head, "Don't. He's bad."

He cowers behind Marvin, who leans down and picks him up. Seth buries his head in Marvin's shoulder. Hank pets Seth's hair and leans close enough to sniff it.

Marvin keeps his temper, barely.

Hank is laser focused on the boy, almost hypnotized, "Nice looking boy."

Marvin steps back a bit, "Sorry, he's timid around strangers."

Hank, back to reality, "That's OK. We'll just have to become friends. Good looking kid like that, he can go places. I know people, I'd be happy to make some introductions."

Marvin, having decided that Seth has had his last audition, "One child star in the family was enough. Thanks though."

Hank shakes his finger at Marvin, "I remember that campaign. You were quite a looker as a kid too. There's just something so appealing about fresh-faced little ones. Innocent, not jaded by the world."

Marvin is stunned at his brazenness.

He's actually saying these things out loud.

Hank laughs as Marvin attempts to put a friendly smile on his face.

Equipment is taken down by several men who shoot glares at Hank behind his back. The Vietnam War is more popular than this guy. Hank turns to observe everything briefly before turning his attention to Seth again. Marvin senses that he's going to touch him and backs up subtly.

Hank, used to getting his way, "Let me know if you change your mind about accepting my help. Or maybe - how about I just stop by sometime since I know where you live."

His grin turns malicious before he turns to leave.

Carey, no worse for wear, hops up onto the porch to join his best friend. He kisses Seth's cheek and nuzzles him to help the boy feel comfortable again.

Marvin seethes, "What a fucking asshole. I'd never let him near my son."

Distracted by the sound of a car pulling into the driveway, they both smile as Jackson gets out and joins them on the porch.

Carey's attendant in the hospital after his accident, Jackson has become more. Aware of the strangers around them, they don't let their feelings show.

Marvin and Carey lock eyes.

I said you'd find someone and I was right.

Carey smiles, having read his mind. Jackson pats Carey's back and heads into the house.

Carey reaches out for Seth, "Come on now, Uncle Harvey is waiting for us. He made your favorite macaroni and cheese."

He turns with a goofy grin to Marvin and makes smoochy noises, "And Diane is staying for lunch. Mmm. Hmm."

Marvin punches him playfully as he takes the child inside.

Carey turns back for a moment and observes his dear friend, the man who saved his life. Marvin stares out into the yard at the director and Carey knows. In that one instant, he knows everything.

Staring at Marvin's back, he knows what Marvin did after his attack. Instinctively. And he doesn't care. It's all in the past.

Carey also knows that Harvey is more than he seems. But he's come to love him as dearly as he does Marvin. Again, he doesn't care.

Another vehicle pulls up. Steven jumps out of his brand new truck and trots up to the porch. Half of his dark hair is gray now but he's also more youthful than before Carey's coma.

As if an albatross, carried for years, had fallen off of his back six years ago. He pats Marvin's shoulder as he passes, grabbing Seth away from him.

Seth squeals with joy, "Hi Pop Pop! We're having macaroni and cheese."

Steven replies, "Well, why else would I be here?"

Seth knows this game, "To see me!"

Steven and Carey share a look of understanding before they all disappear into the kitchen.

Steven turns the boy upside down and walks with him, head down and arms dangling, laughing, "Naw, I don't wanna see you. I'm just hungry."

Seth chortles, "Put on music, Pop Pop!"

Marvin smiles at the arrival of his father and turns to go into the house. He makes it as far as the doorway before he hears Hank berating one of his assistants.

He turns and observes as Hank leans too close to the uncomfortable young man, puts his hand on his rear end and leers as he whispers to him. Hank notices Marvin staring and winks at him.

Marvin, the rage is back, mumbles to himself, "Someone should do something about him."

Harvey, wearing Miss Jezzy's old floral apron, leans in the open doorway right next to Marvin and puts his arm around him.

"You're right, brother."

"For Pete's Sake" by The Monkees blares from the house.

The four wholesome boys sing about this generation, this lovin' time and being born to love one another.

The twins grin sadistically before disappearing into the house for their mac and cheese.

ACKNOWLEDGEMENTS

I wish to thank James Moorer for being my mentor. His faith in me and my work has offered me the opportunity for a new life.

Huge thanks to the whole team at Dark Anthem Publishing.

Shout out to my parents, twin brother, and grandparents who watch over me from the other side and have guided me through this process.

I miss you all and will catch you on the flip side in a few decades.

To my wonderful husband, Mike, who tolerates the tunnel vision and loud playlist that accompanies my writing process. I love you more than anything.

And to my five amazing children - Chelsea, Eleni, Tommy, Kevin and Christopher. You guys continue to be the reason I breathe and raising you showed me that I'm able to do anything I set my mind to.

I'm proud of you all.

And lest we forget, Ryan and Dylan, who tolerate my daughters somehow, thus freeing me up to create.

Finally, thank you God for always watching out for me.

I knew you had plans for me, just didn't realize the route would be so circuitous.